Also by Maggie Sullivan

Christmas on Coronation Street

HarperCollins*Publishers*
The News Building,
1 London Bridge Street,
London SE1 9GF

www.harpercollins.co.uk

Published by HarperCollins*Publishers* 2018

3

Coronation Street is an ITV Studios Production
Copyright © ITV Ventures Limited 2018

Maggie Sullivan asserts the moral right to
be identified as the author of this work

A catalogue record for this book
is available from the British Library

ISBN: 978-0-00-825653-1

Set in Sabon LT Std by Palimpsest Book Production Limited, Falkirk, Stirlingshire

Printed and bound in Great Britain by CPI Group (UK) Ltd, Croydon CR0 4YY

MIX
Paper from
responsible sources
FSC
www.fsc.org
FSC™ C007454

This book is produced from independently certified FSC™ paper
to ensure responsible forest management.

For more information visit: www.harpercollins.co.uk/green

Acknowledgements

Special thanks to my superb editor Kate Bradley and wonderful agent Kate Nash for their continued help and encouragement. To Sue Moorcroft for her help and patience, particularly regarding social media, and to Ann Parker for her character analysis and insights. Thanks also to Shirley Patton, Dominic Khouri and Kieran Roberts for their invaluable specialist knowledge on *Coronation Street*.

To absent friends: Barbara Reid and Renée Byrne

March 1942

Chapter 1

Annie Walker lay in the middle of the generous-sized bed, ready to close her eyes. It was a rare treat for the landlady of Coronation Street's Rovers Return to enjoy the luxury of an afternoon doze, for the pub was the busiest and best in Weatherfield as far as she was concerned. The sunlight that was slanting through the sash window illuminated the dust on the dressing-table drawers and it was almost enough to make her get up and go in search of a duster – but she resisted. Her cold wasn't completely cured yet.

Annie yawned and stretched, lazily grateful that she had been able to persuade her mother to come and look after the children for a few days while she took to her bed.

'You won't have to worry about serving in the pub,'

Annie had said when she'd asked for Florence's help. She'd sensed her mother's hesitation at the thought of having to pull pints behind the bar.

'It's not that, dear,' Florence said, almost too quickly. 'I was just wondering whether you might be better off going to the hospital. This flu that so many people are going down with can be very dangerous, you know, and you don't want to take any chances, not with two little ones running around.'

Annie didn't want to admit that it was probably the two little ones and their boundless energy that had led to her getting so run-down in the first place.

Thankfully, Florence had agreed to come and Annie had been able to indulge in what she considered to be a well-deserved rest. But enough was enough. Now Florence was beginning to irritate her and, grateful as she was for her mother's help, Annie knew it was time for her to take back control of her own household.

Annie closed her eyes, about to drop off, when Florence made an unwanted appearance. She was brandishing the *Weatherfield Gazette*.

'Have you seen what it says here?' she said, waving the paper under Annie's nose. 'There's going to be a special service for Mothering Sunday at the Mission of Glad Tidings.'

'So?' Annie's eyes were already heavy with sleep.

'So, I thought we might go.' Florence began to hum 'All Things Bright and Beautiful'. 'It might be interesting.'

'You can please yourself.' Annie sounded cross. 'But I shall go to Mount Zion Baptist Chapel where I always go. It's where Jack and I were married and where, I believe, I shall be expected.' So saying, she closed her eyes and turned on her side.

Yes, she thought as she drifted off to sleep, it would be timely to go to church and give thanks, if only for the fact that, although German bomber planes continued to fill the skies, the barrage balloons forced them to fly so high it had been some time since the Luftwaffe had managed to drop their bombs with any accuracy on Weatherfield.

After the horrors of the 1940 Christmas Blitz that had laid bare the centre of Manchester and flattened parts of residential Weatherfield, Annie had wondered whether there could be any more bombs left in the Germans' arsenal to be dropped on Britain. But the Air Raid Precaution wardens had warned people to be vigilant because there could still be the occasional air raid even though the Blitz was over. Their advice was to flee to the shelters at the first signs of danger. Annie dreaded the thought of being woken up by the wail of air-raid sirens and having to rush to get dressed and make herself presentable. Regardless of the fact that they were encouraged to leave immediately the sirens sounded and not wait to gather any belongings, she certainly didn't like being bullied by one of the ARPs or the fire wardens into having to seek cover without checking first whether she was decent enough to be seen in public. Annie was thankful she at least had her own cellar where she and any of the staff and customers could flee to whenever necessary. She could not imagine having to run with her two little ones down the street where she would be crammed together with all the neighbourhood hoi polloi who were seeking shelter in the basement of the Mission of Glad Tidings. Even the thought of having to rub shoulders, quite literally, with all those people was more than she could bear.

But, when she stopped to think about it, she was already doing so many things that in the past she would have thought were beyond endurance. Since war had been declared people everywhere, not only in Weatherfield, were suffering hardships and acting in ways they weren't used to, doing things that, until the start of the war, they would not have dreamt of doing. And they had been doing them for so long now it was hard to remember things ever being any different. Not that Annie was a stranger to change and hardship. She had endured sudden loss and a dramatic change of life style when she was a young girl to such an extent that she would have thought it was enough for a lifetime. But even she had to admit that they were now living through some of the most challenging and troublesome times she could remember.

Who would have dreamt that rationing would have become a central and essential part of their everyday lives? Nowadays ration books were crucial for daily living, and shortages and deprivation were the major topics of conversation on the street. Not only were certain foods scarce, but supplies of such basic commodities as clothing, coal, and soap were also becoming difficult to come by, even with the requisite number of coupons. There was little petrol available to fuel the few cars that were on the road, and the scarcity of goods was becoming more widespread each month as different items were added to the list of things that were unavailable or in limited supply. More things were being rationed and restricted items had become even more stringently regulated. Sometimes Elsie Foyle, who ran the corner shop, tipped off the registered customers who shopped with her regularly if she knew something was likely to become scarce, and Annie had been persuaded to buy a few extra tins of powdered eggs, sardines and pilchards before they disappeared altogether from the shelves. However, worrying that they might be considered to be black market items, she made a strict rule that she would never eat any of them herself but reasoned that she had the health of two young, growing children to consider.

Annie was also affected when stocks of the beer she had on tap were running low. She felt a blush creep to her cheeks as memories flashed through her mind of the dreadful and embarrassing time she had had shortly after Jack had gone away to fight for his country. For a brief period the pumps at the Rovers had run dry. She had learned to manage by cutting down on the opening hours from time to time, or even reducing the strength of the beer. On nights when they were not so busy she would call time early, in order to conserve her stocks, and on occasion would open a little later than usual. She had heard it was not uncommon for pubs to run dry all over the country, but Annie was determined to do everything she could to make sure she didn't have to suffer the ignominy of running a public house that didn't have enough beer for its regular customers.

In her thirty-two years Annie had learned how to handle whatever situations she was faced with in life and she had become nothing if not adaptable to her current circumstances. What she did worry about, however, was not about her life now, but about what life would be like for her two young children if they grew up knowing nothing but a state of siege and war. She feared for their future and she wasn't the only one to think like that. One of the main topics of conversation at the bar each night was customers complaining about the difficulties of living with uncertainty; the uncertainty of not knowing what the future might hold.

Annie knew what that was like too. She could never forget the dreadful times that had followed the dramatic downturn of her family's fortunes when she was young and how she had grown used to not knowing what might happen from one moment to the next. She tried hard not to look back, but sometimes it was impossible to avoid the vivid memories and the stinging feelings of humiliation they still evoked. Her life had turned out to be very different from what she had once imagined, and she was determined to do all in her power to ensure her children didn't have to suffer the same plight.

When she woke, Annie lay still for a few moments, gathering her thoughts and unsuccessfully trying to catch hold of the remnants of a dream that was floating somewhere at the back of her mind. Gradually, as the ghost-like images disappeared, she became aware of the buzz of conversation that was wafting up from the public bar below. It sounded busy down there, as it had on previous nights, and yet thankfully they seemed to be managing without her. If they weren't, no one had said so. She didn't move and remained with her eyes closed for quite some time, content in the knowledge that the pub was in good hands. She smiled with satisfaction each time she heard the ping of the till drawer opening and closing.

Lottie Kemp, although several years younger than Annie, was one of her closest friends, and to Annie's delight she had offered to lend a hand behind the bar in the evenings during Annie's absence. As she might have expected, Lottie had proved to be a tower of strength and was totally trustworthy to look after the takings. Sally Todd, who lived on Coronation Street at number 9, could also be trusted as she had worked in the bar on and off for many years and when she offered to work a regular afternoon shift during the busy times,

Annie was delighted. It was good to have such treasured and valued friends at times like this. It was just a shame that, before she took ill, the new barmaid she had hired had felt the need, after working in the bar for only a few months, to join her younger siblings who had been evacuated to the country. A replacement was something she would have to think about as soon as she was well.

Annie pulled the feathery eiderdown up to her chest, glad she had not been persuaded to change her warm winceyette nightdress for the pink lawn cotton one, even though it was prettier. The calendar might be registering that it was officially spring but there was still a definite chill in the March air.

'Would you like me to plump the cushions for you so you can sit up and drink this?' Lottie broke into her reveries when she suddenly appeared at the bedroom door, steam rising from the delicate china cup and saucer she was balancing in her hand.

Now *she's* dressed sensibly for working behind a bar, Annie thought. She liked her staff to look neat and Lottie was wearing a plaid pinafore dress and a fine wool jumper, with her dark hair scraped back into a tidy French pleat.

'I wasn't sure if you'd be up,' Lottie said, beaming, her rounded cheeks spotted pink, 'but I thought you might like this.' She crossed the room to the other side of the bed so that she could put the tea down on the bedside table by the window but she didn't get that far; all of a sudden there was a clatter and a bang and the bedroom door was thrust back on its hinges. Annie lifted her head in alarm, uncertain what had happened. For a moment she couldn't see anybody as she struggled to sit up, only Lottie ineffectually trying to mop up the spilled tea from the satin eiderdown cover with her pocket handkerchief. Then Annie sighed with relief.

'Gosh, darling, you gave Mummy such a fright,' she said, realizing it was three-year-old Billy who had crashed into the room. His fair hair was standing up in spikes and he looked like he had just crawled out of bed.

'Where's Joanie?' he demanded. 'I can't find her.' He ran his hands in exasperation over his hair with the gesture of an adult and Annie couldn't help smiling.

'Have you lost her? Or is she hiding?' Annie asked, humouring him.

'She's hiding, but where is she? Doesn't she know she can't escape?' He threw open the wardrobe doors and the doors of the tallboy, not bothering to close them again. He even pulled out the dressing-table drawers and left them half on the floor. Then he knocked over the wicker chair, heedless of the clothes that had been neatly folded on the seat, and finally he bent down to peer under the bed, flinging Annie's slippers and a pair of shoes out across the landing. And all the time he was shouting, 'Where are you, silly sister? You'll be sorry, Joanie Pony, if you don't tell me where you are. And when Daddy comes home I'll make him send you back to wherever it was you came from.'

Annie laughed when he said that. 'You're the silly Billy,' she said fondly. 'She is only two years old after all, and you do know, darling, that the whole point of hide-and-seek is for you to go and look for her? There's not much point in her telling you where she is. Where's the fun in that?'

One of the things Annie did worry about was how much her mother pandered to the children, especially Billy, unlike Annie who tried to be firm but fair. He was reaching an age when he would really benefit from a more disciplined hand. If she was honest, he needed his father.

Billy turned to Annie and stuck out his tongue, then he pulled a grotesque face aimed towards Lottie who was standing frozen near the window, still holding the cup and saucer. 'I wonder what I've done to deserve that,' Lottie sighed while Annie gave a little chuckle and smiled indulgently. Billy stared at her without smiling back, then suddenly said, 'I want that tea, Mam,' and made a lunge for the half-filled cup in Lottie's hand.

Annie sighed. 'How many times have I to tell you not to call me that, Billy? Remember what I said? It's Mother or Mummy. Mam's so common.'

Billy paid her no heed. It was as if she hadn't spoken as he grabbed the cup and gulped down some of the remaining tea, spilling what was left over his short grey flannel trousers. Lottie made a tapping gesture to indicate he should replace the cup on the saucer but instead he threw it across the room where it hit the doorjamb and smashed into several pieces.

'Oh darling, look what you've done. There was no need for that, you know,' Annie said sympathetically. 'Now poor Lottie is going to have to clean that up. If you're thirsty, why don't you go downstairs and ask Grandma if you can have a proper cup of tea, then you can sit down and drink it nicely. And if you're very good she might even find a biscuit for you.'

'No she won't,' Billy said scornfully, 'because I've eaten them all.' He scuffed his feet over the carpet as he walked towards the door. 'And I didn't let Joanie have any.'

'Oh, and be a love before you go,' Annie called after him. 'Shut the wardrobe doors will you, for Mummy, please.'

Billy looked up and aimed a kick at the wardrobe before jumping over the shattered cup. Suddenly Joanie appeared on the landing from the direction of one of the bedrooms, but Billy just pushed her out of the way, almost knocking her down the stairs as he raced ahead of her shouting, 'Grammy, I'm hungry. I want my tea and Joanie's been naughty so she can't have any. Mummy says so.'

Annie didn't hear her mother's reply, though she could hear the clanging of pots coming from the kitchen. She turned to Lottie apologetically. 'Boys will be boys,' she said. 'He didn't mean any harm. He just doesn't know his own strength.' And she laughed.

Lottie's only response was a deep sigh. She was still holding the saucer that was intact but, ignoring the smashed china, she scooped up Joanie, who was sitting on the landing trying to pair up the stray shoes and slippers, and without a word carried her downstairs.

Annie shook her head and folded her arms across her chest, a wry smile on her lips. 'Children!' she clucked softly. 'They can be such a tonic and a torture all at the same time. I really should be thankful for what I've got. I'm very lucky to have two healthy children living safely with me. All of us together in our own home.' It put her in mind of what her mother had said about Mothering Sunday. She would make it her business to go to church on that day, but the Baptist church not the Mission. And she would make sure she said an extra special prayer of thanks, for she was truly blessed. Not everyone, particularly in Weatherfield, was so privileged.

Her thoughts turned for a moment to the unfortunate children who, for one reason or another, had been separated from their mothers by the war and she felt an unusual prickling sensation behind her eyes. She remembered those who had been sent away when the war had only just got underway. Some, she had heard, had even been sent as far away as Canada and Australia, but most had been evacuated to the English countryside which was deemed to be safer than the industrial cities. She had watched, distressed, from her own doorstep as large numbers of local children from Bessie Street School were rounded up like sheep. Each carried a small suitcase as if they were going on their holidays but she knew that wasn't the case. They had name badges pinned to their coats and they looked lost and bewildered as they were marched off, hand in hand, by their teacher Ada Hayes. Annie would never have let her Billy go away like that, or Joanie. Who knew where they might have ended up? She'd heard some terrible tales and some of the children actually had to come back, their billets were so dreadful. And yet some of those who hadn't sent their children away had undergone dreadful difficulties too, in different ways.

Yes, Annie sighed. She had much to be thankful for. Manchester had suffered terrible damage as a result of the bombing raids during the 1940 Christmas Blitz and some parts of Weatherfield had been particularly badly hit. Whole streets had been destroyed and some unfortunate families had been cruelly split apart, parents or children missing presumed dead, their homes destroyed, the remaining family members left in dire distress. Fortunately, most of Coronation Street had withstood the onslaught and many lives had been saved thanks to people diving into cellars like the one underneath the Rovers or the air-raid shelter below the Mission. But the Blitz was like a wake-up call to the residents who remained, a reminder of the serious implications of the country being at war. People realized they needed to pull together and the residents of Weatherfield wanted to get involved in any way they could.

Most of the young able-bodied men, including her

own beloved Jack, had signed up for the forces as soon as war was declared. Even men like Elsie Tanner's bully-boy husband, Arnold, had joined the navy before he needed to, before any serious battles were underway, even though it meant leaving his pregnant bride to manage as best she could. The local factories that had once been the financial centre to the cotton industry had switched their production skills to war work, employing all the local women who were now being conscripted to work. Instead of being at the heart of the cotton trade manufacturing the fine cotton goods they once had, they now produced uniforms, tank and gun parts and other much needed armaments and munitions.

At the same time, those men who were not eligible to be called up into the forces, or were deemed to be medically unfit to fight, took on other war time responsibilities. Some became fire wardens who issued warnings about incendiary bombs, while others, like Albert Tatlock from number 1 Coronation Street and Ena Sharples from the Mission, became ARP wardens. Their main duties were to watch with a careful eye that no one contravened the blackout laws and to round up residents and help them to reach the shelters in time during air raids. As food became scarcer, and imported goods such as fruit and sugar disappeared completely from the shelves, those who had a patch of spare ground at the backs of their houses, no matter how small, began to create victory gardens where they grew as many of their own vegetables as they had space for. Neighbouring, which had once been a feature of life for those living in the crowded neighbourhoods with back-to-back terraced housing, began again in earnest, as people keenly looked out for their neighbours and frequently popped in and out of each other's houses. After the Blitz, everyone in Weatherfield, from Coronation Street and beyond, began to pull together like never before. No pint of milk was left on the doorstep for long without someone enquiring about why it hadn't been taken in. Annie herself had good reason to be thankful to her neighbours, Albert and Bessie Tatlock at number 1, whenever the sirens sounded for she needed help dressing her two little ones in their siren suits while trying to hurry them down into the cellar.

Annie had never had much time for Elsie Tanner who lived at number 11, dismissing her as common and ungodly, but even she had joined in when the whole street had rallied to help poor Elsie deal with the horrific loss of almost all her family. That event had allowed the swelling number of congregants at the Mission of Glad Tidings to catch an astonishing glimpse of Ena Sharples' softer side and afterwards, when two of Elsie's sisters were found alive, the singing from the Mission could be heard from one end of the street to the other. Sometimes all people could offer was nothing more than a small gesture of kindness, or a shoulder to cry on, but that didn't make their contribution any less valued. The camaraderie and unlikely friendships that were struck during that time helped to bond the whole community. That was when Annie Walker realized, for the first time, that not only her clientele but the Rovers Return itself was at the heart of that community.

Yes, thought Annie, feeling safe and warm as she snuggled under the eiderdown, she would definitely go to church on Mothering Sunday and she would thank the good Lord for finally blessing her and her family with better luck than she'd had when she was young.

Of course, there was one person missing from her family right now; one special person who would have made them complete. A person whose safe return she prayed for every night; a person she wrote to every day and whose photograph she kissed before she went to sleep. Jack Walker, her husband, being the selfless man he was, had signed up for action as soon as he could and was now with the Fusiliers, performing what was considered to be an essential role for his king and his country in the battle against Germany and Japan. Annie understood that what he was doing was important, playing a small part in the greater war effort, like so many others, but it didn't stop tears pricking her eyelids whenever she thought of him bravely battling in some far away corner of the Empire. He was probably cold and possibly even a little afraid, but she would never know. His letters told her nothing about where he was, or what he was thinking or feeling. *Careless talk costs lives* was one of the war's most critical slogans and letters to and from all military personnel were censored to make sure nothing was given away to the enemy that could give them any clues about the where-abouts, movements, or the state of the allied troops. Annie was afraid, but such anxiety had become a part of everyday life, particularly for the women who had been left behind. Sometimes she felt almost worthless, merely standing behind the bar pulling pints, but then she reminded herself that she was fulfilling a valuable role providing solace for those who were unable to fight but who were keeping things going at home until the soldiers were able to return. She could only hope that her letters cheered him a little. She tried not to show her apprehension in any of her daily missives. Instead she gave amusing reports of the children's antics.

At least, she told him about some of Billy's escapades, anecdotes that she thought would make him laugh. Though she hadn't bothered to mention the time last week while her mother was in charge, when the mischiev-ous little devil had locked Joanie into the under-stairs cupboard. The poor little mite had apparently cried herself to sleep in there and had not been found for several hours. Annie saved that story for her own private nightly jottings in the diary she kept. But she liked to send Jack regular bulletins about the welfare of their friends and neighbours in Weatherfield and she eagerly awaited Jack's letters, not so much for their news content, for that was limited, but, if she was being honest, she had to acknowledge that she was afraid

19

that one day there might not be any letters. Like many women in the street she was afraid that her husband wouldn't come back, or that if he did, he might be maimed or wounded. Every day there were stories of people she knew being hurt – or worse. But she knew she had to put her worries aside and for Jack's sake, and for the sake of their children, she refused to let herself dwell on such dark possibilities and she tried to dismiss the wretched images that sometimes threatened to take over her thoughts. She had to stay strong and she had to believe. After all, wasn't she keeping the Rovers going so that he could pick up where he had left off on his return? *Keep the Home Fires Burning*, that was what the song said. And thanks to people like Lottie and Sally she had been able to do just that. Between them they had kept things going and she hadn't had to close the pub for a single day. She couldn't help feeling rather pleased with herself. She did seem to have a knack for choosing loyal and trustworthy friends.

Suddenly Annie heard a piercing scream and she was brought back to the present with a jolt as she sat up sharply in bed. It took her a few moments to realize it was Billy downstairs who had been yelling at his grandmother, demanding that she give him some jam for his bread soldiers. Annie sighed. How could anyone explain to a small child that jam was rationed and that it would probably be at least a week before they would be able to go and claim their next allocation of anything sweet? But if Billy was becoming fractious, then it was definitely time for her to get up, time she went back to work. She sighed. It had been really nice to have a few days off and she had to admit she did feel much better for having had a rest; any longer, though, and it would become an indulgence. She was needed downstairs now as Sally had to go back to the munitions factory where she had been requested to work longer hours and Lottie too would soon be doing extra shifts there. She knew her mother was looking forward to getting back home too. Everyone had been wonderful, covering for her at the bar and looking after the children, but it was time now for her to pull her weight once more. And perhaps a word to Elsie Foyle in the corner shop about getting some special sweet treat for the children would have to be one of her first priorities. She resolved to get up the following morning.

She lay back on the pillows contemplating what she would wear for her first day back behind the bar. Clothes were special to her and she enjoyed planning her outfits. She would love to wear something that would help her make an entrance when she first walked into the bar, even if she did then spend the rest of the session sitting on a bar stool ringing the money into the till. She thought about her limited wardrobe but knew with the current stringency in clothes rationing there would be no possibility of getting anything new. Maybe she could dress up one of her old twinsets with the single row of pearls and matching pearl earrings Jack had given her for her last birthday. Then she could wear her newest pleated skirt that she'd bought just before the war started. She would dab on a little make-up – that always made her feel brighter – and she would tell Jack about it in her next letter, remind him how much she missed him and how much they needed him at the Rovers. She knew he would like that.

Annie stretched and yawned luxuriously. She had had a good few days' rest and she was pleased to say she felt refreshed. But now she was ready to go back to work. For all that Lottie said to reassure her, she worried that they might be struggling a little without her down-stairs and one of the first things she must do was look for a new barmaid. Tomorrow she would surprise the children by giving them their breakfast, but for now she slid down on the pillows and shut her eyes again . . .

Chapter 2

When twenty-year-old Gracie Ashton came to live on Mallard Street in Weatherfield with her mother and two younger brothers she was delighted to find that Lottie Kemp, a young woman of her own age, was living in one of the houses opposite. The Ashtons had moved into a rented house that had become vacant after the Blitz and had been standing empty for some time. The family who lived there before them had flitted to the seaside because they thought it would be a safer place to be when the bombs began to fall. But Gracie didn't really think anywhere was safe, not while the Luftwaffe were still flying overhead. And they were flying with a vengeance, retaliating against the allies' severest bombing yet of Cologne with attacks on all the major British cathedral cities. The house where she and her family had lived had been badly damaged in a bombing raid, and her mother, Mildred, was grateful to be able to move them all at short notice to somewhere that was close to the factory where she worked.

Mildred Ashton had been the family's mainstay while her husband, Petty Officer Bob Ashton, was recovering from the burns he'd sustained when he was with his naval unit somewhere out in the Pacific Ocean. She keenly felt the weight of having to take on so much responsibility for the family's welfare. She had to sort out the details of their living arrangements on her own, even after Bob was fit enough to come out of hospital, and she relied heavily on Gracie's support. In the beginning they had few things to fill the new house with, for most of their furniture had been damaged by a fire started by an incendiary bomb and then further destroyed by the gallons of water the firemen used in their efforts to put it out. Mildred had had to work extremely hard, but at least by the time Bob came home they all had enough chairs to sit on and beds to sleep in. With four sets of ration books, and Mildred's ability to create something tasty from limited ingredients, the family was at least able to eat and they were managing to scrape by. Mildred had also persuaded the two young boys to dig a victory garden before their father came home. There was a tiny square, covered in weeds, next to the privy in the back yard that she knew could be converted with a bit of effort so that they could all benefit from having their own fresh vegetables.

Gracie met Lottie Kemp when she popped out to the local shop early one evening, not long after they'd arrived at the new house. To her dismay, most of the shelves were bare though the queue of hopefuls clutching their ration books stretched out into the street. The two young women got chatting as they stood next to each other in line.

'I've come to see if they've any cigarettes left. It's my only luxury,' Gracie said diffidently. 'They help to keep me sane. My mum and I usually share one between us on a night.'

Lottie laughed. 'You don't have to apologize to me, you know. I'm on your side.' And she held up her left hand to show a homemade roll-up burning down between her fingers.

'We both prefer the tipped ones,' Gracie said. 'They don't taste so strong. But I find smoking does help me to relax, don't you?'

Lottie nodded. She took a puff of her roll-up as if to prove her point and Gracie smiled. She wasn't sure why she felt she had to justify her smoking habits to a stranger and blushed when she finally reached the counter and asked for her favourite brand by name. Relieved that her errand was not in vain, she slipped the red packet of Craven "A"s into her pocket.

'I'm Charlotte Kemp, by the way, known to all as Lottie,' the other girl said. 'I live around the corner in Mallard Street, at number 6.'

'Well, what do you know! We've not long since moved

into number 9, opposite. I'm Grace Ashton, my friends call me Gracie.'

Lottie had exuded such an immediate air of warmth and friendliness as they'd begun to chat that Gracie felt drawn to her already by the time they shook hands. Lottie looked immaculate in her neat, if not stylish, clothes as she stepped forward to receive the newspaper that was usually put by for her father. Gracie couldn't help noticing that her hands were carefully manicured and the French pleat in her hair looked as if it had been freshly pinned. Gracie felt positively unkempt beside her in her wide-legged working trousers, that would keep catching fluff in the turn-ups, and the hand-knitted sweater her mother had made up from an unravelled shawl. As usual, strands of her flyaway hair had worked their way out of the elastic band that was doing a poor job of holding together the ponytail she'd scraped off her face only an hour ago.

'It's really nice to meet you,' Lottie said.

'You too,' Gracie said. 'I was hoping I might meet some younger folk when we moved here, but you can't be sure who's still around, what with all the blokes away in the army and the women working all hours in the factories.' She nodded her head in the direction of the people in the queue who were mostly women of her mother's age.

'I tell you what,' Lottie said, 'why don't you pop round to ours one night, we can listen to the gramophone? I'm working most evenings at the moment, but that won't be for much longer. I'm only helping out a friend, so you can pop in of an evening, any time after tea. I've got a couple of Benny Goodman records we could listen to. If you like swing, that is?'

'I love it. Fancy you having records of *the king of swing*. I'll look forward to that. Thanks.'

'Do you know "Darn That Dream"? It was a number one hit some while back.'

'Yes, I love it. I used to catch it sometimes on the Light Programme.'

'Have you got a wireless? That's something we don't have.'

'Not any more.' Gracie looked wistful. 'We used to have one, before the fire. I miss it. Maybe we'll be able to replace it one of these days. It's good to be able to catch the news without having to go to the pictures to see the newsreels. When my dad was first sent out to the Pacific I was always trying to listen out for news of his ship.'

'Is he in the navy, then?' Lottie enquired.

Gracie shrugged. 'Not sure exactly. He's only just come home from the hospital. His ship was hit by Japanese torpedoes and he got badly burned. We're not sure where that puts him now.'

'I'm sorry to hear it,' Lottie said, adding, 'My dad's at home. Bad eyes and a bad chest. They wouldn't take him on in the first place, worse luck. My sister Maggie and me would both have liked to see the back of him – for a while, at any rate. We might have been able to get out a bit more then. He watches us like a hawk, always wanting to know where we're going and who with.'

'I know what you mean. I used to think the same about my dad, but now I feel guilty for ever having had such thoughts. It's hard on my mum too. I try to do my bit but everything seems to fall on her. We don't know anyone round here. We used to live on the other side of the viaduct nearer to town.'

'I tell you what, why don't I knock on when I'm not working nights any more and let you know when I'll be in? I presume you're not working the late shift?'

'I'm afraid I'm not working at all just yet. I'm on the lookout for a job. I used to work in a school as a dinner lady and I looked after the kids at playtime. But they closed it down when most of the kids were evacuated. Those who stayed behind were sent to another school, somewhere near here. Most of their kids had been evacuated before the Blitz.'

'You must mean Bessie Street, that's the main elementary school hereabouts.'

'That sounds like it.'

'Well, finding you a job shouldn't be much of a problem, if you really want one,' Lottie said.

'Course I do. I need to be able to help out at home. And I've heard they'll be conscripting women of our age into jobs soon; they want to make sure we're all pulling our weight. I'd like to find one of my own before that happens.'

'I do know of at least one job,' Lottie said, then she paused, 'though it's not in a school.'

'That doesn't matter. Where is it?'

'At the munitions factory where I work. They're desperate for women to work there. In fact, there's an empty place on my workbench and it's only up the road. You could probably go down there right now and apply; the office never seems to close.'

'Do you know, I think I'll do that. Thanks Lottie, that's really helpful,' Gracie said when they both emerged onto the pavement. 'I'll let you know how I get on.'

Gracie had only been at the factory for a few days when she realized that munitions work was not for her. But she wasn't sure what she should say to her new friend who had been so kind in trying to help her get the job. She was grateful that the noise of the machinery drowned out the possibility of any private conversations on the shop floor while they were working and it was too sensitive a topic to explain by the mouthing or sign language they had to resort to if they needed to communicate. Gracie waited till the two of them were sitting down for dinner together, with their chunks of bread and slivers of cheese to be washed down by thick mugs of watery-looking tea in a quieter corner of the canteen.

'It's not that I'm not grateful, Lottie,' she broached the subject tentatively. 'I really appreciate all the help you've given me; I want you to know that. Honestly,

I was so pleased when you told me about the factory in the first place, but the problem is, I really can't stand it. It's worse than I thought it would be. I need a job badly and I can't afford just to give it up but I'm going to have to look for something else.'

'What's the problem?' Lottie asked. 'I know it's repetitive and boring as hell, but I reckon that describes most jobs on offer at the moment for the likes of you and me. I don't know any job that isn't tough. It's going to be hard work wherever you go right now.'

'I understand that. It's not the hard work I'm afraid of, it's just that . . .' She wasn't sure how to say it, so she plunged in. 'I hate the idea that we're making guns that are actually going to kill people,' she said.

'But we're not making the guns. The floor manager's always been very clear about that.'

'No, I know. I've heard him say that many times an' all. But the truth is that we're making *bits* of guns and it doesn't really matter that it's other people who are going to assemble them.'

'But they're not the guns that are killing our boys,' Lottie argued, though it was obvious Gracie had made up her mind. 'The guns we're making parts for are going to help to kill the Jerries and the Japs.'

Gracie hung her head and dropped her voice as low as she could while still being heard. It felt important to get her side of the argument across. 'The point is, these past few days, I've realized that I don't care who these particular guns are killing. I don't give a monkey's if they're only killing our sworn enemies. The fact is, they're killing *people* and I don't like that one bit. It's got so's I can't sleep at night. All I can see is the cogs clicking into gear and me pulling the lever that brings the cutter down. And you know what pops out each time I do that?'

'Of course I do. We're on the same bench, remember.'

'Exactly. So it's something we both know is the part of the gun that holds the ammunition. And honestly, Lottie, it turns my stomach. It makes me feel physically sick. When you first told me about the job I jumped at the chance. I thought it would be like any other work. I thought I could close my mind to what I was doing. The fact is, I thought I could handle it and I actually find that I can't.'

Lottie shrugged. 'Someone's got to do it. And if it means we can rest easier in our beds knowing the Jerries are being taken care of by our lads then I'm prepared to be one of them. Frankly, I think it's a small price to pay.' She sighed. 'And as far as I'm concerned it pays my share of the rent.'

'Maybe you'd feel better if we were making holsters, or bren vests,' a stranger's voice suddenly piped up.

'It's a bleeding sight better than filling shells and having your whole body turning bloody yellow, I can tell you,' sniggered her mate.

Gracie looked up angrily. She hadn't realized that two girls had come to their table and had parked their trays close by. She had been so involved in her explanation she hadn't noticed that not only were they sitting within hearing distance, but they were avidly listening in to her conversation. She felt her face flush and knew her cheeks must be scarlet.

'Don't worry,' the first speaker said, standing up from the wooden bench where she'd been sitting next to Gracie. 'There's a part of me agrees with you, so I shan't be saying owt to nobody. And we've got to be getting back now, any road. Come on, Luce.'

The two girls took their trays over to the serving hatch. Lottie looked bemused.

'You must do whatever you think is right,' she said, but Gracie didn't say any more. She didn't like confrontation at the best of times and she certainly didn't want to fall out with Lottie who had done her best to help. But she'd made a mistake. She should never have taken the job in the first place. She hadn't realized how strong her feelings were. The fact of the matter was she didn't like armed conflict, and certainly not wars of any kind, but she had been sucked into wanting to do her bit for the war effort and for her country. She had realized too late that she would have been better with a job that supported the allied soldiers in a different way; one that had nothing to do directly with all the killing. It was a subject they never discussed at home. There was no need. She knew how they all felt. Her father had become embroiled in the war by signing up early on and being assigned to a big ship that had been sent off to the Pacific shortly after the Japanese had bombed

Pearl Harbor. There, he'd ended up fighting an unseen enemy so he didn't think much about it, though he did blame the Americans for his plight when his ship took a hit. She knew that her mother would have joined one of the armed forces too, like a shot, if she could. She often said that if she'd have been younger and didn't have children she'd have gone to fight given half a chance. So would Gracie's brothers. Thankfully, neither of them was old enough to be called up into the services yet, though she knew that didn't please them and she was afraid that if the war continued much longer both Paul and Greg would run off to join up and lie about their age as so many young men had already done.

'I know you don't like war,' Lottie said after a while in a placatory tone. 'No one does, truth be told. But there's lots of men from round here felt they had to fight. There's dozens from this street, Rosamund Street, Mawdsley Street and Coronation Street alone who signed up right from the start, like you said your dad did. And I bet not many of them really wanted to go off and fight if there would have been any other way to defeat bloody Hitler. So I feel I want to try to help them in any way I can.'

Gracie nodded. 'I can understand that, and I realize I have to do my bit now that we are in the war. None of us have any choice, really. I just wish there was a different way I could serve my country than making the actual guns, that's all.'

'Would pulling pints in a pub be more to your taste,

then? How would that suit you?' Lottie sounded as if she was joking and Gracie was glad that the tension of the moment had eased, but then she realized Lottie was serious.

'Down to the ground, I'd say. That sounds like my dream job.' Gracie was not sure how to gauge the sudden switch in the conversation so she added in a jocular fashion, 'In my opinion, it ought to be a protected occupation.' She was surprised when Lottie continued to look serious. Gracie frowned. 'Why are you asking?' she asked. 'Is there a job going? Or are you just teasing?'

'No, straight up, there *is* a job going. Why? Would you fancy it?'

'Course I would. Where is it? Is it local?'

'It's at the pub where I've been working these past few nights. The Rovers Return in Coronation Street.'

'Really? How come you never mentioned it before?'

'I never thought of it before. Probably because I know the factory pays better. But Annie Walker, the landlady at the Rovers, is a friend of mine and I know she's been looking for a barmaid for some time. She's been trying to get someone permanent ever since her husband went into the army.'

'I'd have thought lots of girls would have jumped at the chance to work in a place like that.'

'Someone did, very quickly. A nice young lass called Becky. She was doing all right, but then she suddenly flitted one day. Didn't turn up one dinnertime and left no word, but then Annie found out that she and her family had had enough of the air raids and had moved out to the country.'

At this Gracie laughed. 'Honestly, with all the people who've rushed to get out of town since the war began you'd have thought the countryside would have been full up by now.'

Lottie chuckled. 'By the same reckoning all the cities should be empty. But the fact is, Becky's departure left a gaping hole at the Rovers as far as poor Annie's concerned, so maybe it's a gap you could fill.'

'It could be just the job. How do you know her, this Annie?'

'I used to help out in the bar occasionally before the war whenever she was tied up with little Billy and they needed an extra hand. She's got two little ones now, she only had the one then. But during the Blitz we ended up down in the Rovers' cellar together on several occasions when the sirens went off. Then one night there was a very long raid and we were cooped up down there for ages. Her little boy, Billy, was only a toddler and he was running riot. Poor Annie had her hands full with little Joanie who was still a babe in arms. I suppose you could say I "entertained" Billy. At least I managed to keep him quiet and well out of Annie's way while she coped with the baby and she was very grateful for my help. She always said I reminded her of someone she used to know years ago. I can only assume it was someone she liked because we're very different, Annie and me. But somehow we clicked that night and we've been good friends ever since.'

'So what's she like?'

'She's a fair bit older than you and me and . . .' she paused. 'I'm not sure how to describe her. She's quite a character.'

'How old? Old enough to be my mother?'

'Not at all. I'd say she'd be in her early thirties. I'm twenty-two, by the way. So her clothes are not always at the height of fashion. But then who can keep up with the latest fads when you haven't got enough coupons to get decent material to make anything new. But she dresses very nicely, wears a bit of make-up and I think she must have her hair peroxided and permed a bit. She's very particular about looking neat and tidy all the time, whatever she's wearing. And she likes to keep the bar neat and tidy too. She's got very high standards so you do have to be on your toes. *A place for everything and everything in its place*, she's always saying. And you've got to have a big smile for the customers, no matter how bad you might be feeling. You have to look out not to let things slide. On the other hand, it means that even when the public bar is at its worst – like first thing in the morning before Rose comes in to clean – it's still a reasonably nice place to work although it is still full of the smell of last night's stale tobacco and beer.'

'Why don't you work there full time, then?'

'Mostly because of the money. Which is why I didn't suggest it to you in the first place. And, somehow, I've never seen myself as a full-time barmaid though I do enjoy it and I'm always willing to help out the odd time. Like I say, I've been working there most evenings this past week while Annie was poorly. But hopefully she'll be back by tomorrow so I won't be needed any more.'

'Not if she can appoint someone full time.' Gracie didn't want to sound too eager but she couldn't help feeling enthused by the idea.

'Are you interested in applying, then?' Lottie asked.

'I am. Do you think I'll like her, or more to the point, will she like me?'

'There's only one way to find out. Though I don't see why not. But I don't want to speak out of turn and get any false hopes up. All I can tell you is she'll be wanting to appoint someone as soon as she can. So, if you fancy the job, my advice would be to get in there quick. Shall I tell her you might be interested?'

'Would you?'

'Of course. Though I think it's only fair to warn you that she can seem a bit snooty at times. Sometimes she has this unfortunate way of looking at you as if you'd been dragged in by the dog.' Lottie did her best imitation of Annie Walker arching her eyebrows and looking down her nose and Gracie laughed. 'But she's got a good heart and if you show willing she's a really good person to work for.'

'I suppose if I can manage the girls on the bench at the munitions factory I can handle the likes of Annie Walker,' Gracie said with a confidence in her voice that she didn't feel.

'I tell you what,' Lottie said, 'I'll have a word with her tonight and if she's going to be back at work then maybe you can pop in tomorrow evening before they get busy. Nothing like striking while the iron's hot. Is that all right?'

'That would be fine. I'm sure I can swing something at the factory.'

Gracie was aware that Lottie was looking at her critically. 'You know something,' Lottie said, 'I don't think you'll regret it.'

'No,' said Gracie, determined to be bold, 'I've got a feeling I won't either.'

Annie came downstairs, as she had promised herself, in time to give the children breakfast the next morning and found she had forgotten how much energy it required. Florence, however, had taken her at her word that she would get up in time to see to the children and it was mid-morning before she made an appearance, ordering Rose, Annie's young cleaner, to carry her suitcase down into the hall.

'I asked Neil if he would pop over in the car to pick me up,' Florence said.

Annie was shocked. Neil was her mother's business partner, but it still sounded like a cheeky request. 'Isn't that a bit of an extravagance? Where will he find the petrol?' Annie asked.

'Oh, he'll find some from somewhere, he always does. He knows I'm relying on him to get me back. How else would I get there otherwise? He wouldn't expect me to go on a bus.'

'Why on earth not? It's what most of us mortals have to do.' Annie couldn't hold back her sarcasm but Florence seemed to be immune. She sat down in the kitchen and picked up the *Weatherfield Gazette* to read as she waited for Neil.

As the morning wore on, Annie was surprised how wobbly she felt. She was having difficulty standing for long periods and she had no energy to run after the children. She wondered if it was her imagination that Joanie was even more demanding than usual and Billy was running around so much it made her feel dizzy to look at him. She was very relieved when Rose had finished cleaning in the public areas and was free to watch them. Her mother's departure had left her with mixed feelings. Even though a part of her was glad she had left, she realized how much she had relied on her over the last few days.

'Why don't you sit down and I'll fetch you a nice cup of tea?' Rose said when Joanie was finally settled in the playpen with her teddy and doll. 'And you have no need to worry, Mrs Walker, I won't desert you. I'll carry on here looking after the children till you get your strength back.'

'Thank you, Rose. I must admit I don't feel ready to take over everything just yet. I must have been more poorly than I realized.'

'Well, don't you fret. You just take your time.'

'Why don't you take them out to the park? I know there are no longer any swings or slides left, but at least Billy can kick his ball about and run off some of his energy.'

Sally Todd arrived in time to open the bar for the dinnertime trade. She had been such a help as she knew her way around the bar better than anyone. Annie was grateful Sally wouldn't be returning to her normal daytime job at the factory until the following week.

When she had taken her coat off, Sally proudly showed Annie the till rolls which marked up all the bar takings since she had been out of action. Annie was surprised at how much money they had taken. As far as she was aware, the number of customers had dwindled recently since all but the old men and the wounded were away fighting. To see that the figures had actually increased while she had been away was a pleasant surprise.

'Well done!' Annie said, not usually known for her lavish praise. 'I know that prices have risen a little but there seems to have been a sudden increase in customers. What's brought that about?' she asked. 'Did the army suddenly discharge them all? Or have those left behind been partying every night?'

Sally laughed. 'Nothing like that I'm afraid.' But there

was a mysterious glint in her eye. 'You'll soon see for yourself once we get busy.'

'Welcome back!'

'Lovely to see you again.'

'Good to have you back, though Lottie and Sally have been doing a splendid job.'

Annie inclined her head from side to side in acknow-ledgement of all the good wishes when she finally made an appearance from behind the curtain that separated off her living quarters.

'It's nice to be back.' 'Lovely to see *you* again.' 'Thank you for your kind message.'

She let a gracious smile play on her lips as she greeted each in turn in the way she had seen Queen Elizabeth do on the newsreels as she accompanied King George on their visits round the country. She was enjoying the attention almost as much as when she had been cast in the lead role in the amateur dramatic society before the war and had taken a final curtain call. She hadn't realized how much she had missed seeing all the familiar faces at the bar while she had been ill. She didn't really like being shut away from everything and everybody even if it was only for a few days. She was actually looking forward to being able to take on all the duties of her customary role as landlady once more, including pulling pints, though she would have to try to ease herself back into the job gradually.

It was interesting, she thought, how she had grown

used to being a publican at the Rovers. She had even become quite fond of the place and the job, and it surprised her how pleased she was to be back. Not that it had always been like that. She remembered how she had felt when she had first come here as a new bride. Running a hostelry had not been something she had ever aspired to. She had long accepted that her family's fortunes had really gone and she knew she would never be returning to the grand life she had once known, but when Jack had first proposed and suggested they become innkeepers she had dared to dream of a small country pub set in leafy Cheshire lanes. She saw Tudor-style oak beams, and horse brasses hanging on the walls but for Jack's sake she had been willing to consider the Rovers Return as a sort of trade apprenticeship, a place where she would learn all she could about the hospitality industry. Perhaps one of the most important lessons she learned in the early years was always to greet people with a cheerful smile, even if it didn't reflect how she felt. And that was a lesson that had stood her in good stead. Even when Mr Ridley himself had come to tell them that the brewery had no country pubs available for the foreseeable future she had somehow managed to grit her teeth and smile.

But things had changed since then. *She* had changed and she accepted for now that she would be happy enough to remain behind the bar at the Rovers Return. Not that she would admit that to anyone, especially not to Jack, for she would never give up on her dream.

What she hadn't expected to see on her return to the bar was so many new faces and several different uniforms and for the moment she thought she was in the middle of a Hollywood film set. For mixed in with the locals, whose voices she mostly recognised, was the unfamiliar drawl of American accents.

Sally laughed at Annie's astonished face. 'What do you think to that?' she said. 'I bet you didn't know the Yanks had arrived in full force, did you?'

'I knew there'd been more and more coming since the first batch arrived in January, but I hadn't realized there were such numbers arriving up here.'

Gracie nodded. 'We've got GIs, soldiers, airmen – and some Canadians as well for good measure. They're all over the country now and, fortunately for us, one of their bases is not far from here, in Warrington.'

'Well I never.' Annie didn't know whether to be pleased or sorry.

'Seems like they're trying out all the local pubs in the area and I'm doing my darnedest to make sure this is the one place they want to keep coming back to. And you know what they're saying? "Overpaid, over-sexed and over here".' Annie's eyebrows shot up in astonishment at Sally's choice of language but the young girl seemed not to notice. 'So I reckon we need to make the most of it,' Sally went on, 'because they seem to have access to all kinds of supplies we can't get hold of – cigarettes, nylon stockings, chocolate. They're pretty amazing.'

Now Annie laughed. 'Well, it looks like you're doing a good job of hanging on to them, young lady.' She was looking at the barmaid and actually smiling.

'I think I must be doing something right,' Sally grinned back. 'One of the men told me last night he was even getting to love warm beer.'

Annie looked puzzled at this and pursed her lips, unsure how to take what sounded like a backhanded compliment.

'Apparently, they serve all their drinks poured over ice cubes – "on the rocks", they call it over in America – and they even like their beer to be ice cold,' Sally explained. 'At first, they complained about the Shires being warm, but now I think they're beginning to get used to it.'

'So long as they keep coming back for more, I can hardly complain,' Annie said as she perched on a stool by the till and surveyed the room. She watched Elsie Tanner who was single-handedly entertaining the largest number of GIs and for once Annie was grateful Elsie was a regular customer. She was certainly the centre of attention tonight among one group of Yanks. It seemed that most of them couldn't keep their hands off her and she didn't mind that at all. She was flirting outrageously in true Elsie-style. At least, thought Annie, with so much misery around they're bringing some life and fun into the place. Without them things could easily deteriorate and we'd be left with a pretty dull atmosphere. Thanks also went to Sally, who was confidently pulling pints, serving the customers with a laugh and a joke and generally keeping the clients happy while Annie tossed tanners, shillings, half-crowns and florins into the cash drawer at a steady enough rate to make her one very happy lady.

Gracie didn't know what to wear as she sifted through the hangers on the rail that served as a wardrobe in her bedroom. Not that she had a lot to choose from. Clothes rationing meant she hadn't bought anything new for ages and several of her old clothes were actually worn out. But her real dilemma was whether to wear a skirt or trousers. Since she had taken to wearing trousers at the factory she had felt more comfortable in them and normally wouldn't have thought twice about wearing them when she was popping into a pub. But from what Lottie had told her about Annie Walker she began to worry that they might appear too casual for the landlady who sounded a little prim and proper. She discarded each thing onto the bed as she tried it on. Both the straight, pencil-line skirt with the side pockets and the slightly flared skirt with the patch pockets still looked to be in reasonable shape, whereas the trousers did look rather shabby. In the end, she settled for her cream pleated skirt because it went well with the coffee-and-cream-coloured jumper that she loved, even though she would have to remember not to lift her left arm for that would show up the darn there. The outfit made her feel more grown up and ladylike with its set-in sleeves that were gathered in tucks at the shoulders so that they looked like shoulder pads. It would give her a boost of confidence at what could prove to be a difficult meeting. She drew a stub of bright red lipstick across her lips, pinched her cheeks and looked at herself in the mirror. She smoothed down the tendrils of hair that persistently escaped from her ponytail and twisted this way and that to try to see her back. 'It will have to do,' she said out loud and ran down the stairs.

'Let's be having a look at you.' Mildred stopped her as she went to open the front door.

'I've no time now, Mum. I'm already late. I can't afford to give a bad impression. I'm scared enough without having to worry about that.'

'What on earth are you scared about? You'll knock 'em out.'

'Yeah, but you don't know what the landlady can be like. Lottie's been telling me and I can't help worrying: what if she doesn't like me?'

'Of course she'll like you. Everybody will.' Her mother gave her a kiss. 'Just be yourself and she can't fail to love you. But slow down for a moment. You know what'll happen if you keep rushing about. Your hair will fly out of its band for a start, and in no time at all you'll be looking a mess.'

'Oh, thanks a lot for that!'

'You didn't let me finish. What I was going to say was that at the moment it looks lovely. Just make sure to keep it that way.'

'And from what Lottie says, I must remember to smile,' Gracie said giving her mother a big grin. Mildred laughed.

'When do you not smile? Now go. And good luck.'

'Punctuality. That is what counts at all times, my dear,' was the first thing Annie Walker said, glancing up at the clock in the bar. Gracie's heart sank. As far as she understood they hadn't set a specific time for the inter-view but Annie had the bit between her teeth. 'Always remember that our clients expect us to open the doors on time and we have, by law, to close up on time. Fortunately, the bar is not officially open yet so we do have some time to talk before the rush begins.'

'Yes, Mrs Walker,' Gracie finally got an opportunity to say. 'I agree. I'm quite a stickler for timekeeping myself.' She didn't want to explain that she might have come sooner if she hadn't been dithering about what to wear. Annie smiled at her but there was no warmth in it and Gracie wondered for a moment if she had made a mistake in coming. Maybe this job was not for her after all. But she took a deep breath and calmed herself down. Then she lifted her chin and began to answer Annie's questions.

'And tell me, my dear, do you have a sweetheart away in the forces?' Annie said finally.

'No, I don't,' Gracie admitted. She was surprised by the question and wondered if that was going to make any difference to the outcome. But Annie merely looked directly at her and this time gave her a warm smile.

'I married mine,' she said unexpectedly. 'And now he's gone away, fighting abroad.' She looked so wistful Gracie couldn't help feeling a little sorry for her, but Annie quickly became businesslike again as she handed Gracie a pen and a piece of paper.

'Now, if you wouldn't mind writing your details on here and then working out the answers to the little sums that I've written out on the back . . .'

Gracie hadn't expected a test, though she supposed it was the best way to make sure she could read and write, and make the correct change if she had to handle customers' money. So she did her best approximation of the neat copperplate-style handwriting they had been taught in school, and wrote down in figures, as quickly and as accurately as she could, the solutions to the arithmetic questions. She took a deep breath while Annie was scrutinizing her answers and nervously tucked away the stray tendrils of hair that she could feel had escaped from her ponytail. Annie was reading carefully and didn't speak for several moments. When she looked up, Gracie stopped breathing for a second or two.

'When would you be free to start if I were to offer you the job?' Annie asked.

'Tomorrow,' Gracie said without hesitation. 'Does that mean I've got it?'

Annie's face finally creased with pleasure and the warmth of her expression at last reached her eyes. 'I would like to offer you a week's trial,' Annie said. 'At the end of that time we'll both be at liberty to call time on the offer, if you'll pardon the pun, if things haven't worked out. But I feel sure they will.' She put out her hand. 'I look forward to working with you, Gracie,' she said. 'I presume I may call you Gracie?'

'Yes, of course, and thank you very much.' Gracie grinned. She was surprised to find Annie's handshake was warmer than she had expected.

'And I'm Annie,' the landlady said. But the softness in her voice suddenly sharpened as she added, 'Although I prefer to be referred to as Mrs Walker in front of the customers.'

Annie was pleased she had managed the interview so soon after coming downstairs from her sickbed. It would certainly make her life easier to have a permanent barmaid in place. But then, she had always prided herself that she had learned how to gather good people around her, and it was an essential attribute at a time like this when she was running the pub and bringing up the children single-handed.

The only person she had been unsure of hiring was Ned Narkin, who had turned up as a potential potman, in answer to her ad, shortly after Jack had joined up. It was not an easy job to fill as all the young able-bodied men were abroad, fighting for the cause. Even those who weren't fit enough to join the forces, like Albert Tatlock, had taken on civic duties and become firefighters, ARP wardens or joined the Home Guard, jobs which occupied them full time. She had been forced to take on the only man who had shown up in response to the card she'd placed in the window. From the moment she first saw him she wasn't sure she trusted Ned Narkin, for she thought he had a shifty look about his eyes. He was too old for the army and he came with no references but she had no choice but to take him on. She needed a man about the place and she was pleased when he set to work in the cellar almost immediately, heaving the crates and barrels that were too heavy for her to lift.

Then one day, in a crisis, she had seen a different side to Ned. He surprised her when he'd fearlessly challenged two youngsters who were hanging around by the back door. They looked as though they were up to no good and he'd actually been injured when they took on his challenge and picked a fight with him. Annie warmed to him after that and she had to admit she felt safer during working hours having him about the place.

But hiring Gracie, of course, was a different matter. She seemed like a nice class of girl, very much in the Lottie mould, and she sounded to come from a decent family so Annie had a good feeling about her right from the start. Annie was sure she would be staying long beyond the week's trial she had offered her. When Sally and Lottie left, it would be a great comfort to have a bright young person like Gracie about the place.

Gracie forgot to walk with any kind of poise as she made her way back to Mallard Street and every few steps she did a little skip, followed by a hop, a step and a jump. She would have to mind her Ps and Qs with Annie, she could see that, but the idea of working behind the bar was so much better than being on the workbench in the factory. Wait till she told them at home. They might not be pleased about the cut in wages she'd had to agree to, but her mother, at least, would certainly understand that she would be much happier. She hoped Lottie would be pleased too. It would be hard work, she would be on her feet most of the day, but she wasn't afraid of that. And she'd have a chance to get some time off if they weren't busy. She had always been conscientious and having decided she really did want the job she would do her best to make a good impression from the start.

The only problem she could anticipate was the little tearaway she had seen several times being shooed out of the public area. He didn't look to be more than three, but the cleaning lady, Rose, had to chase him out of the bar several times even in the short time Gracie'd been there. When Annie proudly introduced her son, she seemed very relaxed about his behaviour but all Gracie could think was that Rose was a saint for putting up with his antics. Gracie's younger brothers had taught her all there was to know about mischief-making and she would hate to have to work with a little terror like that running round her feet. All she

51

could hope was she wouldn't have anything to do with him while she was working, for a public bar was certainly no place for such a little boy.

By the end of the week Annie was surprised how tired she was, given that she had spent much of her time perched on a bar stool by the till while her new barmaid, Gracie, ran around after the customers. But the constant buzz of conversation and the fog of smoke that permanently filled the atmosphere had given her a headache. Tobacco was supposed to be in short supply but there was no shortage of cigarettes among the American soldiers who were distributing packages of tens and twenties generously.

One afternoon Annie felt in desperate need of a rest and longed for a chance to go back upstairs for a brief break. As they weren't very busy, she signalled her intentions to Gracie and got down from the bar stool. She was about to slip away behind the curtain that separated the vestibule to her living quarters from the public bar when she saw a young girl, with long blonde hair straggling over her shoulders, push her way through the double doors of the street entrance. Her greasy-looking fringe almost covered her eyebrows and her eyes were virtually invisible as she tried to peer out from underneath. Her clothes were even shabbier than most of the young women who came into the Rovers these days. The last time she had seen such a young girl in the bar was when Elsie Grimshaw, now Elsie Tanner, living at number 11 Coronation Street, had first put in an appearance when she was not yet of an age to be drinking alcohol. Not that this girl had Elsie's poise, or the touch of glamour that had somehow surrounded Elsie even in her darkest days. The appeal and charm Elsie exerted over others was obvious right from the start, so that when Annie had insisted she be served only lemonade she knew for certain that Elsie's friends were slipping her the odd shot of gin. This one looked even younger than Elsie had been then and Annie could feel her hackles rising. She stepped down from the stool ready to do battle.

The fair-haired girl glanced about her almost furtively as she stepped nearer to the bar and, when she caught Annie's eye, it seemed as if she might turn and run out again. But then a resolute look crossed her face and she made a strange sight as she walked up to the counter in a determined manner. Large black shoes flapped out beneath a blue serge skirt, so that it looked like the old-fashioned Edwardian style. The skirt's coarse material was gathered at the waist under a stiff buckram band that seemed to be cutting her in half and the whole thing looked like a hand-me-down because it was too big and much too long for her, far longer than the current fashion dictated, given the limited availability of fabric. A tight, rib-knit jumper with several holes in it flattened whatever there was of her breasts. The girl's hands were hidden from view, plunged into the two side pockets, and a small wooden box was tucked under one arm.

'Can I help you? Annie asked in the most superior voice she could muster. Now that she was close to, she felt as if there was something familiar about the girl's face. Was it the unusually high cheekbones that didn't seem to have much flesh on them, or the narrow chin giving her a diffident, almost impish, look that Annie was sure she had seen before?

'I've not come to drink,' the girl said, 'if that's what you're thinking.'

Annie's laughter was steeped in sarcasm. 'I should hope not, young lady. I don't know who you are, but one thing I do know is that you are far too young to be in a pub at all. Now I must ask you to leave or they'll be after my licence.' The girl glanced down. She had released her hands from her pockets and was twisting her fingers awkwardly, only stopping now and then to pick at the cuticles. Her hands looked red and sore; Annie's response had obviously unnerved her and she suddenly seemed unsure.

'You'd better leave quietly before I get cross.' Annie made a waving motion in the direction of the door but the girl didn't move. She plunged her hands back into her pockets.

'I'll go as soon as you've answered my question,' she said, her voice suddenly strong.

'Oh, and what question is that?' Annie sounded amused.

'Is your name Anne?' she asked. 'I'm looking for someone called Anne.'

Annie's first reaction was to raise her eyebrows in astonishment. As the landlady of the Rovers Return she was not unknown in these parts, but she would never have expected a young girl to march in and ask for her by name like that. Then she frowned. She tilted her head trying to get a closer look at the girl's face; there was something familiar about those cheekbones . . .

'And who . . .' Annie began. But the girl cut across her.

'Did you used to work at Fletcher's Mill?' the girl asked.

Now Annie's jaw fell open and for a moment she was speechless. Nobody knew about the time she'd worked at the mill. Except for her mother and Jack, of course, but the shame of it would preclude Florence from ever disclosing the fact to anyone. She glanced round the room. Quite a few of the locals and several GI soldiers still lingered, though to her relief no one seemed to be listening to what the girl was saying.

'I think you'd better come this way,' Annie said abruptly, her voice stiff and unnatural, and lifting the velvet curtain she led the way through the little vestibule that lay behind it, and into the living room.

Gracie had seen the young girl enter the bar and was unsure what she should do so she was pleased that Annie had not yet gone upstairs and was still around to deal with her, but she was surprised to see Annie usher her into her private quarters. Annie had been looking tired before the girl appeared and was looking even more so after speaking to her. Gracie wondered who she was. She collected all the dead glasses and went to attend to Mrs Sharples, who had just banged her pint pot on the counter demanding immediate attention in her customary way. Gracie recognised the girl's face. She had seen her hanging round outside on her way into work but when Gracie had tried to smile at her she had quickly looked away. She had been carrying a small wooden box with her then and she was carrying it now. What could she want with Annie Walker, she wondered? What would she give to listen at the living room door in the vestibule!

'A pint of stout when you've finished dreaming.' It was Ena Sharples. Her reputation went before her and Gracie was anxious not to cross swords with her.

'Oh, sorry,' Gracie said. 'What can I get you?'

Ena shook her head at Gracie's forgetfulness, but for once she just pointed at the row of black bottles and didn't say anything.

Annie gathered herself in the time it took to usher the girl into the room and settle her in to a chair. It took a few moments but finally her breathing rate returned to normal. She would have welcomed any excuse to leave the room while she collected her thoughts. But she knew she couldn't do that.

She sat down opposite the girl and entwined her fingers so that her hands lay passively in her lap.

'Now then, young lady,' she said and smiled benignly, 'who are you exactly? And what is it you want to know?'

'I want to know if you're Anne Beaumont. It's not such a difficult question, is it?' The girl lifted her chin and tried to sound defiant but it was obvious her bubble of initial confidence was beginning to deflate as Annie's gaze didn't flinch. 'My name's Annette, Annette Oliver,' she added looking away.

Annie's brows knitted together. The name didn't immediately mean anything to her, but the similarity to her own name was not lost on her. 'Am I supposed to know you?' she asked.

The girl shrugged. 'Dunno.' She looked as if she was going to say something else but then changed her mind.

Annie's eyes were then drawn to a white lawn handkerchief Annette was pulling out of the box that had been under her arm. She could clearly see the initials that had been embroidered in the corner in red silk thread. AB. Now it was Annie's turn to look uncomfortable. She visibly blanched. 'Where did you get that?' she asked, her voice sharp now.

'It was in this box the orphanage gave me now I'm old enough.'

She passed it to Annie, who held it loosely in her fingers as if she were afraid to touch it. Then she let it fall into her lap. Even though her eyes had misted she could recognize the unevenly embroidered stitching and the sight of it brought back floods of unwelcome memories. She looked at the girl from under hooded lids. Annette was almost twelve years old, she'd said. Annie did some quick arithmetic and sat back in shock. She looked again at the handkerchief and her breathing quickened. Then she looked at the girl. There was something familiar about the girl's face, though she couldn't quite put her finger on what.

'I grew up in the orphanage, no one ever knew my mum or dad.' It was Annette who broke the silence. 'And for some reason they thought I should have the box on my twelfth birthday. It was the only thing that was left with me, apparently, when I was aban-doned in a shopping basket outside the gates. I was only a baby, just a few days old, one of the staff once told me, but no one had any idea where I came from.'

'That's very sad,' Annie said.

'I suppose it is, but it's all I've got. That handkerchief's my only clue, really. You recognize it, don't you? I can tell the way you was looking at it.' The girl was staring at her disconcertingly and Annie began to feel uncom-fortable.

'There was a dummy and a rattle in the box as well,' Annette went on. 'But they had no marks on them to say where they came from. Or where I came from, for that matter.' Annette stopped and stared directly at Annie. 'I was hoping the rattle might be silver so's it could make me rich.' She shook her head. 'No such luck, though.' Annette gave a little smile. 'It's shaped like a man in a funny hat and it's got bells hanging from it. Mean anything?'

Annie looked at her, her expression blank. She didn't know what to think. She shook her head slowly. Though she was still wracking her brains about what was so familiar about the girl's face.

'The box has a letter in it too, telling me to go look for Anne Beaumont. I haven't had much time lately because I've started working after school and most weekends as a scullerymaid in Grant House on the edge of the big park in Cheshire.'

'But that's miles from here.' Annie lifted her head and looked with pity at the young girl.

'I know. But whenever I gets a day off I goes looking. And though I save what I earn to help pay fares, I usually have to walk most of the way so it takes me a while. But I do what I can. I really wanted to find you.' She hesitated. 'That's supposing . . . you are Anne Beaumont?' She peered directly into Annie's face, as if she was hoping to recognize something, some specific feature.

Annie didn't answer. She looked down into her lap and fingered the white lawn square. What was Annette reading into this, she wondered? She shifted uncomfortably in her seat, feeling agitated and unsure. How did Annette think she was related to AB?

'Do you want to see the letter?' Annette stood up and carefully unfolded the fragile piece of paper into Annie's lap. Then she stood behind her so she could read it over Annie's shoulder. 'See?' She pointed a red, swollen finger. 'See there, it says I'm to contact Anne Beaumont from Clitheroe. That *is* you, init? I know I'm right.'

Annie picked up the delicate letter by the corner. It looked as if it had been torn from a notebook. She turned it over but there was nothing written on the back. The letter wasn't signed and she didn't recognize the tiny scrawl. Finally, she gave a little nod.

'Yes, it is me,' she said. 'Beaumont was my maiden name. But . . . but I don't know how my handkerchief ended up in your box. I . . . I don't know anything about your mother,' she said softly.

Annette stiffened.'

'The trouble is . . .' Annie hesitated. 'I don't know how you think I can help you.'

Annette didn't reply.

'Do you know who wrote the letter? You do realize it could have been written by anybody?' Annie said.

Annette hung her head. She sighed and her shoulders dropped as she turned away and slumped back into the chair.

'I've been looking for you for ages,' was all she said then.

'But the fact that your letter mentions me by name is no proof that I've any connection with your mother,' Annie said, 'or that I even know who she is. For all we know, it could be a different Anne Beaumont entirely.'

'I suppose so.' Annette sounded dejected. She leaned forward and put out her hands in a pleading gesture. 'But I've got to find out about her. I've got to know where I come from and the letter says you could help . . .' Her voice cracked and a tear plopped onto the carpet.

'Are you sure you—' the girl tried again, but Annie cut in sharply, 'The letter is wrong.' Her voice was firm, but then she saw the despondent look on the girl's face and Annie had to look away. 'I'm truly sorry, Annette,' Annie said sadly, 'but I'm afraid I can't help you.'

Gracie was pulling a pint of Shires for Albert Tatlock when the bedraggled young girl finally came out from Annie's living quarters, the small wooden box still tucked under her arm. Gracie watched her make her way to the door, her shoulders slumped. Annie was only a few steps behind her, as if to make sure she didn't turn to come back into the bar. Gracie thought Annie looked a lot paler now than she had before and somehow even more weary, though her jaw seemed set in a kind of grim determination. Neither she nor the girl spoke so Gracie was left to wonder who the stranger was and what she had wanted.

As soon as Annette had gone, Annie climbed the stairs as fast as her unsteady legs would carry her but she stood uncertainly on the landing for a few moments, remembering the feel of the handkerchief, seeing again the words of the letter. Her legs were trembling and she had to work hard to control her breathing as her mind was flooded with memories. She gripped hold of the bannister and opened her eyes wide, hoping the sight of the vase of silk flowers tucked into the recess on the landing would help to shut out the images that assailed her.

Annie felt sorry for Annette. How dreadful not to have any idea who your parents were. She had seemed a nice enough child, but Annie really hoped she would never have to meet her again. For Annette, even in her short visit, had managed to rake up so many painful memories of heat and lung-filling dust, memories of long, uncomfortable hours in a loom shed; memories Annie would rather forget.

Chapter 3

1927

Annie was eighteen years old when she went to work in Fletcher's Mill; not something, even in her wildest imaginings, that she had ever thought she might be doing. Her dreams had been of stage and screen stardom. She had assumed she would be living the life of a lady, once she had secured a good marriage to some rich eligible young man, someone who matched the standing of her own prestigious background, and she had never thought beyond that. But then their family fortunes had changed dramatically and their status and upper-middle-class life style had disappeared overnight.

When she saw her parents being unceremoniously dumped out of the back of their erstwhile gardener's old wagon and left at the front door of the two-up, two-down terraced cottage on the poorest side of Clitheroe, Annie rushed out of the house to greet them. She could see at once how hard this was going to be for them to grasp that this was, for the foreseeable future, to be their new home.

'They can't expect us to live here!' Edward Beaumont stood, shoulders hunched, amid the straggling weeds on the moss-ridden flagstones. The bowler hat he was clutching seemed so out of place he didn't try to put it back on and he scratched his almost bald head in puzzlement.

'Who's "they"? Annie asked wearily. She knew what her father would say, but she thought that hearing him put voice to the words might help all of them to make sense of their plight.

'The authorities . . . the mill owners . . . Oh, I don't know. Whoever owns these kinds of places.' He gestured towards the front door in exasperation.

Annie shrugged. 'Why shouldn't we have to live here? It's no worse a house than lots of people live in.' She was feeling wretched and deflated but was determined not to show it in her parents' presence.

Having arrived first and already explored what she could only describe as a doll-sized house, she felt helpless and knew they would too. She had never been to this part of the town before and now she was here she knew why. Inside herself she was feeling as lost as her parents were. They were all still trying to make sense of what they had been reduced to, to work out how their fortunes had turned so completely around, but Annie thought it politic to try to put on a brave face.

'I've had a little time to have a look around before you came,' she said, 'and from what I've seen and heard from the neighbours I think this one's a step up from what some people have to put up with round here.'

'What do you mean by a step up? We would never have let one of our tenants live in a hovel like this, never mind us. This is nothing but a working-class slum that should have been cleared years ago,' her father blustered.

'I suppose even the working classes have to live somewhere, and if they don't have enough money to do them up—' Annie began.

'But we're not like those lower sort of people,' Florence cut in, 'and we can't live in a place like this.' She sounded most indignant. 'We can't be expected to live amongst them.' Now she was openly dismissive. 'Just because we have no money doesn't bring us down to their level, you know.' She flapped her arms vaguely, as if to dismiss the whole neighbourhood. 'It doesn't matter what our financial situation is, we could never be considered to be the same as the labouring classes. They are of a completely lower order. That is just the way it is.'

There was an old lady sitting on the doorstep of one of the terraced houses opposite, with some tired-looking knitting in her lap. She must have thought Florence was waving and she waved back.

Florence tossed her head in disgust and turned away. But Annie waved to their new neighbour and gave her a tired smile. 'That's Mrs Brockett, that old lady over there,' Annie said. 'She's lived here all her married life. She's actually very nice.'

Florence peered down her nose and looked at Annie as if she was mad. 'How on earth did you come to that conclusion? The poor old thing looks like she's a permanent fixture in that chair.'

Annie laughed, trying to lighten the mood. 'You're right there, Mother. I think she sits out on the doorstep every day unless it's raining, but I had a chance to chat to her before you arrived.'

'Did you, indeed?' Florence didn't look impressed and she actually shuddered.

'As long as we're stuck here she might turn out to be a very useful lady to know. She seems to know most of what goes on in the street,' Annie said.

'I hope you didn't tell her any of our affairs?' Florence's reprimand was as swift as it was sharp. 'I know I certainly shan't be giving her the time of day.'

Annie ignored her mother. 'She thinks we're very fortunate that we have our own lavatory and she says we should be grateful we have a tap for water actually in the kitchen.'

'Grateful? For a lavatory and running water? Are you mad, girl?' Now her father spoke up. 'This is the end of the 1920s. Surely everyone has water and water closets these days?'

'It seems not,' Annie said carefully. 'Not round here at any rate. But, apparently, it's a real bonus having our own lavatory, just for the family's use. Although . . .' She hesitated, thinking of their old home. 'It is outside.' She tried not to pull a face as she said this for she didn't want to tell them just yet that it would need a jolly good clean before any of them could think of using it. 'Apparently,' she thought she'd better add, 'many of the houses in these terraces have to share a toilet with half the street. And there are several who have to carry their water indoors in buckets that they fill from some kind of communal standing pipe in the yard.'

Annie thought her mother was going to faint when she said this, so she quickly pushed open the front door and ushered them inside. But that didn't improve either of her parents' demeanours. Florence looked so lost and bewildered standing in the middle of the single downstairs room that was to serve as a living room-cum-kitchen for the three of them that Annie almost felt sorry for her. But when Florence wailed, 'We can't possibly live here! There's no room for anything,' Annie thought she would lose patience. She watched Edward and Florence as they stood regarding the few meagre items they had begged to salvage from the bailiffs, while the rest were ignominiously sold, together with the bedding they had been allowed to keep. The few selected items of clothing they had clung on to had been bundled up like rags and lay discarded by the front door.

'At least there's two separate bedrooms upstairs,' Annie said quickly, hoping to distract them. 'They're off a small landing.' She indicated the stairs at the back of the room.

'And where will the servant sleep?' Florence enquired.

Then Annie's patience snapped. She felt so exasperated at her mother's inability to grasp the magnitude of the tragedy that had befallen them that she thought she was going to scream out loud. She herself was struggling to understand what had happened to them, but how could she get it into her mother's head that life was never going to be the same as it had once been? When Florence began to cry, it was all Annie could do not to strike out and hit her. Surely she, as the child, was the one who needed her parents' support?

'Shall I show you the bedrooms?' Annie said, gritting her teeth. 'Then you can see for yourself exactly how much room there is.'

Florence shook her head. 'Not just yet, dear. I haven't the strength.'

There was a wooden table and a bench and two chairs that had been left by the previous tenants by the window in the front room. Florence wiped the seat of one of the chairs with her white lawn handkerchief and sat down. She also tried to wipe away the powdery film of dust that covered the scratched wood of the table, but when she leaned against it the table wobbled back and forth, so she pulled back, sitting up as straight as she could. Edward sat in the other chair without paying heed to the dust that was being transferred from the splintered wooden seat to his best Crombie overcoat. Annie kept her back as erect as possible when she took a place on the bench.

They all stared in the direction of the window, though it was too grimy to see out of it. Suddenly, there was a wailing sound that made Annie jump.

'What's going to become of us?' It was Florence who had cried out. 'And what's going to happen to our lovely home? Who's going to look after it until we're ready to go back?' She prodded her husband who was sitting beside her, looking bemused. 'We can't desert it now, Edward. It's been in your family for generations.' She shook her head from side to side as though in disbelief. 'The beautiful summerhouse and the old oak tree down by the lake . . . I know how much you love it all, Edward. Will the gardener really look after it while we're away? How much will he do if you're not there to prod him and remind him?' She covered her face with her hands for a moment.

'You can ask my father about the house and the estate when you next see him,' Edward growled angrily. Scowling, he kicked a piece of garden rubble from where it had stuck to his shoe to the other side of the stone floor.

'Don't be disrespectful of the dead.' Florence sounded horrified.

'What respect did he show me when he left me the legacy of all his debts? Don't call me disrespectful,

69

madam, when it's me who's had to sacrifice the family inheritance to pay off his creditors. When it's me and my family who've been reduced to this.' He looked round the room in disgust. 'How can you respect someone who, despite his years, still had no idea what made for a good business deal and what made for a bad investment?'

'I always thought Grandpa was rich,' Annie intervened, for she recognized the expression on her father's face as one that meant they were in for a long harangue.

'He was when I was a young lad. But I was too young to understand that money was leaking out of the estate faster than it was coming in. As I grew older, if ever I questioned anything, he always found ways to cover up his incompetence.' Edward closed his eyes and took a deep breath. 'I can't say I blame the family entirely for turning their backs on us. I suppose we must look like a piteous lot.'

At this Florence had a fresh outburst of tears. 'Not one of them put out a hand to help. I wouldn't have expected the bailiffs to show much sympathy, but Edward, your own brothers? I ask you.'

'I know.' Edward sounded resigned. 'Charity begins at home, I told him. But that meant nothing to him. He was too busy feeling smug about how he had managed to hang on to his own fortune that, fortunately for him, had nothing to do with the family's money.'

'Uncle William was in the same position but at least he did find you a job,' Annie chipped in.

'Doing what?' Edward was scornful. 'As a clerk at a mill?'

'A senior clerk,' Florence corrected him.

'A clerk nevertheless,' he repeated. 'At Fletcher's Mill. In the worst part of Clitheroe I've ever seen.'

'At least Uncle William was true to his word,' Annie said as patiently as she could. 'You said the mill does have a job for you?'

Edward nodded. 'I suppose that's something. I understand there's not much work about these days.'

'I know,' Annie said. 'The country is still struggling from the disastrous financial effects of the war and it's affecting everyone.'

'But what do I know about cotton mills?' Edward was still grumbling. 'I've never done a day's work outside of the estate in my life. All I know is about managing smallholdings and woodlands, supervising the gardeners, and collecting the rents from the tenants' cottages. That's my line of work. Not cotton mills.' He got up and stomped round the room.

'At least it's a clean job and it's honest work,' Annie said.

'Well, Daddy certainly couldn't have entertained getting a manual job like those dreadful men we passed on the way here. They looked so rough.' Florence was trembling as she spoke. 'Really low, working-class men they looked. They probably spend half their lives in a pub,' she added contemptuously. 'You must never forget, Annie, that regardless of what has happened to

71

us we are not like the common people of the lower orders.'

'At least whatever wages you get will put some food on the table,' Annie said to her father who seemed to be preoccupied peering into cupboards.

He stood up. 'As I see it, most of whatever pittance of a wage I earn will be going in rent. Imagine, we have to pay rent for this . . . this hovel.'

'Don't worry, Daddy,' Annie said encouragingly. 'I'll go to work too. Just as soon as I can find a job.'

She thought that would please him, but instead of looking happy her father shook his head. 'That's wonderful. We are descendants of the line of the great Beaumonts of Clitheroe; we can trace our roots back to William the Conqueror and we're used to having nothing but the best. We should be enjoying servants to make our lives comfortable as we get older and instead my only daughter is talking about going out to work.'

'Not just me. Mummy, you will have to work too,' Annie said, though she was not sure how that would be received.

Her father raised his eyebrows and Florence looked aghast. But Annie sounded determined. 'Don't you agree, Mummy? I suggest you make it known among the neighbours that you're an extremely able needle-woman. It would help enormously if you could begin to take in some sewing.'

Florence looked shocked. 'You seem to have an answer for everything, young lady,' she admonished.

'So tell me, who's going to do all the cooking and cleaning, not to mention the shopping? We'll need to get someone in to see to all of that. Small as it is, the house will still need to be looked after, not to mention that we'll need someone to look after us. You've already told us there are only two bedrooms, so I imagine the servant will somehow have to sleep down here.'

Annie looked at her mother with pity now, but Florence was following a new train of thought as she looked round the dismal room.

'Those wretched bailiffs have allowed us to keep so few possessions that I don't know where to begin, but I need to start making a list of what we'll need to buy and what the servant will need to do.' She sniffed. 'Not that there's sufficient space to bring in much in the way of furniture.' There was barely enough room for the few bits they had been allowed to salvage from their old house. Annie thought back to the morning of the previous day when she'd watched helplessly as the bailiffs piled their few bags onto a wagon that the horses then drove away. By some miracle, the boxes were waiting for them when Annie had first arrived, but they didn't actually amount to much. Annie stood up. She couldn't sit here and listen to more of her mother's delusional ramblings. There were things to be done – and even if it hadn't dawned on Florence yet, Annie understood that she and her mother were the ones who would have to do them.

She looked at the ashes in the grate that must have

heated the range at the back of the room near the stairs. Perhaps the first thing she needed to do was to learn how light a fire. Not that it was cold, fortunately, but as long as there was no fire, she now realized, there wouldn't be any hot water for tea. She went into the back yard and then into the alleyway beyond to look for some kindling and old scraps of paper which she had seen their kitchenmaid turn into a fire at home. She collected what she could and went back inside.

'And who's going to do the shopping and the cooking? You haven't answered me that one.' Florence was trailing round after her now, following her into the scullery where Annie was searching for any usable pots. 'We've lost cook and the butler and all the servants,' her mother was wailing. 'I don't know how we shall begin to replace them.'

To Annie's disgust she thought her mother was going to cry again. Instead, Florence whined, 'Who's going to feed us?' And she sat down again by the table once more, only this time with her head in her hands.

'Sadly, we need to wake up to the fact that nobody but us is going to feed us, Mother.' Annie had tried to be gentle but now she spoke more sharply. 'We'll have to learn how to feed ourselves.'

At that, Florence jerked up her head but before she could say anything Annie jumped in. 'The fact of the matter is that you and I will have to learn some new housekeeping skills. I've already spoken to Mrs Brockett, the old lady we saw before, across the road.' She held up her hands before her mother could respond. 'Not that I've told her much about our exact position but she has agreed to try to help us. In exchange for the odd loaf of bread, she'll give me some cooking lessons.'

Florence looked bemused. 'Where will we buy the bread from to give her?'

'Oh, Mother!' Annie became exasperated. 'That's the whole point. We won't buy it. We'll make it ourselves. She'll show me how to do it and how to cook a few simple meals. She'd help you too if only you'd agree. She has very kindly said she'll tell me what ingredients we have to buy and where to get them and then she'll show me how to cook them over the fire.'

Then Florence did begin to cry in earnest. She had barely been inside the kitchen in the grand house in Clitheroe except first thing in the morning when she used to check in with the housekeeper and issue orders for the day's meals to the cook. But Annie had no time for her.

'Oh, really, Mother, do pull yourself together.' She could no longer hide her exasperation. 'Here, have a look at this.' She threw the *Clitheroe Echo* down onto the table. 'Maybe you can find yourself a job this way. I know there's not much around at the moment, particularly for women. These are depressing times, as Daddy said. The men claimed back all their jobs after the Great War so there's precious little available for ladies right now. But you never know.' The front page was filled with classified ads and she had ringed a few items. 'I'm hoping I might have something lined up pretty soon. I shall be going into town this very afternoon to at least one shop where I believe there's a vacancy.'

Florence looked up. 'Really, darling! Some of the things you say. The very idea of it. Are you trying to shock me or something?'

Annie stared at her mother in disbelief. 'What do you mean?'

'I mean, how can you say such a thing? A daughter of mine even thinking of going out to work in a shop. You can't seriously want to do that – what on earth would people say?'

Annie shook her head and gave a disdainful laugh. 'It's not a question of wanting to, Mother, but it's needs must when the devil drives, you have to know that.'

'Annie, for goodness sake. I do hope you're not implying that it's the devil that's driving you.'

Annie held her breath for a moment before replying. She was afraid her mother really didn't understand the seriousness of their situation. 'I fear I am, Mother,' she said eventually. 'But the trick is: we can't allow the devil to win.'

'But what will you do in this "job" of yours? Where have you decided to work?' Florence made no attempt to look at the paper. 'I can't read in this light without my glasses.'

Annie sighed. 'It may not be a question of choice.' Annie was trying to be practical and realistic, though she had no doubt about her ability to carry out any one of the first few jobs she had marked. 'Obviously, I shall look for as good a position as possible but I may have to take whatever I am offered.'

Florence looked horrified, so Annie went on, 'My preferred position would be as a saleslady in one of the fashionable hat shops in town. See, I've noted the first one here.' They were brave words, spoken with more confidence than she felt, but Annie was frustrated that neither of her parents seemed to understand the gravity of their predicament. If her father's wages would only cover the rent and she and her mother didn't find a job quickly they might well be in danger of starving.

Upstairs, in the tiny bedroom under the roof, the one with the single bed, Annie crouched over the laundry bag of clothes she had managed to bring with her. Most of them she now realized would be completely unsuitable for the kind of life she would be leading in the future, but maybe she could persuade her mother to put her skill with a needle to good use in her own home first.

She picked out the smartest of the dresses she had been able to keep. It was in a soft blue wool and she thought it would be very suitable for working in a milliner's shop. It had three-quarter-length sleeves and a nipped-in waist and she knew it was very stylish. Fortunately, only a few weeks before the bailiffs had come, she'd bought a pert little felt hat from her own milliner's that matched the blue of the dress perfectly.

She might as well wear it for the interview before she had to go through the whole shaming process once more of selling her clothes, or worse still, having to pawn them. The blue hat was really cute with a sideways-tilting brim and a small ostrich feather slotted into the petersham ribbon that ran around the base; it sat on top of her blonde sausage-curls in the most flattering way. She was glad she had thought to keep it when she had had to sell all her other lovely clothes. She didn't know how long she would be able to hang on to it but for now at least it seemed like the perfect outfit for a job interview.

Annie set off into town where the shop was located. She didn't have enough money for the bus fare both ways so decided she would walk back and took the bus to her destination, not wanting to appear hot and flustered even though that was how she was feeling. The sign above the door said Elliott's Fine Millinery in gold script lettering. As she pushed open the door a bell tinkled in the distance and an older lady popped out immediately from a room behind the shop.

'Good afternoon and how may I help you? I'm Mrs Elliott.' The woman beamed at her as if she were a customer and looked prepared to show her an array of hats.

Annie thought she should come right to the point. 'Good afternoon. I am here about the vacancy,' she said. 'I saw from your advertisement in the *Clitheroe*

Echo that you have a retail position available. I hope I am not too late to apply?'

'Not at all,' Mrs Elliott said affably, although her smile faded a little, but her eyes examined Annie from top to toe. Annie met her gaze; she felt equal to any such scrutiny.

'May I ask how old you are?'

'I'm eighteen.'

'That's perfect,' the older woman agreed.

Annie began to feel more confident. The job would be hers, she was sure of it. 'Perhaps you would be kind enough to fill out this form.' Mrs Elliott produced an official-looking piece of paper from under the counter. 'It's so that we may have your details on file.'

Annie thought this sounded promising until she actually began to write. No sooner had she written her name than she hesitated on the next line. She was tempted to give the more impressive Clitheroe address of her former home, but what if they tried to contact her and found out she no longer lived there? She took a deep breath and, with a flourish, wrote 16 Alderley Street, Norwesterly Clitheroe, before handing it back across the counter.

Mrs Elliott looked at it, the smile never wavering from her face, but when she posed her next question the eagerness had gone from her voice.

'And what previous retail experience do you have, Miss Beaumont?' she asked. 'Is it in millinery or in some other commodity of ladies' fashion wear?'

Annie felt her own smile begin to fade. 'I-I don't have any such experience, I'm afraid. But I'm an extremely quick learner,' she added eagerly.

'I don't doubt it. But perhaps you have some other working experience that may be relevant?'

Annie realized, with dismay, that saying she had no experience of work of any kind would not be to her advantage. She wracked her brains but could think of nothing she had done in the past, other than being a valued client, that would prepare her for working in a hat shop. It hadn't occurred to her that just being Annie Beaumont late of Clitheroe Town might not be sufficient recommendation, as it had been in the past, for whatever she decided to turn her hand to.

As the silence lengthened, Mrs Elliott said, 'I'm afraid we must insist on taking on someone with prior experience and impeccable references as I'm sure you understand. The job calls for a trained saleslady who would be able to step in and pick up the reins immediately. We don't have the time to train someone up.'

'May I ask how I'm supposed to gain this experience if you won't give me a job where I could learn?' Annie could hear the desperation in her voice and hated herself for it. It sounded almost like begging.

Now Mrs Elliott's smile was positively condescending as she said, 'I'm sure there are plenty of small local shops where you could gain an invaluable apprenticeship. Although not, perhaps, ones in the immediate vicinity of Alderley Street. They may not offer the kind of experience we would be looking for. I mean you could hardly expect a—'

Annie didn't wait to hear the rest. 'Thank you for your time,' she said with as much dignity as she could muster. And she turned on her heel and walked out, trying to hide the burning tears of humiliation that stung behind her lids.

She had been so convinced she would be offered the job at Elliott's Fine Millinery she hadn't bothered to write down the addresses of the other retail positions she had seen advertised in the local paper, though she had noted they were all within walking distance of each other. So, after her initial disappointment, she set off scouring the neighbourhood to see if she recognized the names of any of the shops and if they matched the shops that had advertised they had positions available. She found two more milliners' shops and a retail dress shop that had placed ads in the paper and at first her hopes soared when she found them. But when the shopkeepers' reactions were similar to Mrs Elliott's, she soon began to feel deflated. Even if they didn't balk visibly when she gave her address as Alderley Street, Norwesterly Clitheroe, in what she now realized was the slum heart of the working-class neighbourhood, they were not prepared to overlook the fact that she had no retail experience, or indeed, experience of work of any kind. After each interview, she began to feel so disheartened it was difficult to pick herself up again ready for another one. Even when she found two more shops, one selling ladies' underwear and one selling ballgowns, that had not been advertised in the *Echo*, but which had discreet postcards propped up in the window, the result was the same. After the initial question and response routine exposed her lack of experience, she turned on her heel and walked away. By the time she had visited all the retail shops that she could find that required staff, it was getting dark and she thought about the long walk home. As she turned in the direction of Norwesterly, she accepted there was no point in trying for any more similar jobs. It was time to admit defeat and look for something else.

There had been one other job in the *Clitheroe Echo* which had caught her attention but she had initially discounted it as not the kind of work she wanted. However, after such a fruitless day, she now realized that unskilled labour might be the only kind of work she was fit for. She knew where Fletcher's Mill was, even though she hadn't actually been there, for it was where her father worked in the administration offices. Not that their paths would cross if she did get the work, for the job on offer was for a loom operator, to work in the loom sheds which involved longer hours than any clerical job. The ad had said there would be training available and that, despite the long hours, she would be earning a pittance of a wage. She knew her mother would not find it palatable that any daughter of hers should have to be nothing better than a mill girl, and in this instance she wondered what her father would have to say about it too. Not that it mattered; she had tried her hardest to find more genteel work but it seemed obvious to her now that no matter how hard she tried there would be nothing forthcoming on the retail front.

The following morning, when Annie first set eyes on the sprawling complex that was Fletcher's cotton mill, she was appalled. The only word she could think of to describe it was 'Victorian', but it was a far cry from the wealthy Clitheroe kind of Victorian buildings she was used to. This was a forbidding-looking compound surrounded by high walls that looked more like a prison. It was old-fashioned and out of date, a relic of the industrial revolution. As she approached the grimy, red brick buildings with the tall chimneys belching foul-coloured smoke she didn't change her opinion. It was like taking a step back in time and she couldn't believe she was about to put herself forward for a job in such a place. What was she thinking of? If only Mrs Elliott had been able to see beyond her lack of experience.

Fletcher's Mill was quite some way out of the town centre in Norwesterly and the only thing in its favour, if she could get the job, was that she wouldn't have to spend precious pennies, or too much time, travelling to and from work each day. No longer so confident that she would even be offered a job, she approached the man at the gate cautiously and asked to see the manager.

The first thing that hit her as soon as she entered the building was the hot, steamy atmosphere. There seemed to be no ventilation and, as she inhaled the dense, foggy air of the main looming shed, she knew she was making a mistake. She wanted to turn and run away while she still could, back to the fresh air and sunshine outside, but she had no choice. She desperately needed this job, any job, and for a moment she was rooted to the spot. It was like entering an alien world. The air was dense with cotton dust so that it was hard to see through the haze, and the heat and humidity made it very difficult to breathe. The fibres caught the back of her throat and made her cough.

The other thing that struck her was the noise, for what assailed her ears even before the doorman let her into the shed was the din, the like of which she had never heard before. The clatter and racket of the machinery, pounding down hundreds of times a minute, was compounded by the ceaseless whirring of a million hissing wheels rendering any kind of conversation almost impossible. As the sore, bloodshot eyes of the loom operators turned towards her momentarily, she fancied she could hear wolf-whistles even above all the cacophony. At least, she could see many lips pursed into whistle shapes as men and women alike eyed her up and down, eyebrows raised.

She was wearing what she thought of as her interview

outfit and suddenly felt foolish. It might have been suitable for impressing Mrs Elliott, but it certainly wasn't appropriate for the interview she was about to have. She wished she had thought to wear something more appropriate. But then she straightened her back and stood as tall as she could when she saw the manager coming towards her. As he negotiated his way down the narrow passageway between the looms she could see him chastising the floor workers with a flick of his finger, indicating they should be watching their machines rather than watching her. Then he directed her to the glass booth at the end of the shed that served as his office. When he closed the door, she was aware that it only shut out the highest decibel level of noise and she still had to strain to hear what he said.

Annie sat down and fanned her face with a cotton handkerchief she kept in her pocket now that she had relinquished all her leather handbags. It was unevenly embroidered in red silk with her initials. 'Is it always so hot in here?' she asked.

'It's got to be, unless you want the thread to keep breaking,' he said.

'Oh.' Annie felt dismayed, but what could she say?

'How do you like the racket?' Mr Mattison asked, grinning as he shouted louder than necessary.

'I don't,' she said. 'But I suppose you get used to it.' Annie's throat already felt sore from shouting.

He shrugged. 'There are five hundred sodding looms out there thumping down two hundred times a minute, so it's no wonder they make such a bloody racket. And that in't going to change either.' He laughed a mirthless laugh, then he began to bark some basic questions at her. Annie shouted back her answers, hoping he could hear them. Then after only a few moments, she thought he said she could have the job. Under the circumstances, she wasn't sure whether she'd heard him correctly.

'Are you offering me the job?' She thought she'd better ask for clarification.

'Yes!' he shouted, nodding his head. 'As you're here, you can have it. When can you start?' He answered his own question before she had a chance to consider. 'Right this minute couldn't be soon enough for me, though I can see you're perhaps not quite prepared . . .' His eyes appraised her from top to toe. 'But that's the bugger of it. The job that were advertised int' *Echo* were filled yesterday night. That were to replace the stupid bitch that's got herself pregnant like she seems to do every other bloody year.' His face registered disgust. 'She's away more than she's here. She's like a bleeding bitch on heat that one, I'm telling you. Not a thought for anyone else, I don't know why we keep having her back. But then, would you believe, one of our best girls suddenly went off sick this morning, without any warning. So we're another one down and I'm having to cover while that poor old sod Marjorie out there,' he pointed towards the other end of the shed, 'is having to watch two frigging areas at once.'

Annie was horrified to hear such language. She'd

never heard the likes of it addressed to her before, and the words he used were getting cruder each time he opened his mouth. It was all she could do not to reprimand him. She had half a mind to remind him she was a lady who was not used to hearing such vulgar words, but when she remembered the looks of disdain she had received as she'd walked down to his office she thought better of it. This was a new world she was descending into, rather like Orpheus had descended into Hell. And as Rudyard Kipling had once said, she must learn to bite the bullet. If this was the price she had to pay to save her family, then so be it. She would somehow have to close her ears to the foulness that seemed to flow so readily out of this man's mouth and do whatever it was she had to do. At least she wouldn't be able to hear him while she was on the shop floor.

'I could start tomorrow if you like,' Annie said, 'although you are aware that I've had no experience with any machinery like this?' She had no wish to be caught out and humiliated again.

'Pay no mind to that, you needn't sweat over it cos we'll train you. The work's not hard. If them buggers out there can do it, then sure as hell you can.'

Annie looked out at the tired-looking women who were etching grease and grime into their faces each time they swiped their glowing foreheads. Some of them looked as if they could hardly lift their arms to adjust the looms or load fresh yarn. Their legs were no longer straight and looked as though they wouldn't support their meagre bodies much longer. The poor souls looked about ready to drop. Annie sighed. She wanted to ask him what he meant by 'not hard' but thought he might interpret her query as sarcasm.

'It's six days a week, one week off when the place closes down for wakes week in summer.' Annie bit her tongue as she accepted his offer of a pittance for wages. It was demeaning, but she knew she had no other choice. No doubt the pay would be in line with all the others out there, only hers would reflect her novice status. Annie stood up and prepared to leave. She decided not to offer her hand in a farewell greeting but she felt impelled to shake his calloused fingers when he shot his hand out in her direction.

'See you tomorrow then,' he said. 'Sharp at seven, mind. You clock on by the main gate as you come in. Your time starts ticking from there. Time wasted for whatever reason is time docked off your pay. So if you arrive late, knock off a minute early, take too long a dinner break or go to the lav too many times, you can expect a smaller pay packet. You don't get to clock off till six.'

Annie wished she could at least have taken her hat off as she once more ran the gauntlet and dodged between the huge machines. But it was too late for that now. She would no doubt be recognized by all those who had watched her coming in. It was difficult to imagine that by tomorrow she would be one of them and she would have preferred not to leave herself open to even more ridicule. She noticed many of the women were wearing trousers and she wondered how quickly her mother might be able to run up a pair from an old skirt for her. Maybe Mrs Brockett would be able to give her some advice on how she could knit a cardigan or a warm shawl if she unpicked one of the jumpers that she had salvaged, and turn it into something more fitting for getting to and from a loom shed. She drew herself to her full height so that she could leave with some dignity, but as she walked out of his office she felt his hand spanking her so hard across her bottom she knew his fingers must have left print marks. She spun round to find he was laughing.

'Like that, did you? Play your cards right, there could be plenty more. Pretty girl like you.' He winked at her. Astonished and appalled, Annie didn't know how to respond, so she turned on her heel and walked away as fast as she could, relieved to realize that he hadn't followed her out.

Things went badly from the first moment she started working at the mill. On the first morning she arrived in good time at the front gate but she put her card in the wrong way round and caused an angry queue to form behind her as the overseer tried to sort it out. She knew, without being told, that she and everyone in the line behind her would see less of their wages come Friday night for not clocking on, on time, even though it hadn't been their fault.

'God, it's bloody her,' she heard someone in the crowd say. 'The frigging goddess in the crazy hat. She was bloody looking down her nose at us yesterday night. Yer might have guessed she'd cause trouble soon as she got here today. What idiot thought she was up to the job?'

Annie knew immediately they were talking about her but she didn't make eye contact with anyone and tried to keep her face neutral, as if she hadn't heard. She had been hoping she wouldn't stand out from the crowd today and had deliberately worn an old skirt and blouse covered with a sort of overall that her mother had quickly fashioned out of an old sheet. She'd covered her hair with a headscarf she herself had cut and hemmed from the same sheet, as she'd been advised to keep it out of the way of the machinery. She knew that dreadful, sometimes fatal, accidents were all too frequent in mills such as this and she'd rolled it in the mud patch in front of the house then rinsed it through several times to make it look old and worn, hoping she would look no different from the others, but she was perturbed to find they quickly found other ways to single her out.

'D'you mean the one that was sat like a stuffed dummy in old Henry's office?' someone else chimed in.

'My dear, do you mean Mr Mattison?' another one queried, trying to make her voice sound terribly posh.

'Don't tell me she's bloody well going to work here?'

'As what? That's what I'd like to know?'

'Not a bleeding supervisor?'

'Don't be so sodding daft. How could she supervise? She doesn't look like she's ever done an honest day's work in her life,' someone else said and everyone round her guffawed.

'Aye,' others agreed. 'She looks sodding useless.'

'I don't know,' a young man's reedy voice piped up. 'I wouldn't mind having her picture on my bedroom wall. Reckon I could get off on that of a night.'

Raucous laughter broke out as he said that but what hurt most was that they were speaking as if she wasn't there.

'Do you fancy she'd be up for a bit of you know what, then? A bit of how's your father?'

Annie saw him make a pumping gesture with his arm. She wondered what on earth that was about and didn't really want to guess. Neither did she want to hang around to find out. As soon as the supervisor indicated the machine was working again and her card was satisfactorily punched, she walked purposefully down the long corridors, hoping she would find the right shed without having to ask. She saw – or rather smelled – the lavatories on the way in and hurried past as fast as she could, determining then that, no matter what, she would never use them. She had just about got used to the outside privy at home that she shared with her parents after she'd spent hours scrubbing it clean, but she drew the line at having to share such facilities with a bunch of women, most of whom she was sure rarely washed. She pulled open the door marked Shed One and was relieved to find it was the one she had been in yesterday. She hurried to Henry Mattison's office as he had told her to do to receive her first instructions.

By the time Annie went for her well-earned dinner break she was aching all over. She didn't know how she was going to get through the remainder of the day, and then do it all again for the rest of the week. But ten hours each day was what she had had to agree to. It was the length of shift most of the girls did, from what she'd heard, and one way or another she would have to get used to it. On her way to the dinner room she passed girls clustered in small groups, leaning against the wall with cigarettes dangling out of their mouths. Fortunately, she didn't smoke and she didn't know how they could either. She had only been in the shed for a few hours and already her throat felt so sore she could hardly speak. But if the women's conditions were bad, she wondered how the men fared, for she had seen some of them stripped to the waist, struggling with the same hot and damp conditions, and with cotton dust flying everywhere. They were stoking the boilers, heaving hefty boxes from one shed to another and, worst of all, were sorting the raw cotton which made most of them sneeze and cough till she was sure they must bring up their lungs. She didn't know exactly how much they earned, but it couldn't be much more than the women. Worst of all was the children. No longer the very young ones, thank goodness, like the pictures she had seen of them going down the mines or up chimneys. But some of the boys and girls who dodged between the looms and crawled around the floor to correct a foot pedal or pick up a dropped spindle could only have been a few days over the statutory school leaving age of fourteen.

Once she began working, after her so-called training, she also understood why the women had looked so pale and red-eyed in the scene she had witnessed yesterday and would no doubt witness every day she worked there. For her arms were aching from the constant stretching and reaching across the looms and, as the morning wore on, she found it became harder and harder to lift the bales of yarn. Her legs ached too and she began to understand how they could become deformed from all the standing, not to mention the walking, that they did all day long, back and forth, following the machine carriages. She was sure she must have walked several miles already that morning. How many miles would she walk if she stayed in the job for any length of time?

At dinnertime she sat alone in a corner of the canteen. She was starving, but she tried not to look at what anyone else was eating for all she had was a piece of dry bread. She had given what little cheese there was to her father and instructed her mother to see what she could scrounge from the butcher for their tea and tomorrow's dinner; she said not to mind even if it was old, so long as it wasn't on the turn. And she prayed Florence would use some initiative and go looking for some sewing work as Annie had begged her to do, so that they could afford to buy more food for the next few days.

All Annie wanted to do now was to keep her head down so that she wouldn't be noticed by the others, several of whom had been staring and pulling funny faces at her during the course of the morning. She had managed to ignore them most of the time, feeling thankful that in the noisy shed no normal conversation was possible. There were three young girls, however, who were the worst culprits. Two, who looked like they might be twins, had carroty red hair straying out from under grubby-looking headscarves that were tied up at the front, turban-style. They both had extremely pale skin that was almost yellow and they looked as if they were severely undernourished. The third one was possibly their older sister because she looked a lot like them, except that she had dark hair. She was even thinner than the younger two and never seemed to stop coughing. All three of them had red-rimmed, watery eyes so that they looked as if they were permanently crying.

Annie had been aware that they had been mouthing and pulling weird faces at her, like children, for most of the morning. They had also been signing to each other in such a way that even she, as a new girl, was in no doubt what they were saying. Although she had to admit she didn't understand all of what she assumed to be rude gestures. When the dinner break was signalled, she had followed them out as they made their way to the dining area and when she saw them sitting together under the window she went to sit at a table far away in a dark recess on the other side. But it was not possible to escape them entirely. As soon as they saw her, they left their table and made a beeline for where she was sitting. They sat down and huddled close to her until they were almost touching. They then proceeded to talk about her as if she wasn't there.

'I wonder if she speaks as la-di-da as she looks?' one of the twins said, looking directly at Annie.

'I know what's wrong with her,' the other twin said. 'She's got a poker up her arse.'

They collapsed into paroxysms of laughter.

'That must be what Mattison the octopus, that bleeding excuse for a man, likes about her bum. I couldn't understand what he thought was so special about it and why he couldn't keep his hands off it yesterday.'

Annie wanted to protest that she had hardly invited his unwanted attentions, but she thought it more prudent to remain silent and play them at their own game, pretending they weren't there.

'Do you think she's dead?' one of them said. 'Maybe if I give her a poke . . .' Without warning, the speaker reached across and prodded Annie's hand with her fork.

Annie gave a squeal of pain. 'Do you mind!' She spoke without thinking. 'That hurts.'

Once more, the girls seemed to find this hilariously funny and laughed out loud for some moments as Annie stared at them questioningly.

'Do you mind?' each of the girls imitated in turn; responding to each other, 'Yes, I do bloody mind as a matter of bleeding fact, don't you?'

That set them off into fits of more giggles. They then proceeded to pinch Annie's already aching arm and went through the same ridiculous routine several times. Were they mad? Annie thought. Or was it her fault for coming to work among such common girls in such a dreadful place? Annie, trapped now into the corner at the end of the table, was unable to move.

'Do you think we should tell someone about this poker? After all, it could be fatal?' They had hold of something they couldn't bear to let go now.

'Maybe we should tell Mister fucking Mattison.' The older one feigned a posh voice as she said this, despite the coarseness of her language. She exaggerated what might have been a fair imitation of Annie's voice even though Annie had barely spoken half a dozen words.

Annie looked around the room desperately, but no offer of help was forthcoming. It was a dimly lit room but if anyone had seen what was going on they were choosing to ignore it for no one met her gaze. Either they didn't see or no one was prepared to make eye contact. Annie felt helpless. She had seen girls teased and bullied at school in Clitheroe but she had never before been the butt of such cruel jokes.

'Where's that cute little hat, I wonder?' The trio were off again but she didn't even look to see who had spoken as they pretended to look around for the missing item.

'Oh bugger, it's disappeared.' As she said this, the older one with the dark hair whipped off Annie's head-scarf. She rolled it into a tight ball and knotted it before she threw it to one of the twins. It was then tossed around the table like a snowball until it eventually unfurled and fell into a mug of cold tea that had been left by a previous diner. This caused endless mirth with the girls falling about with helpless laughter. But then suddenly one of them stood up. She looked at the clock that was above the serving hatch.

'Bloody hell!' she said. 'We'd best be getting back if we don't want the old ogre on our backs.' The twins stood up quickly and, turning to Annie, belched loudly in her face while the older one actually spat at her. Then they fled the room as quickly as they could. Annie was so relieved to be left alone she would have been pleased to sit there for several more minutes. But a voice in her ear made her jump and brought her back into the room.

'If you don't get back this instant I shall be docking your wages.' It was Henry Mattison. She looked up.

'Yes, of course, Mr Mattison,' she said, and she hurried back to the shed, not sorry that dinnertime was over. It had been the longest half hour she had ever known.

When the hooter sounded for the end of the shift Annie didn't know whether to be glad or sorry. She was glad that she now had a whole evening in which to rest her throbbingly painful limbs, and she was delighted that the stretching and bending and endless walking was over, at least for today. But what she dreaded was the fact that, before she could set off home, she would have to run the gauntlet of those dreadful girls again. She could see they were gathering their few belongings and abandoning their looms as quickly as they could, and she worried that they would be lying in wait for her. She had no chance of leaving the shed before them.

Annie was jostled and pushed as she made her way out to the clocking-off area. She was trying to keep a lookout for her tormentors so that she wouldn't be caught unawares, when she felt someone pulling at her arm and she reacted instinctively, slapping the offending hand away. Feeling emboldened that the day was done and she was no longer on mill time, she turned to address her attacker. To her surprise, it wasn't one of the bullies from this morning. It was a fair young girl with her hair knotted into two plaits that were piled up on either side of her head.

'Hello,' the stranger said. Her lips parted in a huge grin, though her grey eyes looked too tired to join in.

'My name's Lilian Vickers. Me and my friend here, Nancy, thought you might like an escort.'

To Annie's astonishment a pretty, young-looking girl suddenly popped up beside her on the other side and grasped hold of Annie's other arm. She had short dark hair that had been cut into a straight bob with a fringe that threatened her eyebrows. Despite just having finished a long day shift the blueness of her eyes sparkled from within the red frames of their lids. She nodded her head. 'Nancy Warburton,' she said. 'Pleased to meet you. We saw what them dreadful Bradshaw girls were doing at dinnertime and thought you might need some 'elp.'

'You sound like you know them,' Annie said, re-assured by the warmth of the girls' linked arms.

'Aye, we do,' Nancy said. 'They're sisters and they're well known round here. Them's troublemakers.'

'Someone tried to get the older one sacked once,' Lilian joined in, 'but she managed to worm her way back in. If you haven't already guessed, the carrot tops are twins. When they're all together they're shockers. And they're always like that with new girls. See them as easy game.'

'They come from a very large family. They're very poor and they live in one of them old Victorian slum houses, the ones that share a privy and have no inside taps,' Nancy said. 'They seemed 'armless when we first met 'em but they've got huge chips on their shoulders 'bout anyone as they thinks might be better'n them.'

'It's not just that they call yer names, but they say loads of 'urtful things too.' Lilian joined in again. 'Sticks and stones and all that. But they can get real nasty.'

'We saw what went on in the dinner room but we didn't like to interfere because you were pretty well hemmed in and they'd 've made 'ell for us an' all,' Nancy said. 'But we thought we could at least see you 'ome safe. Show 'em we mean business. There's safety in numbers out here.'

'Where do you live?' Lilian asked.

'Alderley Street,' Annie said without thinking. She was surprised to realize she was beginning to accept that Norwesterly Clitheroe was her home now. 'My name's Annie. Annie Beaumont. And thank you very much. It would be really good to feel there was someone on my side.'

The next morning Annie was surprised and pleased to find Lilian and Nancy standing at the corner of the street. They looked as if they were propping up the corner shop as they leaned against the wall, smoking.

'Are you waiting for me, by any chance?' Annie asked.

They both grinned.

'How do you manage to smoke?' Annie wanted to know. 'I see most of the mill girls do it. But what with all that dreadful heat and the cotton fluff and the dust it just makes me want to cough all the time.'

'I suppose you get used to it,' Lilian said. 'It's summat I've always done, since I were at school. You know, there's nothing quite like that first drag of the day.' She took a long puff as if to prove her point then stubbed out the butt on the dusty paving stones.

Annie wondered what her new friends had been doing since they'd last met, for they looked much perkier and brighter than she felt, but she didn't like to ask. Maybe they'd just eaten better than she had. When she got home she had expected her mother to have prepared a meal for the three of them. But all Florence had said when Annie challenged her was, 'I've had a bad day and I've not been able to stir out of the house.'

Annie exploded when Florence said that. 'All the more reason why you should have had a hot meal ready for Daddy and me when we've both been out working all day,' she shouted. 'Do you honestly expect us to have to come home and cook as well?'

But at that Florence had merely run upstairs and the next thing Annie heard was the bedroom door slamming shut. Thankfully her father had managed to buy some sausages on his way home and the two of them had cooked them together on a toasting a fork over the fire when they had finally managed to get it going.

'I didn't have a very good night,' was as much as Annie felt able to confess to her new friends. 'It's funny, when you left me I thought I was tired enough to sleep for a month. But I hardly slept at all.'

'It 'appens. You can get overly tired,' Nancy said, 'that 'appens to me, often like.'

'The problem is, I'm tired now, before we even start,'

Annie said. 'Goodness knows how I'm going to get through the day.'

'Mebbe the Bradshaw sisters'll keep you entertained,' Nancy said. 'Some of their miming antics can be quite funny once you get used to their language.'

'I'm not sure I want to,' Annie said. 'Some of it looked very crude to me.'

'Oh, but it is. That's what can make it so funny.'

'We'll 'ave to give yer some translation lessons,' Lilian said and at that they all laughed.

Annie was glad to have the support of Nancy and Lilian, for the Bradshaws refused to leave her alone. Her new friends picked her up in the mornings and escorted her home in the evenings and every dinnertime they made sure they sat together. But the terrible sisters still took every opportunity to bully her. They tried to steal Annie's food, meagre though it was, and they would slash her coat or cardigan or any other item of clothing she wasn't wearing if she made the mistake of hanging it up in the cloakroom. Annie learned to keep all her possessions with her as much as she could, once even wearing her coat despite the heat in the shed rather than risk having it trashed.

Annie's health had begun to suffer as a result of working in the mill. Her cough grew worse and she lost a significant amount of weight. She had learned from their neighbour Mrs Brockett to cook a few simple dishes but her father had had some time off recently as he'd been sick, so that his pittance of a wage packet was seriously reduced. They still couldn't afford much in the way of decent food and her skin took on an unhealthy pallor. Her blonde hair, which once used to bounce and shine, looked dull and hardly seemed to grow at all. Her eyes were permanently red-rimmed and watery, the way she had noticed in others, and when she looked in the mirror she was horrified by the skeletal mask that stared back at her.

'You should at least put a little make-up on. If you haven't any left I can give you some of mine,' her mother offered generously. 'You mustn't let yourself go, you know. We might not have any servants at the moment, but imagine what they would say if we did.'

Annie couldn't help giggling. Somehow her mother still managed to come out with the most ridiculous remarks. Annie was working like a slave and all her mother could think about was how it would look to the servants! As if they were ever likely to have any ever again.

'No, don't laugh,' Florence admonished and she was obviously serious. 'Every morning I think: what would cook have said if I'd gone into her kitchen looking like a ghost? It's very important to take care how we appear to the outside world. It's all too easy to let things slide. If there's one thing I've come to understand it's how important it is to put a good face on things and to keep up standards.'

Annie wasn't sure her mother always adhered to the

ideals she espoused, but she admired the maxim nevertheless and resolved to try to live by it, even though
she found it hard to motivate herself sometimes. It was
more difficult in the winter, once the cold weather set
in. When the wind whipped the snow into high banks
under the front windowsill and she had to scratch with
her fingernails at the rime of frost that had collected
on the inside of the glass in order to be able to see out,
Annie didn't want to get out of bed in the mornings
to go to work. She dreamed that the factory was closed
and at the end of the week someone magically appeared
with her wage packet. But that never happened. The
snow covered the cobbles, making walking hazardous,
but the three girls still had to pick their way over the
treacherous pavements each day.

The Bradshaw sisters delighted in the heavy falls of
snow that blanketed the neighbourhood. They would
lie in wait for Annie even when she was with Nancy
and Lilian. Then, as the three friends turned the final
corner before they reached the mill gates, they pelted
them with small hard snowballs that were packed so
tight they stung painfully on impact. When they split
open, large stones or lumps of coal were revealed that
had been tucked inside.

These days Annie never seemed to be free of pain.
She permanently ached all over from the hard physical
labour of working the looms, the soreness being deeply
embedded in her bones. If the pain wore off a little
one day it was only so that it could come back with

a vengeance the next. She hated her life and wondered if there would ever be any reprieve.

The only day she enjoyed was Sunday, when she and her mother went to church. It was old Mrs Brockett who had first introduced them to the Baptist church in the village and Annie had to admit the singing, particularly before the sermon, did lift her spirits if she was feeling down. Her mother must have felt the same way, although they didn't speak of it.

For Annie, going to church was a welcome diversion. Weekdays were hard, particularly as she felt that Florence still wasn't taking it seriously that she was in charge of their greatly diminished household. Many a time Annie came in exhausted and hungry from work to find no meal prepared, far less cooked. Each morning she would leave Florence a list of food to buy and she was grateful when her mother completed the shopping. But it was frustrating when Florence found some excuse for why she hadn't felt able to cook a meal as well. It was the same with the washing. Annie lost count of the number of times she found the blouse or the underwear she needed for the morning still rolled up in the laundry bag so that, tired as she was, she had to wash it and iron it herself. And there had been numerous occasions when she had found Florence curled up in bed, saying she hadn't felt well enough to clean the house that day, small as it was. It was as if Florence lost touch with the world around her sometimes, and as if she couldn't appreciate that her effort was required just as much as Edward's and Annie's if the household was to run efficiently. But however many lapses she had, on a Sunday Florence seemed to rally and begin to take an interest in things once more. Annie, in her attempt to forgive her mother, began to attend church with her regularly. They got to know a few members of the congregation who were their neighbours and the vicar always stopped to have a few words each week. Sundays became a real day of rest to Annie, a symbol of freedom; a time when, if only for a few hours, she could make believe life was as it used to be.

She would begin the day lying in bed, pretending she was back in their old home in Clitheroe Town. Then she would dress in what she still called her best dress, though in fact now, having sold or pawned most of her other clothes, it was her only dress and it was showing signs of wear and tear. She still had the hat that had given her so much grief when she had worn it at the mill and this also became a ritual part of her Sunday outfit. When the service was over and they greeted their neighbours she would allow herself the indulgence of remembering the old days and how she had smiled and nodded to the servants who used to line up in the spacious mansion hallway and bob a curtsy as she and her parents swept by.

Annie tried to persuade her new friends from the mill to join her in church but Lilian was adamant she wanted nothing to do with anything religious.

'I don't bother God and I don't expect him to bother

me,' she said when Annie asked her one Saturday night if she would join them the following day.

'It's just that it's Mothering Sunday tomorrow, so I thought you might like to come. Maybe you could bring your mother?' Annie said.

Lilian spluttered. 'Not bloody likely. Over 'er dead body, like as not as she'd be telling me.' She could always be counted on to express her opinions in a forthright manner. 'The only time she set foot inside a church was when she got wed and then, apparently, she didn't stop grumbling about it. Only did it cos o' my gran. She insisted. I like my bed on a Sunday morning and that's where you'll find me tomorrow an' all.'

'It will be a special service with flowers all over the place. And there'll be lots of singing; there are some really nice hymns,' Annie tried to tempt her.

'I might like to come, if you'd be 'aving me.' Nancy spoke softly. She was by far the most diffident of the three. 'Though I'm not so sure about my mam, either. Not because she's agin church but she's alus run off her feet of a Sunday morning, trying to organize the kids for Sunday dinner. What with all my brothers and sisters running around, they drive her potty; and there's little enough room for her to cook, any road.'

'That would be lovely if you'd like to come, Nancy.' Annie was genuinely delighted. 'We can go together. Why don't you pick us up? It's on your way. And you've already met my mother.'

They reached the church well before the time scheduled

for the service and were surprised to find the vicar standing at the arched oak door, anxiously checking the congregants as they arrived.

'Good morning, Mrs Beaumont, Miss Beaumont, and Miss . . . ?' He hesitated politely. 'Warburton,' Nancy supplied and the vicar nodded his head and smiled a welcome. 'Forgive me if I don't stop to chat right now,' he addressed Florence, 'but I'm looking for Mrs Bland. She's promised to play the organ today in the absence of Mrs Denham our usual organist who's gone to spend Mothering Sunday with her daughter in Manchester. But her next door neighbour fears Mrs Bland may be ill and unable to come today. As you may imagine, I am most concerned that we may not have an organist for our special celebratory service.'

'Oh, you don't have to worry about that, vicar,' Annie was surprised to hear her mother say. 'I can always play the organ for you. I'm more used to a piano, of course, but I have been known to manage the organ if pushed. Though at such short notice I'm afraid I'd need a copy of the music.'

The vicar's eyes opened wide. 'I had no idea, Mrs Beaumont.'

Florence laughed in a way Annie hadn't heard her laugh in a long time.

'Hidden talents, my dear man,' she said. 'Hidden talents.' And she swept inside as if she were a maestro going to play a concert recital.

Annie didn't know whether to laugh or cry at the

brilliance of her mother's virtuoso performance. It wasn't just about the way Florence had come alive and played the instrument as if she had practised every day; it was the way, as Annie listened to Florence playing with confidence and finesse, that her original, accomplished mother, the mother she remembered from her childhood, had appeared once more in front of her eyes. It was a very different Florence from the one who so often now, since their life had changed, flapped ineffectually around the house. And the more Annie thought about it the more she realized that there was no point in getting upset about Florence's behaviour in the house, for no amount of nagging was going to change it. There were many times when her mother appeared uncaring, inadequate and incapable of carrying out even the most mundane of tasks, but it was futile for Annie to expect her to take on the role of holding the family together like she once had. Annie realized now that since their move, that role had more naturally fallen on her own shoulders. Sometimes her father was able to help her out but at times he became depressed too and abrogated his responsibilities. As she listened to her mother pulling out all the stops and filling the little church with the swelling music, Annie finally understood it was time to forgive Florence her shortcomings. Annie had taken on the mantle of homemaker ever since disaster had struck the family and now she must continue to wear it.

'That was amazing, I'd no idea your mother could play the organ like that,' Nancy said to Annie as they waited outside the church for Florence to appear. It seemed she was being stopped by each congregant in turn to congratulate her on stepping into the breach.

'Neither had I,' Annie confessed. 'I'm more used to hearing her on the piano. She used to play a lot at home. She was very good at that. She loved her piano so much.' Annie spoke without thinking and realized Nancy was staring at her.

'She played at home? Where on earth did you put it?' Nancy laughed. 'You don't 'ave it now? I imagine there's not much space even for any kind of musical instrument,' she teased, 'except mebbe a flute.'

Annie felt the blood rush to her face. 'Actually . . . I didn't mean this home. I meant the house we used to live in in Clitheroe before we . . .' She paused, not sure how to go on. 'It was . . . it was much bigger than where we live now.'

'It'd need to be,' Nancy said, then stopped. 'I'm sorry. Is it summat you'd rather not talk about?'

Annie was grateful for Nancy's sensitivity, and for a moment she was sorry she had mentioned it. It brought back so many painful memories: of Clitheroe, of their former life, of very different ways of spending Sundays. She looked at her friend whose face was showing concern. Maybe it was time she talked to someone about it, to someone she considered to be one of her closest friends. Nancy and Lilian were surely the two people in this world that she could trust with her story. Without pausing to think any more about it, Annie told Nancy about her early life, the dramatic downturn in the family's fortunes and their migration to Norwesterly Clitheroe. She couldn't look at her while she was talking and she fiddled with her hands, taking them in and out of the pockets of her dress.

When she had finished, Nancy didn't say anything for what felt like the longest time. Then she said, 'I'm so sorry, I'd no idea. Though it does explain lots o' things. It must've been very hard for you all.'

Annie looked at her friend now, finally meeting her gaze. 'It still is, in some ways. But it always amazes me how adaptable human beings are. How we're all learning to cope with it, even my father.'

At that moment Florence appeared in the church doorway. She waved at the girls as she descended the steps like she was waving to a fan club. 'Well, I think that went very well indeed, for my debut appearance, don't you?' She was beaming and her eyes sparkled as she linked arms with her daughter and they set off walking home.

'Mrs Beaumont!'

Annie stopped when she heard the vicar calling after them. 'Mrs Beaumont, I meant to give you these.'

He looked so flustered as he thrust a huge bouquet of fresh spring flowers into Florence's arms that Annie felt sorry for him. 'They were intended for Mrs Bland, but under the circumstances you must have these and I shall send her some other flowers to wish her well.' Florence looked delighted as he gave a little bow. 'I am only too pleased to be able to present them to you to thank you so much for saving the day. I don't know what we would have done without you.'

'It was a real pleasure. Really. Any time, vicar,' Florence enthused.

'You may regret saying that, dear lady.' He wagged his finger in a jocular manner. 'But for now, I hope you have a beautiful Mother's Day.'

Chapter 4

May 1942

'Penny for them. Isn't that what you say over here?'

Gracie looked up at the sound of the American drawl that she was becoming familiar with in the Rovers. New York? Texas? No, she wasn't able to distinguish. To her, all the GI servicemen sounded the same and there seemed to be more of them arriving each day. They certainly outnumbered the locals in the bar at the moment. There were few enough Weatherfield residents around, except those who were too old or too decrepit to be called up into the services. There were certainly no young men of any interest drinking in the bar these days, as far as she was concerned, so in a way it was refreshing to see some young faces, even if they were foreigners. This one had some gold markings on his uniform, though she had no idea what that meant, but he was quite good-looking so she wondered she hadn't noticed him before. She'd been mopping up the beer puddles on the countertop when he spoke to her and the surprise at the sound of his voice must have shown on her face.

'Sorry if I startled you,' he said. 'I've been sitting over there, minding my own business, and didn't realize everyone had gone home. I was writing a note to send to my mother.' He pointed to one of the booths with the pen he still held in his hand. She could see the half-written air letter lying on the table. 'It's Mother's birthday quite soon, I thought she deserved a special letter.' Then he smiled sheepishly. 'Well, although I really was trying to write to my mom, if you must know I was actually watching you, though I didn't want to embarrass you by saying so.'

Gracie felt a flash of annoyance and glared at him, cross that he'd felt it necessary to make up such a cock-and-bull story. She had never been terribly inter- ested in GIs in the first place and such stories didn't help their cause. But he was a customer and she had to be polite. Outside of that she was happy to leave them to the likes of Elsie Tanner, who never seemed to tire of their company. For Gracie, there was no point in getting to know any of them personally for she would never dare to take one home; her father wouldn't stand for it. He was still dead against anything or anyone connected to the USA. She had hoped he'd get over it, but he still suffered pain from being badly burned when his ship was hit in the Pacific and by some twisted logic he blamed the Americans' involvement in the war for that and his being invalided out of the navy. She knew this made no sense but her father's personality had changed since he'd been sent home and now she was afraid of the dreadful things he seemed capable of doing in anger if he was crossed.

The soldier was still staring back at her, chewing gum and manoeuvring it round his mouth in expert fashion. He put out his hand. 'Second Lieutenant Charles Dawson, United States Army. But my friends call me Chuck.'

Gracie wasn't really interested in knowing his name, though she had to suppress a giggle when he announced it. Should she tell him that in Weatherfield 'chuck' was a term of endearment? She draped the dish towel she'd been using over the beer taps and offered him a weak handshake in return. He had the smooth, strong fingers of an office worker and she wondered whether he had a desk job in the army. They enveloped hers in a cool, firm grip. He seemed to want to hold on to her hand longer than was necessary so she withdrew it abruptly.

'Gracie Ashton,' she said.

'I hope I'll be seeing a lot of you from now on, Gracie.' His voice was deep, flattering.

'No doubt you will if you carry on drinking here,' she said, deliberately sounding tart. 'I work most nights.'

'Have you worked here long?' he asked.

'A couple of months. Is this your first night here?'

'At – what do you call it? The Rovers? Yes, it is. Though it's not my first time in an English pub.'

'How long have you been in England, then?'

'Four days and eighteen hours,' he said. 'And this is not only my first night in this pub but my first in Weatherton.'

'Weatherfield,' Gracie corrected him.

'Sorry,' he said immediately. 'I didn't mean to insult your home town. At least, I presume it's your home town.' She nodded. 'And from what I've seen of it so far, I like it. Though to be honest, I've only seen it in the dark.'

'That's probably when it's at its best.' Gracie suddenly giggled. 'Though only we locals are allowed to say that.'

He put up his hands, palms out. 'No need to worry. I wouldn't dare criticize. Not when the British people I've come across so far have been so good to me and the guys already.'

'Glad to hear you appreciate our hospitality,' Gracie said.

'We've been billeted down by the gas works – me and one of the other guys in my outfit. He has a date tonight already, can you believe it? He sure is a fast worker.' He paused and Gracie was aware that his gaze had never left her face, though she refused to look at him. He began to smile slowly. 'Although I wouldn't say no to going out with you, one night.' At that Gracie scowled, though she didn't respond. She picked up his empty glass and carried on with her cleaning. Really, the arrogance of the man! Who did these Yanks think they were?

'Maybe I could walk you home?' Chuck offered. 'You can show me the bits of Weatherfield I've missed.'

Gracie stared at him. Were all GIs so forward? No wonder they had a reputation. She'd have to watch out for hers.

'You don't have to worry, thanks all the same, I don't live that far,' she said.

'No? Well, that'll be fine and dandy as it makes it a whole lot easier. I can walk with you and then you can point me in the right direction to get me back to the gas works.'

Gracie felt an instant of alarm when she realized he had followed her behind the bar and into the kitchen and, for a brief moment, she wondered if she should call Ned, the potman, up from the cellar where he was fixing a new Shires barrel to the tap ready for tomorrow. But, to her amazement, the young lieutenant picked up a cloth and began to dry the glasses she had already piled onto the draining board.

'Here, let me give you a hand with those,' he said.

Gracie was angry at his presumption and was about to snap out a refusal, worrying for a moment what Annie Walker would think of his behaviour. Then she hesitated, for it seemed rude to refuse his offer.

Annie Walker had long since gone upstairs to bed

asking Gracie to close up, so when all the glasses were wiped and put away Gracie shouted down to Ned that she would be leaving shortly, and when she heard him slip out of the side door she hurried over to bolt it behind him. Then she began to go through her locking-up routine. She was proud that she had been entrusted so soon with a set of keys and was conscientious about following the safety procedures as she'd been taught. She was a member of the Women's Voluntary Service in her spare time and so was particularly conscious of the importance of taking all necessary air-raid precautions. The windows had been boarded up at the start of the war and had not been opened since. The blinds had been drawn since nightfall to make sure the blackout was total, so all she had to do was to make sure all the lights were off before she opened the door to let the two of them out into the street. Then she carefully locked it behind them and dropped the keys to the bottom of her bag.

'Well, goodnight then,' she said. 'And thanks for the help.' She turned away and set off in the direction of Mallard Street. To her surprise, Chuck fell into step beside her. When she stopped, intending to shoo him away, he stopped and she soon realized how impossible it was becoming to shake him off. She was getting annoyed and was anxious not to engage him in conversation. The last thing she wanted was for him to come with her as far as the house, but she had difficulty ignoring him when he seemed so determined to talk.

'So, tell me, Gracie,' the lieutenant said as they began walking again, 'do you like dancing?'

'Doesn't everyone?' she said.

'I'd wager there are some that don't.'

'Then I'd say they're pretending. I know lots of girls who say they don't like it but that's only like a sort of insurance in case they don't get asked to dance.' Gracie suddenly became animated. 'But the moment they get to the dance hall they can't wait to grab hold of the blokes that come over to ask me to dance.'

'And I bet there's tons of those,' Chuck said.

Gracie ignored him. 'You wouldn't believe the way some of them cut in, like they were in the middle of a Paul Jones or a ladies' excuse me or something.'

'Wow,' Chuck said.

'Which part of America are you from?' Gracie asked.

'I'm from New York. The Big Apple.'

'The big what?'

'Hey. Will you listen to that?' Chuck put his hand on her arm and they came to a halt. 'What's all that singing I can hear? Are they trying to signal to the German pilots where Weatherfield is?'

At that Gracie laughed. The Mission of Glad Tidings was in total darkness so that it did seem like the music that was belting out must be purely to signal its location. The disembodied voices sounded almost eerie in the pitch-black of the night.

'It's coming from the Mission House.'

'It's a bit late for a Bible meeting, isn't it?'

119

'It won't be a religious meeting at this hour of night. More likely the end of a whist drive. Any excuse for a sing-song to keep their spirits up. Even when there's an air raid and they're down in the basement it doesn't stop them singing. It's Mrs Sharples, one of our Rovers' regulars, who's in charge of the place and she eggs them on.'

They walked the rest of the way in silence until Gracie stopped in front of a row of houses.

'This is where we say goodnight,' Gracie said.

Chuck frowned. 'This looks pretty much the same as the street where the pub is. What's that called again?'

'Coronation Street.'

'That's the one. Are you sure you haven't just taken me round in a circle? Seems to me like we're back where we first started.' She could see Chuck grinning in the pale moonlight.

'These houses were built for the mill workers so you're right, all the terraces round here look the same, back-to-back, two-up two-down with an outside privy round the back, if you want the local lingo.'

'Whoa!' he laughed. 'You're way ahead of me.'

'All I'm saying is, the houses may look the same, but they *are* in different streets, I can assure you. And this is my street. So, thank you for your company,' she said.

'My pleasure. And I'm living where?' He told her the name of the street and then spun around three hundred and sixty degrees.

'That way.' Gracie pointed. She fumbled in her pocket

for her house key. She wanted to cross the road and let herself into the house without any fuss. What would her father say if he knew she'd been escorted home by a GI? He'd said enough rude things at breakfast about, 'those damn bloody Yankees', calling them 'arrogant buggers'. 'They're only after one thing and they think our girls are easy pickings.' He never let the topic alone.

To the best of Gracie's knowledge her father didn't know any Americans personally and had probably never even met one, but he blamed the torpedoing of his ship out in the Pacific on the fact that the Americans had allowed themselves to be dragged into the war in the first place. According to him they should never have got involved in the fighting, even after Pearl Harbor. Gracie knew his arguments made no sense but she knew better than to tell him about the increasing number of GIs who were now drinking at the Rovers. Thankfully, it was not his pub of choice.

'Oversexed fatheads who think they can buy their way into our girls' knickers by flashing free this and free that; silk stockings, cigarettes, chocolates, soap, you name it. Anything they can get their hands on that might turn the girls' heads. I'd like to tell them where they can stuff them.' That was the unprovoked tirade he'd treated his family to over breakfast.

'Bob, please mind your language at the table,' was all her mother had said. Gracie didn't see the harm in a girl getting the odd luxury item in return for offering a few home comforts, as long as you knew where to draw the line, but she would never have admitted that to her parents. However, now that Chuck had seen her all the way home she had to confess that a part of her was a little disappointed that he'd made no move towards her. It might have been fun fighting him off. All he'd done was to grasp hold of her hands and draw her towards him so that he could give her a chaste peck on the cheek.

It was then she heard her father's voice give an angry shout that carried across the street and she pulled away quickly. She rushed over and put the key in the lock as quickly as she could. She was in time to see Chuck on the other side of the road turn and wave and begin to walk away.

'Is that you, our Gracie? Why are you so bloody late?' Her father's voice boomed into the night before she had the chance to get the door shut and she hoped Chuck hadn't heard. The last thing she wanted was for him to come back to see if anything was wrong. She closed the door as quickly as she could and leaned her back against it, surprised that she suddenly felt a little breathless.

'What were you up to out there?' her father yelled.

'Nothing, Dad,' she shouted back.

'Who is he?'

She cursed under her breath. Did her father have a sixth sense or something?

'He's no one.' She sighed. 'Just one of our customers who offered to walk me home, that's all.' She knew better than to deny Chuck's existence completely.

'A Yank?'

Gracie was astonished. What had made him say that? He couldn't possibly have known. 'I hear they're over-running our pubs. They're certainly all over the Three Hammers. I'm warning you if I ever catch you . . .' he began as she started up the stairs. Gracie sighed again, only more loudly this time. 'Let it rest, Dad,' she said. 'We've had our fair share of them at the Rovers, an' all.' Before he could question her more closely she climbed the stairs and threw herself, exhausted, onto her bed.

She closed her eyes and to her surprise she could still feel the lingering warmth of Chuck's lips on her cheek. She brushed her hand across it. Next time she'd make him leave her by the Field rather than bring her so close to her own front door. She frowned. What was she thinking of? It would be much less complicated if she made sure there wasn't a next time.

Annie remained troubled by Annette's visit and was not sleeping well. She didn't tell Jack about the girl turning up unannounced and she didn't talk about it to anyone else, even those who must have seen the girl coming through to her private quarters. The only place she recorded her thoughts was in her private diary. She did this most nights and afterwards found herself tossing and turning as an assortment of memories of the three worst years of her life kept flashing in front of her in a jumble of disorganized images. The memories they

123

evoked were clear and shocking, but no one aspect of those dreadful times was any more vivid than another. She remembered equally the drudgery of the work, the wearisome poverty and the inability of her parents to rescue her from their dire situation. Then there was the frightful bullying and the teasing that never seemed to stop. But she also recalled some of the friendships she had forged, initially out of need but which became attachments she had then pledged forever. Recent events had caused her to add a new face to her gallery of recollections, however. One that she really didn't want to be reminded of: the memory of her first love that she had tried so hard to forget.

Chapter 5

1928

Archie Grainger was one of the young mechanics in loom shed one where Annie worked. It was his job to maintain the machines and to make sure they continued to run smoothly. He was expected to sort out problems as they arose or, better still, to prevent them from happening in the first place. He would run from one machine to another, spanner in hand, tightening nuts, oiling creaky joints, sometimes risking his life when he had to squeeze his large frame into the small space underneath or between the looms to untangle the fine yarn or free the cogs from cotton dust.

He was a pleasant sort of fellow, lips always pursed, which Annie assumed meant he was forever whistling, even though no one could hear him above the din in the shed. Unlike many of his grumpy older colleagues he was big and brawny and always willing to lend a hand if any of the women were having trouble lifting a bale of yarn or handling a bolt of cloth. He often went about shirtless and his glistening body gave off a glow that Annie, she was shocked to discover, found attractive. When she had first noticed him he was fixing some of the machines and she had feigned disinterest when he tried to engage her in a pantomimed conversation. But he seemed so determined to attract her attention that soon she found herself unable to resist responding to his antics, and even laughing at them. There was no denying he was a big, handsome young man, and when the Bradshaw sisters began to tease her about his obvious interest they did it from a distance, as though they were afraid to tangle with him at close quarters. They were not afraid, however, to spread wicked lies about him and Annie, though Annie was determined not to let their vicious nastiness get her down.

She still walked home with Nancy and Lilian each night and one evening after work, as she was waiting for them to appear, Archie came out before them and came over to where she was standing.

'Annie Beaumont,' he said, 'are you three so permanently attached there's no room for anyone else to join your little clique?'

'They say there's safety in numbers,' Annie teased,

but there was a flirtatious glint in her eye as she met his gaze. 'Why don't you join us? That might make it even safer.'

'Because it's you and you alone that I'd like to walk home with. Nice as I'm sure your friends are,' he added quickly.

Annie blushed. No man had ever approached her like this, not since the days when her dancing card was filled for the evening at the formal balls held by her parents and their friends. Now, she was no longer the same confident young woman and she wasn't sure what Archie saw in her. She knew she didn't have the same good looks she'd once had, even though there were no mirrors in the house these days. But she knew, without looking, that her eyes must be as red-rimmed as those of the girls she worked with for they felt sore and tender. She didn't know quite what to say. Fortunately, Archie was never at a loss for words.

'I tell you what,' he said, 'I'll offer you a compromise.'

Annie raised her brows. 'Oh?'

'If I leave you alone to walk home with your friends tonight, then you must promise to come for a walk with me later on this evening.'

'Oh,' Annie said again, only this time more coyly. 'Where would we go?'

'Why don't you tell me where you live and I'll come by and pick you up at eight? I'll think of somewhere for us to go by then.'

Annie suddenly felt all of a flutter, even if he was

only a lowly mill worker. But there could be no harm in going for a walk . . . She told him where she lived and wondered what her parents would make of him. She was trying to explain how he should find the house when Nancy and Lilian arrived.

'Never mind,' Archie said, 'I'll find it. Good evening, ladies,' he said as the girls approached. He made a gesture of doffing his cap although he wasn't actually wearing one. 'Pardon me if I leave you to your own devices. I shall see you anon,' he said, looking straight at Annie, and then he strode off in the opposite direction to where the girls were headed.

'Can't even find a man to take you home. What a shame.' It was the eldest of the Bradshaw sisters shouting as she passed by. 'If you let him into your knickers he might be persuaded.' The three bullies cackled together. Annie turned away and ignored them as she and her friends set off in the direction of home, arm in arm in solidarity as they always were.

'You don't think I intend being a mechanic in a rotten mill all my life do you, fixing bloomin' looms day after day?' Archie shook his head until his long fair curls had rearranged themselves, then he drew in his breath. 'I think that would just about kill me off.'

'I must confess I hadn't thought much about it. It's never really crossed my mind. I just accepted that you were a mechanic and that's what you do. I suppose most of the men seem to be grateful enough to have a job of any kind. I'm not sure they question what they're doing.'

'You're right there. And it's true, times are hard and I am grateful to have a job right now. But it doesn't mean I don't intend to better myself soon as I can.'

'I must admit I feel very much the same way, but then it doesn't take much skill to operate a loom whereas you seem to be really good at your job. You're very skilled. You've certainly kept my decrepit old machine going longer than it deserves. Maybe it would have been put out on the scrap heap long ago were it not for you.'

Archie did a little dance in front of her and took a deep bow. 'Thank you kindly for your praise, ma'am. You've no idea how much that means to me.'

Annie giggled, something she had not done for a long time. 'Now you're making fun of me.'

'Not at all. The thanks were sincerely meant. I can assure you, any teasing is in far better humour than what those wretched girls at the mill mete out. They're forever going on at you.'

'You've noticed?' Annie was surprised.

'I can't help but see it and hear all their malicious gossip, I'm afraid. They never miss a trick. I've seriously thought about putting them over my knee and giving them a good spanking. I tell you, I wouldn't be sorry if one of them disappeared under a loom.'

Annie tried to look shocked, but she echoed the sentiment, even if she couldn't bring herself to express her feelings in words. 'I suppose I've learned to live with it. It's as if they are the cross I have to bear at the mill. But tell me, Archie, what else would you like to have done if you had your time over?'

Now Archie sounded shocked. 'You make it sound like that's it, like I'm stuck here forever – when let me tell you I'm not. I'm not waiting for my time to come around again. I intend to do something about it at the first time of asking. I'm not going to wait for hell to freeze over first, if you'll pardon the expression, but I'm sure you know what I mean. I'll be gone from here as soon as I can get together enough money to see me through for a short while. I'm going to do something about changing my life just as soon as I possibly can. I shall be off and out of here at the first opportunity. I'm going to be a pilot,' he said proudly. He folded his arms across his chest and planted his feet solidly on the ground as he stood in front of her. 'I intend to go wherever you have to go to learn to fly an aeroplane, so I want to get myself into the best possible shape first.' He flexed the muscles in his arms to demonstrate his strength and they did indeed bulge through his shirt. 'That's what I intend to do and I can tell you it won't be long now,' he said. He was staring up at the sky and beaming. Annie felt that he was no longer aware of her presence as he spread his arms and spun round slowly enjoying all he could see. She couldn't bring herself to tell him that the RAF would never be inter-ested in a working-class boy like him. They believed that only public schoolboys were the right material for such work. 'I want to be up there in the sky.' His voice was full of wonder. 'Imagine being so free that you can just flit from trouble to a place where you're so far away from all this mess down here, that all you can see are birds. Imagine being in a place where the air's so clear there can never be any danger of filling your lungs with so much dust and fibres that you can't breathe. And if you should happen to bump into a cloud you can take off again and fly in the opposite direction where the air's just as clear and you're not afraid to take a deep breath.'

He sounded so passionate that, when he paused for a moment, Annie burst into spontaneous applause. She couldn't bring herself to spoil his dream. 'Bravo,' she said, 'that was a wonderful speech. You make me want to be up there with you.'

Archie, however, did come down to earth very quickly when she said that and looked a little embarrassed. But Annie had seen how his face had lit up as he spoke, his green eyes shining as if he had already been transported hundreds of miles away. He looked at her shyly and began to walk on.

'How about you?' he said. 'Do you reckon you're stuck here till the end of your working life?'

'Goodness me, no,' Annie answered immediately, without even thinking. 'I'll never allow that to happen.' Then she hesitated. She didn't want to tell him too much about her past. At least, not now. There would be time enough for that later – if there was ever to be a later. 'I intend to get out of here at the first available opportunity, though I am not quite sure yet how I'm going to do it.'

'Marry some rich bloke,' he joked.

'Maybe that too.' She felt comfortable enough with him to be able to join in the jest. But she knew she was not going to rely solely on marriage to change her situation. 'There's something I'd like to do first. Something I've dreamed of doing ever since I was a little girl.' She wondered if she should tell him but she was surprised how easy he was to talk to and decided to take the plunge. 'I used to live on the other side of Clitheroe where I belonged to the amateur dramatic and operatic society,' she said, though she didn't tell him she'd had only one starring role. 'The thing is, I would love to go on the stage or be a film star – I don't mind which. I've always longed to be an actress of some kind. There now, I've never told that to anyone before.'

She let out her breath and looked at his face, dreading that it might be filled with amusement. But he had a serious look as he turned to her and said, 'Your secret's safe with me.'

It was almost dark when they arrived back on her front doorstep and, as Annie watched him go, she realized her feelings were in deep turmoil and she was unsure what to do. She really liked Archie. He was good-looking, he was exciting and she was impressed by his ambitions. But would he ever amount to anything? Would he really be accepted by the RAF, or was he just flying a kite full of dreams? She must proceed with caution. It would not be wise to form a deep attachment to someone who might remain a mere mill worker all his life. After all she had been through, she could never allow herself to get involved with someone who might prove to be totally unsuitable.

Chapter 6

June 1942

Although she lived outside Weatherfield, in Easterly, Ethel Simpson was in charge of the Weatherfield branch of the WVS, the branch where Gracie offered her services, helping people in need and supporting the home defence team whenever she had some time to spare. Gracie had never seen the older woman in the Rovers before so she was surprised to see her striding towards the bar one night.

'What can I get you to drink?' Gracie asked politely.

'Nothing at the moment, dear, thanks all the same,' Ethel said. 'I've actually come about these,' and she placed a wodge of quarto-sized leaflets on the counter. 'I wondered if the landlady would mind you putting these up in the bar. for us?'

Gracie picked up one of the small posters to see they were advertising a dance that was to be held in the community hall on Friday night.

'Sorry for the short notice, but we have to do the best we can,' Ethel said.

'When was this decided?' Gracie asked.

'It came up as an any other business item at the end of Monday's meeting. Of course, you weren't there, were you?'

'No, I was working that night.'

'Well, we decided we should organize something quickly. Essentially, it's for the overseas servicemen to welcome them to Weatherfield. But as it says, everyone's invited to come. In fact, we'll be relying on all the locals or the poor men will have no one to dance with.' Ethel gave her telltale cackle.

'I'm sure Mrs Walker won't mind advertising it,' Gracie said. 'She'll understand, what with her own husband being away overseas. But I'll ask her, to be on the safe side.'

'I'll leave you with a bunch of them leaflets,' Ethel said. 'Perhaps you could hand them out to any soldiers who drink in here. Tell them to pass them on to all their mates. Now, I've got to get off, I've all this lot to distribute before the night's out.' Ethel indicated the large bag she was carrying that was filled with leaflets. 'Spread the word best you can,' she called over her shoulder. 'Tell all your friends. I'll see you there on Friday night.'

Annie Walker had no objection to displaying the leaflets and distributing them to the clientele but, as Gracie suspected, she wasn't interested in going to the dance herself.

'I don't think they really want someone like me there spoiling the fun. A mother of two? I'm an old lady in their terms,' Annie laughed and Gracie made all the right noises to assure her she wasn't old and it would be perfectly respectable if she fancied the odd dance with a soldier. 'Thank you for your kind words,' Annie said, 'but I really can't leave the bar on a Friday night, not if you're wanting to go, which I happen to think would be much more appropriate. In fact, why don't you take the evening off? I'm sure I'll manage on my own.'

Gracie capitulated without further ado. 'Thanks very much, that would be lovely. Though I won't need to go too early. I could come in here for the first hour or so. It's not as though I'll know anyone there at the dance.'

'But isn't that the point, to mingle with all the new faces? In any case, you'll probably know some of the Americans who've taken to drinking in here, and you always say you enjoy a good dance. I happen to think you should go early if only to see the soldiers while they're still sober.' Annie grinned.

'That's true,' Gracie said, and she suddenly thought about Chuck. Would he come, she wondered? She'd thought she would have seen him again after their first meeting but that was several weeks ago now and he hadn't come into the Rovers since. How would she feel about seeing him now, believing as she did that he'd been avoiding her? She thought she should not show herself to be too keen if he was at the dance. 'Perhaps I will go early, thanks,' she said.

'You might even be able to persuade Lottie to go with you,' Annie said. 'She could do with being taken out of herself for a bit. You'll have to see what you can do. Look, she's here now so you can ask her.'

'What do you think?' Gracie asked Lottie when she'd given her time to peruse the leaflet.

'I can't say it fills me with any great excitement,' Lottie said. 'But you know me, I'm always game to give it a go, if I can get out of the house before my dad says owt. And I'm always ready for a free sandwich.'

'Now that's a great motivator if anything is,' Gracie said with a grin.

'Well, I'm sure it'll help entice many people who're finding rationing hard to deal with. And if the Yanks have anything to do with it, no doubt they'll be handing out some of their own motivators an' all – the odd pair of stockings or a bar of soap won't go amiss for most of us.'

Gracie laughed. 'We could think of it as our contribution to the war effort,' she said.

'I think that's one of Elsie Tanner's lines, isn't it? Her excuse for having a good time,' Lottie said.

'Well, and why not? I can't say's I blame her. If the Americans joining in the war can help to bring it to an end sooner, then it will all be worth the effort. So, if you come here about seven we can go together. I don't think the Rovers will be too busy if we're all down at the hall dancing the night away.'

'Maybe you'll see that fella who walked you home once. Do you think he'll be there?'

'I don't know. He's obviously not interested in me, though. I've seen neither hide nor hair of him since that night I first met him and that was weeks ago.'

'You mean you wouldn't dance with him if he asked you?' Lottie teased.

Gracie's cheeks reddened. 'I don't know about that. I'll have to see.' She tossed her head. 'I've only met him the once and it's not as if I really fancied him.'

'Though you might have, if you wouldn't have been so worried about your father's reaction?'

'Not at all,' Gracie protested.

'Okay. We'll see,' Lottie said and she laughed.

By the time they got there on Friday night the dance was in full swing. It was a warm evening, with no expectation of rain. Ethel and her small team of organizers had been super-efficient at their task and, with some passable homemade decorations and a few balloons, had managed to make the hall look festive. At the beginning of the evening the windows were wide open and there was a gentle breeze wafting the net curtains. The resourceful women had gathered enough rations to be able to lay out a small table with light refreshments and had stacked some drinks behind the bar. They had also managed to get a few musicians together at short notice. The combination of an energetic bandleader and the live music was enough to encourage many of the dance-goers onto the floor before any serious drinking began, though most of them only walked through the steps or jigged about to the music instead of dancing properly.

Gracie had hardly set foot inside the hall when Chuck Dawson approached her. She wasn't sure why, but she suddenly felt shy and her first instinct was to turn around and exit the door as quickly as she'd entered. The American stepped in her path.

'May I have the pleasure?' he said bowing slightly.

'Oh, hello.' She stumbled over his feet. 'I didn't realize it was you.'

'Well, now that you can see that it is, how about a dance?'

'I don't really know how to do this one,' Gracie said, and she looked at Lottie as if hoping her friend would rescue her. But Lottie nodded her head in encouragement and smiled. Then she walked away.

'Allow me to show you,' Chuck said. 'It's not too complicated, you just follow my lead.' He held his arms aloft, ready to clasp her in an embrace as they stepped onto the dance floor and he began to guide her into something resembling a quickstep.

Although he maintained a respectable distance, it felt strange suddenly being close to him and Gracie fancied she could feel the beating of his heart, though it was probably her own. Indeed, her pulse rate noticeably increased as he smiled down at her, his blue eyes meeting her gaze.

'I was hoping you'd come,' he said.

'Really? I thought you must have changed your allegiance and gone drinking elsewhere.' She tried to keep her tone light.

'I did, that's exactly right. In fact, I've been down in London ever since we last met so I've not had a chance to get back to your pub.'

'Oh.' Gracie couldn't believe the relief she felt. He hadn't been ignoring her after all. 'I thought you were in Manchester permanently?'

'It's complicated,' he said, 'but I often have to go down to London.' From the tone of his voice and the expression on his face she gathered the subject was closed.

They danced without pause through several sets of music and without further conversation, because as the hall became more crowded and the music grew louder they couldn't make themselves heard. At the end of the last set, when they finally pulled apart, Chuck still held on to Gracie's hand, as if he was reluctant to let her go.

Gracie was feeling extremely hot and needed some air. She extracted her hand and moved towards the door.

'Can we sit down outside for a bit?' she said. 'There's some tables and chairs out here and I'd love a ciggie.'

'Sure. Let me get you a drink first, though. And here, I've got a fresh pack of Camels.' He reached into his breast pocket and handed her a full packet of cigarettes. She hadn't tried American ones before.

Chuck ordered a beer for himself, and Gracie asked for a lemonade shandy.

'How does it feel to be on the other side of the counter for once?' Chuck asked.

'Strange, I must admit. I've never been much of a drinker. Before I got the job I rarely went into a pub, so I was amazed how quickly I felt at home behind the bar in the Rovers.'

'And a wonderful bartender you make,' he said, 'if I may be so bold as to say so.'

That made Gracie laugh. 'Well,' she said, 'the purpose of holding this dance is to help you lot feel at home. So, is it working?'

'Sure is,' Chuck said. 'I'm really beginning to feel at home here in England. Well, as much as you can when you're so far away from your real home and caught up in doing things you'd rather not be doing.'

'And how do you like Weatherfield?' Gracie asked.

'I can't speak about Weatherfield in particular, I've not been there long enough, but I guess I'm slowly getting the hang of how you Brits tick generally. That's the only problem with my line of work – I never know how long I'm going to be in any one place.' He laughed.

'I go wherever I'm sent and, at the moment, I'm thankful no one's actually fighting the war on British soil.'

Gracie was intrigued about the mystery that seemed to surround his work and was about to ask him more about what he actually did, but once again Chuck's expression indicated 'no more questions'. He asked her to tell him about her childhood and began to regale her with stories about his own. Then the music struck up and people began to drift back inside as the final set of dancing was about to begin.

They finished their drinks and stubbed out their cigarettes and Chuck led Gracie back to the dance floor where the music and the mood had changed from fast to slow. Gracie felt a tingle of electricity as Chuck embraced her more closely than before and she didn't resist when he pulled her face towards him so that her cheek rested on his shoulder. She felt almost sad when the bandleader announced it was time for the last waltz. It felt perfectly natural, as the lights dimmed, that he should tilt his face towards her and she didn't object when his lips brushed lightly over her mouth. It was in that moment she realized that she couldn't be aloof with him. She wasn't wary about him at all – in fact, she quite fancied him. Without thinking, she responded immediately at his touch, moving her head so that she presented her lips more fully to his. He needed no second invitation, for he pressed down hard and every nerve in her body seemed to tingle as she felt his tongue touch hers. She gave herself to the moment but then suddenly she stiffened. What was she thinking of? This man was an American soldier, a man whose existence she could never acknowledge at home, whose name she would never be able to mention for fear of catching a clout off her old man, and yet here she was allowing, even encouraging, him to kiss her.

Chuck stopped. 'Anything wrong?' he whispered anxiously in her ear.

Gracie shook her head, unable to find the words; after all, what could she say?

As soon as the dance was over, Gracie looked round in search of Lottie. She had lost track of her friend after Lottie had walked away at the beginning of the evening but she assumed that when she was ready to go home, Lottie would seek her out. Then she saw her on the other side of the dance floor in the arms of a fair, closely-shaven British soldier, and Gracie wondered if Lottie had been with him all evening. More importantly, she needed to know whether he would be seeing Lottie home. Gracie didn't want to desert her friend but she was hoping she might be free to accept Chuck's invitation to see her back to Mallard Street. Well, as far as the Field. She was going to have to tell him how her father felt about Americans so that he wouldn't think her rude or inhospitable at not asking him in.

Gracie hadn't had a chance to talk to Lottie since the dance, so she was delighted to see her when she came into the bar early the next evening.

'Come and talk to me, at least until I get swamped with customers,' Gracie said. 'I can be setting things up as we talk. Mrs W says you can have this on the house, by the way.' She placed a small glass of orange juice in front of Lottie. It was a very pale orange colour because, thanks to rationing, it was much diluted.

'Thanks very much,' Lottie said.

'Now, I want to know all the details,' Gracie said. 'Who is he? You looked well-involved when I last saw you.'

'So did you,' Lottie retorted. 'I presume that was the same Yank you've been talking about? The one you said you didn't fancy?' Lottie guffawed when Gracie nodded her head.

'No, well . . . A girl's entitled to change her mind.' Gracie's look was coy.

'You won't hear an argument about that from me,' Lottie agreed. 'I thought he looked rather nice. And he's certainly keen on you.'

'He was very nice once I got talking to him properly,' Gracie admitted. 'I really enjoyed his company.'

'I could see that even from where I was standing,' Lottie quipped. 'So, when are you seeing him again?' Her face looked serious.

'We're going out dancing.' Gracie couldn't help beaming. 'He's taking me to the Ritz, on Friday. He said he'll tell me the time and everything when he's next in for a drink. He'll come and pick me up at the Rovers.'

'Ooh, how thrilling. Are you excited?'

Gracie nodded eagerly. 'And scared,' she admitted. 'How will I sneak out of the house dressed up without my dad seeing?'

'Tell him there's summat special on at the Rovers,' Lottie suggested. 'That's what I always say when the old man creates about me going out.'

'Good idea. Now, never mind about me, tell me about you and that soldier. You looked as if you were enjoying yourself an' all.'

'I most certainly was.' Lottie chuckled. 'Much more than I thought I would, at any rate.'

'I've never seen him before. I presume from his uniform that he's English? But he looked too young to be in the army – in fact, he didn't look as if he was old enough to shave.'

'I know, he's got very fair skin and a sort of boyish smile, but he's not as young as he looks. He's worked in a bank for several years since he left school and he's got ambitions to be a manager one day.'

'Where's he from? What's he doing up here?'

'His name's Tim Lucas,' Lottie began her story eagerly, 'and he comes from Portsmouth. All his family are still down there.'

'So why didn't he go in the navy?'

'That's what I said, but he wanted to go into the army and they sent him up here to do his basic training. He's only been in Weatherfield a short while so he hasn't made it yet to the Rovers.'

'You should encourage him to come.'

'Oh, I did. But he reckons they might not be here that long. He thinks they'll be shipped abroad pretty soon.'

'Where to?'

'He seems to think it'll most likely be North Africa. He doesn't seem too mithered either way. I fancy they like to keep them guessing as long as they can so no one can give away any secrets to the Germans.'

'At least he'll get better weather, wherever he goes. And some nice scenery,' Gracie laughed.

'But I don't suppose that can really compensate for having people sniping at you or rolling out tanks and things. I suppose all you can really think about is that you could be killed at any moment. And that's not much of a picnic, is it?'

Gracie sighed. 'It's easy enough for us to joke, I suppose. It's about all we can do. But, in the end, we've no real idea what it feels like to be on the front line.'

'And I hope we never do.'

'Will you be writing to him if he gets posted abroad?'

'Yes, he asked me if I would, even though we'd only just met. But he seemed keen.'

'Well, he certainly looked keen enough last night, even from the other side of the room.'

Lottie looked diffident now. 'Well, it's mutual. I liked him too. It was really fun to be with him so I don't mind being a sort of pen pal.'

'Go on,' Gracie teased. 'Your faces said you'd both

like to be more than mere pen pals. You looked really smitten.'

'I suppose I was, if I'm honest. I don't get too many opportunities to meet boys like him. And it was flattering that he seemed to like me.'

Gracie lowered her voice. 'How far did you get? You know.' She nudged Lottie's arm with her elbow and winked.

Lottie flushed. 'He kissed me, if that's what you're asking. And very nice it was too,' she said a little primly. 'Look, as I say, I really do like him. I'll make no bones about it. And I'd love to see him again. But it's very hard to think of more than one night at a time with this bloomin' war and everything. What's the point of thinking beyond that with someone who's about to be shipped overseas? I mean, I don't know if he'll ever come back, do I?' she added, and her voice quivered.

'I hadn't thought about that. Chuck never talked about going away. But I suppose we have to grab what we can, when we can. This crazy war puts a different perspective on things. Why else would you be thinking seriously about blokes you've hardly had time to go out with?'

She saw Lottie was nodding her head in agreement. 'I know,' Lottie said, 'but I don't want to jump the gun and do something I might regret, so writing letters is okay.'

'What did your parents have to say when he saw you home?' Gracie asked. 'I presume you invited him in.'

'Oh yeah, about as fast as you did.' Sarcasm dripped from Lottie's voice.

'Oh? But Tim's not American. Your dad can't object to a British soldier?'

'He can and he does. He can object to anybody that crosses our threshold when he's got a mood on him. For some reason he hates Madge and me going out and enjoying ourselves. I think he can't bear the thought that we're not around to wait on him hand and foot. He could never bear for either of us to get wed.'

'Well, you know my situation's even worse. If my father so much as caught a whiff of New York outside the door he'd be having poor Chuck's guts for garters. I don't dare mention his name, or the fact that I know him, let alone take him within a mile of the house. But I've decided that I won't let that stop me going to the Ritz with him or anywhere else if he asks me out. I like him and I intend to take every opportunity to get to know him better.'

Gracie waited eagerly for Chuck to put in an appearance at the Rovers every day that week, to tell her about the arrangements for going to the Ritz ballroom on Friday. She was excited and looking forward to going out with him. But he didn't come and none of his friends seemed to know where he was. Or, if they did know, they weren't saying. She began to worry that he had been posted elsewhere and hadn't had the heart to tell her and, having convinced herself that was true, she felt hurt that he was so cowardly that he had not even found a moment to say goodbye.

He didn't come until the middle of the following week and by then she felt angry and let down. When she saw Annie Walker step forward to greet him as he finally entered the Rovers she was tempted to turn her back and ignore him. But she knew she couldn't. He looked so weary and had dark circles beneath his eyes that she felt she had to hear him out.

'Good evening, ladies,' he said. 'May I have a pint of your best beer please and whatever you would be drinking?' His tired smile included them both.

'That really won't be necessary, but thank you,' Annie said graciously. 'Although I think Gracie here might appreciate a quick break as she's been on her feet all night.' Gracie turned to face her and Annie smiled. 'Perhaps I can get you a sherry, my dear. It'll help to revive your flagging spirits.'

Gracie felt she couldn't refuse Annie's carefully worded offer and knew she would indeed welcome a few moments of privacy. Her stomach had somersaulted when she had first seen Chuck arrive and she realized how anxious she had been about him; she hoped the sherry would calm her down. She went around the counter and sat down gratefully when Chuck found a couple of chairs in a quiet corner of the bar. He pulled two cigarettes from a pack in his breast pocket and lit them both before handing one to her, exactly as she had seen Humphrey Bogart do in the cinema.

As she looked across the table at Chuck, she could feel a lump rise in her throat. It felt like all her bottled anger and disappointment and she was afraid to talk for fear of saying something she didn't mean. So she sat for several moments puffing on the cigarette, waiting for him to speak first.

'I really do have to apologize,' he said eventually. 'I never should have promised you a date.'

'No, you shouldn't,' she said. 'Not when you had no intentions of keeping it.'

'Oh no, that's where you're mistaken,' he countered quickly. 'I had every intention of keeping it, you must believe me, but knowing the nature of my work I should have suspected that something would get in the way. I should never have been so specific about the particular day.'

'What difference did that make? You disappeared completely after the dance and I haven't seen you or heard from you for over a week.' Gracie made no attempt to disguise the frostiness in her voice.

'I told you before, I think, that I'm required to go down to London fairly frequently. The meetings I go to usually come up at very short notice and I was ordered down there the day after the dance and then, believe it or not, I had to go up to Scotland. I had no telephone number for you and I didn't dare write to you as I know your father doesn't approve of GIs so I wasn't sure how best to communicate. I thought Mrs Walker might consider it presumptuous of me to contact you at work.'

He sat forward when Gracie didn't respond, as though eager to make eye contact, although Gracie continued to stare down into her glass. 'Well, can you forgive me?' he said at last. 'I'm truly sorry for messing you around, though believe me, I had no choice. Whatever, I'd like to make amends.'

'I must admit I didn't know what to think,' Gracie said quietly. 'But I do know these are strange times and strange things do happen.'

He put his hand out on the table, palm upward, inviting her to put her own hand into his. 'So, am I forgiven?' he asked.

After a few moments Gracie smiled. 'Just this once.' And she felt her nerve endings firing in all directions as she put her hand in his.

'Do you think you might be able to get tomorrow afternoon off? I have somewhere special in mind I'd like to take you.'

'Tomorrow? But—'

'Please say you'll at least ask Mrs Walker. I can't promise I'll be in Weatherfield any longer than tomorrow.'

Gracie's feelings were in turmoil. They were only just getting back to an even footing. 'You mean you're going away?'

'Only for a short while. But I'll still be in this country.' He laughed. 'Don't worry, I'll give you more notice than this if I'm being posted elsewhere, that I think I can promise. If you'll agree to tomorrow I could pick you up about fifteen hundred hours.'

'You mean three o'clock?'

'Yes, of course, I'm sorry. I forget you civilians don't use twenty-four-hour clocks.'

She finally met his gaze and smiled. 'Why don't I go and ask Mrs Walker now?'

Chuck arrived at three o'clock exactly, as promised, and Gracie greeted him excitedly as Annie had agreed she could take the afternoon off. He had told her to dress smartly and she had managed to slip out of the house with her coat on, despite the warmth of the afternoon, before her mother had noticed what she was wearing.

He was dressed as neatly as usual in his uniform, although his boots looked as if they had had an extra wax and polish. Gracie proudly took his arm and they set off to catch the tram into town.

'Can I ask where we're going?' she said as they took their seats.

'Aha, you'll have to wait and see,' he said. 'It's in the centre of Manchester, that's all I'll say.'

The tram dropped them by the cathedral and Chuck strode off full of confidence in the direction of Deansgate.

'I'm so impressed. You really look as if you know where you're going,' Gracie said. She almost had to run to keep up with his long strides.

'Oh, but I do. This is one part of Manchester I am very familiar with now, having been here many times for one reason or another. Or should I say one meeting or another. Do you come into this part of town much?'

'Not really, not now that I'm working full time, and we have enough shops locally to get all I need. Not that there's much to buy these days. Things are either out of stock or you need more coupons than my whole family gets.'

They continued walking along Deansgate and, when they reached King Street, Chuck turned left. Gracie followed him, it was not a street she had been to before and as she gazed in awe at the shop windows that had not been boarded up she could see why, for they seemed to be displaying either exclusive items of ladies' clothing, none of which showed a price tag, or fur coats which she would never have been able to afford.

Halfway along the street Chuck turned towards a little arcade that formed a quiet passageway from King Street into St Ann's Square. They emerged in a tranquil location behind St Ann's church and Chuck stopped outside a shop with a large plate glass window fitted into an ornate, dark wooden surround. Despite the criss-crossing of tape over the glass she could see people sitting at tables, drinking tea, looking as if they were framed in a painting. Gracie stopped and looked up. Meng and Ecker, the sign above the window said.

'Here we are, madam.' Chuck gave a mock bow. 'A genuine old English teashop.' He grinned. 'I'm not sure how old it is but it's certainly a teashop.'

Gracie gasped. 'Oh, my goodness it looks so posh.'

'That's because it *is* posh.'

'But how do you know about it? You've hardly been

in Manchester more than five minutes. I've lived here all my life and I've never been here before. I didn't even know it existed.'

'You obviously don't mix in the right circles,' Chuck laughed.

'And you obviously do.' Gracie laughed too.

'Of course. But allow me to escort you inside. We've not come just to watch other people through the window. We're here to partake of the delicacies ourselves. In fact, we have a table booked.'

As she stepped inside, Gracie was struck by the soft murmurings of muted conversations and the smokiness of the atmosphere, mitigated by the sweet smells of different teas. Several men were smoking pipes or even the odd cigar while the women were holding long, extravagant-looking cigarette holders. Although everyone seemed to be animatedly talking, Gracie was struck by the calmness of the atmosphere. People were talking quietly and the tables were far enough apart for private conversations to remain private, not overheard by everyone else. She glanced round and noticed a number military personnel among the clientele. But despite being in uniform they seemed to blend into the crowd. It was a place where people could escape the noise and bustle of the shops and conduct their business privately, eating and drinking without being disturbed. Gracie had never been anywhere like this before and she was glad she had put on her best outfit. A waitress helped Gracie into her seat and proffered a menu listing names of teas she had never heard of: Darjeeling, Assam, Lapsang Souchong, with the warning note – as available – beside them. A waitress passed by with a tray full of pastries and fancies and it made Gracie drool at the sight of such luxury items.

'How on earth did you get to know about a place like this?' she whispered.

'I work under Captain Roy Farnworth and he told me about it. You might know him, he drinks at the Rovers. All the senior officers seem to know about these kinds of places. They often have informal meetings here. So I was introduced to it pretty early on.'

The waitress came and, without asking, Chuck ordered a pot of tea for two. Exactly what kind of tea she didn't quite catch but he ordered some pastries as well.

'Don't you have to present ration books?' Gracie asked.

'Don't worry about that. Being military, I can cover it.'

Gracie chose her cake from the tray when the waitress came to their table and she was eagerly awaiting the arrival of the tea in a silver teapot with matching milk jug and sugar bowl, the like of which she had never seen before. She sat back to enjoy the surroundings and Chuck's company. This was fun. She was glad she had come and she felt proud to be seen with him. They chatted easily and comfortably while they were waiting and Gracie began to relax. Chuck was certainly interesting and she felt she could talk to him about almost anything. She loved to hear him talk, just to hear his accent, and he seemed to have a different take on life with different priorities about what was and wasn't important. He definitely wasn't like anyone she had ever met before and each time she saw him she wanted to know more about him.

'I hope this makes up for us not going dancing,' Chuck said eventually.

'It more than makes up for it, thank you,' Gracie replied sincerely. 'After all, I've been to the Ritz before, but I've never been anywhere like this.'

'No, it is rather special, isn't it? I find it so . . . so terribly English.'

'I agree. It's special for me too.' Chuck sat forward when she said that and Gracie gave him a diffident smile, suddenly realizing what she had said.

'Perhaps, if you've forgiven me, we can go dancing some other time?' he said.

Gracie looked up. Chuck was smiling at her. Their eyes made contact and Gracie found it impossible to look away. She felt the blood rush to her cheeks and her pulse quicken. 'I'd like that,' she said, sounding almost breathless, and for a moment a stillness settled around them and it was as if they were the only two people in the room.

A whining noise that at first sounded like a klaxon horn suddenly disturbed the tranquil atmosphere and Gracie thought it must be a car or a bus that had come into the square. But after the initial blast the pulsing whine continued and everyone sat up and took notice. Gracie looked round. Several people in uniform were on their feet and together with their guests rapidly exited the door. When a civilian shouted wildly, 'It's an air-raid siren. We've got to get out of here fast. Evacuate,' there was a sudden rush to get out. For a few moments the alarmed crowd were wedged together by the door so that no one could get out. Chuck stood up quickly. 'No need to panic, folks.' He raised his voice to be heard over the din of the horn and the hubbub of conversation that had risen almost immediately. 'Keep calm, everyone, and we'll all be okay. We can all get out if we just take it easy.' He pushed his way over to the door and took command, dispersing the group that had inadvertently blocked the exit and ushering people out in single file.

The staff seemed to have their own drill and after a while the grateful manager took over from Chuck quietly escorting the remaining customers and waitresses out into the street. Gracie, seeing Chuck was safe, joined the crowds who seemed to be making for St Ann's Square.

'Where do we go?' she called to him as he was hurrying to catch up behind her.

'We follow the crowds. There must be some designated shelter nearby.' And sure enough, in an arcade in the square, people were following one another down into a cellar beneath the shops.

The whole experience was terrifying. It had been some time since there had been an air raid in Weatherfield, and Gracie had to work hard to stop her mind from going into overdrive, but all she could think about was: what if they were blown up when she was so far from home and no one knew where she was? Gracie was thankful she was not on her own. In fact, she was extremely glad she was with Chuck. He had a calming influence as he held her hand and spoke to her softly and although it was hot and uncomfortable in the arcade basement she found his closeness re-assuring. He gave her an encouraging kiss and she found herself suddenly wrapping her arms around him and weeping quietly on his shoulder.

'Hey,' he said when he realized, 'what's all this? No need for tears, everything's going to be okay.'

'I'm sorry, but it suddenly all felt a bit . . . over-whelming,' Gracie sobbed not caring who could hear her.

'I know. But it's all right now.' He brushed away her tears with his finger and smoothed back her unruly hair. 'I won't let any harm come to you, ever, I promise,' he added in a whisper.

After a few moments he reached into his pocket. 'Here,' he said, 'I've got the very thing to cheer you up. I've been told all girls love them.'

The cellar was dark so it was difficult for her to see what he was holding in his hand but as soon as she felt the cool smoothness of the material she realized it was a pair of fine silk stockings.

'Are these really for me?' she asked.

'I don't see anyone else around here who deserves them, do you?'

That put a smile on her face. 'Thank you so much, I'll treasure them.'

'I was rather hoping you would wear them,' Chuck quipped.

'I'll do that too,' she said and she touched her finger to his lips.

They were down in the cellar for another half an hour. When they heard the all-clear sound, people filed out of the temporary shelter as quickly as they could, and Gracie took a deep breath of the wonderful fresh air.

'Shall we go back to the café?' Chuck asked. He lit two cigarettes and handed one to Gracie. 'Here, this will calm you down.'

She took it and inhaled deeply. 'I'd rather not, if you don't mind,' she said. 'The treat sort of got spoilt, didn't it?'

'Some other time, then,' Chuck agreed. 'That air raid was quite some experience.'

'Have you not been caught in one before?'

'No. But I suppose you get used to it.'

'Unfortunately, yes. I lived through the Manchester Blitz in 1940 and that was not something I would want to go through again. When I heard the alarm just now it brought it all back.'

'Do you want to go for a walk now instead? Clear your head a bit.'

'Not really. It'll mean having to walk past all the bombed-out parts of town. If you don't mind, I think I'd rather go home. It's bad enough having to see all the bomb sites on Deansgate.'

Chuck went to settle the bill at the café and then they walked slowly back to the cathedral, ready to catch the tram home.

'Well, that was a bit of a disaster. I'm really sorry about that,' Chuck said as they waited at the stop.

'It was hardly your fault.' Gracie grinned. 'But I enjoyed the bit before the alarm. Thank you.' Gracie realized just how much she had enjoyed his company and the opportunity to get to know him better and without thinking she reached up and kissed his lips lightly.

Chuck responded immediately by hugging her close. 'Me too,' he said. 'And we will do it again, only properly next time. But I'm not going to make any promises that I can't keep, so I won't fix the date for when next time will be.'

'How about we write to each other if you have to go away again?' Gracie suggested. 'Then you can tell me when you expect to be back.'

Chuck frowned. 'Where would I write to?'

'Care of the Rovers. Mrs Walker won't mind if I explain, I'm sure.'

'That sounds ideal, if you think she won't mind.'

'It will be fine. I'll sort it out with her as soon as I can.'

Chuck held her tightly against him while he looked down at her face and smiled. Then he pushed hard against her lips, flicking her tongue with his so that she was hardly able to catch her breath. He didn't let go of her until the tram arrived. 'Do you know something, Gracie Ashton?' he said reluctantly pulling away, 'I think you're definitely my kind of girl.'

Gracie didn't have time to ask him what he meant before they got on to the crowded tram but her lips tingled and her mind was racing throughout the long ride home.

They managed to meet several times after their interrupted visit to the tearooms, although Gracie was constantly wary that Chuck could be called away or could cancel their arrangements at the last minute. While the weather was still warm as Weatherfield basked in an Indian Summer, they managed a successful picnic in Heaton Park that was merely a tram ride away. Then, when the town was firmly in the grips of an autumnal chill, they opted to stay indoors and went to the cinema instead. They always sat in the back row where all the young couples sat. What usually started with Chuck putting his arm round her and holding her close, ended with them kissing and petting until, in good humour, Gracie felt obliged to gently prise herself away. On the way home they would share a bag of fish and chips while they tried to piece together the snapshots they had managed to see of the film.

In between what Chuck referred to as their 'dates' he kept his promise and wrote to Gracie care of the pub. He wrote in flowery, elegant language unlike the more matter-of-fact way he spoke when they were together, and although she loved to read it, flattered by his glowing and often affectionate words, she tried to keep her language grounded and to the point. But it didn't matter how she framed it, or what words she chose to use, the more Gracie saw of Chuck, the more their friendship grew, and Gracie realized that she was becoming very fond of him.

The hardest part of what she thought of as her budding romance was deceiving her parents and she wondered how much longer she could continue the subterfuge, not even mentioning his name at home. She was longing to talk to her mother about Chuck but, at the moment, she knew that was out of the question. She needed to be more certain of her own feelings before she could tell them about Chuck. It wasn't worth the risk of tipping her father over the edge when he could be physically violent. So for now she and Chuck would still say their affectionate goodbyes at the Field and then silently part when he finally left her at her front door.

Chuck came into the pub most nights when he was in Weatherfield, but it was several months before Gracie found a last-minute note suggesting they went dancing at the Ritz. She was thrilled, for she loved dancing with him, and she was grateful when Annie Walker said she could have the evening off. Chuck picked her up at the Rovers and it was a magical evening spoiled only by having to keep her outfit hidden under her coat when she finally arrived home.

The following day Annie expected to see Gracie tired from being out late dancing, so she was surprised to find the barmaid bright and perky and arriving early for the dinnertime shift. Despite the dark shadows beneath her lids, her eyes still managed to sparkle.

'I thought you'd be flaked out,' Annie joked. 'Did you not stay to the end, then?'

'No. We left about eleven.'

'That's late enough, by the time you got home. Are you not feeling tired?'

'I suppose I am a bit,' Gracie admitted, 'but there's a part of me that feels sort of excited; I imagine that's what's keeping me going.'

'Excited about what, may I ask?' Annie had a knowing look. 'Or can I guess?'

'You can probably guess.' Gracie said, a coy look on her face.

'I'm not a complete stranger to romance, you know,' Annie smiled. 'I've had my own share of it in my time.'

Gracie smiled back, though she looked uncertain for a moment, unsure how much to say. 'The thing is, nothing has actually happened, but it was just such a special evening given that I've had to wait so long for it to materialize. We danced almost the whole time apart from when he bought me a drink and we stopped for a smoke. A couple of blokes tried to butt in at one point, but he was having none of it.'

'That all sounds very promising, then. A sensible young man.'

'I think so. I now think my first impressions of him when we met in the Rovers that night were all wrong.'

At that moment there was a bang and a blast of cold air as the door into Annie's private vestibule was flung open. Annie leapt out of her chair. 'Billy!' she shouted. 'Come here this minute. What have I told you about coming into the pub?' But Billy's only response was to run around all the chairs and tables, at least three steps ahead of Annie, shouting, 'You can't catch me, I'm getting free.'

Eventually, unable to catch him, Annie sat down again on a bar stool. She was out of breath and shook her head in anger. 'Honestly, that boy. I don't know what I'm going to do with him. I'm only glad there are no customers here. I could lose my licence.'

'Can I get him for you?' Gracie offered.

'That's very kind, but I think we'd be better ignoring him. All he wants is some attention and I haven't got the time right now. He'll soon get tired of it and go and play with his toys. Now, where were we? I'm so sorry.'

'I was just saying the more I get to know Chuck, the more I like him. He's really nice and he's easy to talk to.'

'There's nothing wrong with that.'

'No, of course not. He's different and he's exciting. I like him a lot. The only thing I don't like is the way he keeps disappearing so I never know where I am with him. But at least, since that first dreadful time, we can now write to each other when he's not around.'

'I presume it's his work keeps him away?' Annie asked.

'So he says, though he won't talk about his job.'

'Did it occur to you he might be in intelligence? In which case, he wouldn't be able to talk about what he does.'

'No. I never thought of that. You could be right. It would make sense.'

'Has he told you much about himself?' Annie wanted to know. 'Do you know what kind of life he leads back home?'

'Yes, he's talked a lot about his parents and his sister in New York. He'd been living at home with them before he was drafted. He even talked about wanting to take me over there to meet his family, one day,' Gracie said, though now she sounded confused. 'But I told him, I can't be thinking of such things right now.'

'Hmm,' Annie muttered. 'That's all very nice but you're quite right to be a little cautious.' Annie nodded and as she spoke she saw Billy crawl across the floor and disappear through the door. Gracie saw him too, but made no reference to the tiny figure sneaking away. 'You know, men aren't always to be trusted where matters of the heart are concerned,' Annie continued as if the Billy incident hadn't occurred, although as she spoke she got up once more from her chair and wedged the door closed. Then one by one she picked up the trail of Dinky cars Billy had left in his wake. 'I would be particularly wary of one whose vision might be a bit skewed because he's so far away from his home and family. He might say things without thinking. He might mean them at the time, but in my experience men rarely think things through.'

'He's been very respectful,' Gracie said. 'He's certainly not taken advantage, if that's what you mean?'

'That's good to hear.'

'Though I know he's a believer in grabbing whatever happiness he can, wherever he can get it. At least, as far as his own happiness is concerned.'

'That's exactly my point. For most of the time such men don't consider the possible consequences of their actions.'

'But you can't blame him entirely.' Gracie defended Chuck now. 'I think war does that to you. I feel a bit that way inclined myself. We none of us know what's going to happen next.'

'I don't disagree either. *Carpe diem*, as the saying goes,' Annie said.

'Whatever that means,' Gracie laughed.

'It's Latin and it means "seize the day", exactly what you are describing.'

'Okay, *carpe diem*, then. What with all his comings

and goings I never know what each day's going to bring. And I think: what would I do if I never saw him again?'

There was a catch in Gracie's voice and suddenly she began to cry.

'Isn't it time you told your parents about him?' Annie said gently.

'I'd love to be able to talk to them, honestly, but I can't just take him home and introduce him, not when my father has threatened to throw me out or worse if I ever go out with an American. He can be violent when he's a mind. And Mum's none too keen on them, either.'

'Are you sure they still feel that way? The war has changed many people's ideas. I mean, they don't even know him. Maybe if you asked them you'd find they would like to meet him.'

'Not if he's a Yank, they wouldn't. My dad reckons you should steer well clear of anything or anyone to do with the USA and not a day goes by that he doesn't say so.'

'Maybe you should start by trying to get your mother on your side then,' Annie suggested.

Gracie blew her nose noisily on a handkerchief she brought out of her pocket while Annie was thoughtful for a few moments. She drummed her fingers on the countertop and had to clear her throat before she said, 'Whatever happens, I do hope you'll be sensible, Gracie. Don't get tricked into doing something you don't want to do.'

Gracie looked up, her eyes questioning.

Annie continued, 'Girls, particularly these days, need to be extra careful if they don't want to get into trouble. Remember, if he gets sent abroad, it doesn't matter what he's promised you. When push comes to shove you'll be the one who's left high and dry.'

'Oh, but Mrs Walker, we haven't. I wouldn't . . . I couldn't . . .'

Annie sighed. 'All I'm saying is that you must take care of yourself. And never give away cheaply your most precious commodity without protecting your reputation. Once lost, you can never get either of them back.'

Gracie was shocked to hear Annie speaking so personally, but she knew the advice was well meant. Neither of them said anything for several minutes and, as they sat there at the bar, Gracie could sense Annie getting more and more agitated and she began to wonder whether she had been alluding to something from her own life when she had issued her caution. She wanted to press her to say more but Annie was looking thoughtful, locked away with her own thoughts and memories.

Gracie suddenly thought back to the week she had started working at the Rovers and wondered if such warnings might in some way be connected to that mysterious young girl, Annette, who had appeared apparently out of the blue. That was something she hadn't made connections with before, though she had thought of the girl often and wondered who she was. Now her mind began racing. Could Annette be . . . ? Gracie threw out the idea almost as soon as it came into her head. Surely, it was unthinkable that Annie could have strayed like that? But the more she thought about it, the more she was convinced that Annie had definitely been hinting at some cautionary tale from her past; something that remained a secret and was therefore a mystery to those around her. Gracie would have loved to know more but didn't feel she could ask. She could sense Annie's reluctance to say more than she already had. She could see it in the tightness of Annie's posture as she hunched over the bar stool, and the rigidity of her hands as she locked and unlocked her fingers.

Gracie sighed. 'How will I know, Annie?' she said at last, needing to break the tension.

'Know what?' Annie was surprised out of her reverie.

'How will I know if someone I like is the right one for me? How will I know if I am really in love?'

'That really is a tough question to answer, you know, my dear.' Annie released her fingers and rubbed her palms together as if to warm them. 'I suppose I could say you'll just know, but that's not very helpful, is it? I think, basically, I would urge you to follow your instincts in all matters of the heart, but do for goodness sake err on the side of caution.'

'How did you know when you met Jack that he was Mr Right?' Gracie asked boldly.

Suddenly Annie laughed. 'Oh goodness, I didn't.' She chuckled. 'My first meeting with Jack is not something you want to emulate, I can assure you.' She paused. 'But then, ours was what you might call a very unconventional meeting.' Annie smiled then, remembering the first time they met.

Gracie shook her head. 'Really? I would have imagined you two being friends from school, or something.'

'No, it was nothing like that.' For a moment, a dreamy look came into her eyes as she was reminded of his actual proposal, but then she threw back her head and laughed. 'We met when he knocked me down one day while I was standing on a bridge over the canal.'

'Knocked you down? You mean by accident?'

'Oh, no. He meant to knock me down. He said it was to stop me from flinging myself into the water. But the silly thing was, I wasn't about to do that at all. He'd got completely the wrong end of the stick.'

'What were you doing there, then?'

'I was only trying to see if there were any fish in the water.' Annie laughed. 'But suddenly I heard the sound of someone running hard. By the time I looked up, this young man was lunging at me and it was too late to dodge out of his way. I tried to sidestep him but he was coming too fast, then he threw himself at me and the next thing I knew I'd been knocked to the ground. I was pretty shocked, I can tell you, and he badly winded me.'

'Weren't you hurt?' Gracie interjected.

'I suppose the worst that happened was that I jarred my back as I fell, but thankfully I could still move my arms and legs and even my fingers and toes.'

'I bet you were cross.'

'Cross? I was so angry I wanted to hit him. In fact, I was convinced he had run away so I was surprised to find he was bending over me looking very concerned. Not only concerned, but extremely anxious. And the other surprise was that he was only a slip of a boy, about my own age, but he was checking me over to make sure I was all right.'

'What did he say?' Gracie wanted to know.

'To my amazement, he apologized. And he kept asking me if I was sure I was okay. Then he said, "Thank goodness, thank goodness, I'm so relieved, I'm so glad", over and over until I began to think maybe he was the one who wasn't all right. And when I asked him what on earth he thought he was doing, he said that a few cuts and bruises were far better than the alternative.'

'What was the alternative?' Gracie was puzzled.

'It seemed he thought I was going to jump. "Things can never be that bad you know," he kept on saying. "I'm sure if you'd talk to someone you'd find they're not as bad as you thought. You could even try talking to me if you're desperate."'

'What happened next? Did he leave you there?' Gracie asked.

'Well, he helped me up and then I remember thinking

that he actually wasn't bad-looking. He looked rather serious, which I thought might be a good thing, though I wondered whether that was just the effect of his glasses. They'd been knocked off in the fall and before he put them back on I couldn't help noticing that he had kind eyes and seemed to blush easily. Both of which I found rather attractive,' she added coyly.

'Did he tell you his name?'

'Yes, of course, and when I was upright again he offered me his hand to shake. He told me he came from Accrington but worked in Weatherfield with his brother, Arthur.'

'Did you tell him your name?' Gracie asked, determined to glean every last detail of the unusual encounter.

'Yes, I did. Not that it meant anything to him. It was a well-known name in Clitheroe, where the family hailed from, but not in Weatherfield. I must say he acted like a gentleman throughout and he offered to see me home.'

'To which offer you said . . . ?'

'I said, yes.' Annie gave a self-satisfied smile. 'So we had a lovely leisurely walk down Canal Street.'

'And that's how it all started?'

Annie nodded.

'All very romantic,' Gracie concluded.

'I suppose it was, in the end,' Annie agreed. 'Though it certainly didn't start out that way. But once we started stepping out together I gradually came to realize how much I loved him and we began courting seriously. He has a great calming influence on me and always seems to be there if I need rescuing in any way. Not that I need rescuing very often, but he does like to negotiate on my behalf if he thinks I've got myself into a difficult situation.'

'Did you know what he worked at? Did he tell you that right away?' Gracie was interested.

'Yes, indeed, he did tell me that he was working in a pub with his brother in Weatherfield. And that was where he was learning the trade. He also told me that he hoped to be offered his own tenancy very soon by the brewery. We had hoped it might be something in the countryside, but that obviously wasn't to be.' Annie sighed. A wistful expression was on her face and for a few moments she seemed to be lost in her own thoughts.

'What happened when he asked you to marry him?' prompted Gracie, determined to hear every bit of the story.

'Oh, my goodness, was that ever romantic? Down on one knee, with his grandmother's ring in a black velvet box in his hand.' Annie looked down at her hands where the only ring that would fit her spreading fingers now was her wedding band. But she had enjoyed wearing the family heirloom while her finger was still slim enough for it to fit. 'And we've been working together ever since.' She smiled. 'A very interesting job it's turned out to be. Until the war intruded, that is, when of course my Jack, being the selfless man he is, signed up straight away to fight.'

The two women sat in silence for a few moments, then Gracie plucked up the courage to ask, 'So he hasn't let you down in any way? You've never had any kind of bad experience with him except for him knocking you over?'

Annie looked surprised by the question. 'No. No problems at all. Why do you ask?'

'Because I was just wondering . . . who . . . ? Gracie wasn't sure what exactly she was asking. 'I thought you said . . . it was just that you seemed to understand what it means to be let down.' Gracie felt the blood rise to her cheeks and wondered if she had asked one question too many.

Annie's face changed. She answered calmly, though there was a slight quaver to her voice. 'I do understand. But that wasn't because of Jack. It was someone else. And it was all a long time ago.' She put both hands on the countertop and lifted herself up from the stool. 'I think it's time we opened the bar, don't you?' Her voice was brisk now. 'Oh, and here's Lottie popping in for a Saturday drink. The two of you might be able to pinch a moment for a catch-up on last night before the rush begins.' Then, to Gracie's amusement, before she went back into the kitchen to retrieve some glasses, Annie winked.

Chapter 7

When Roy Farnworth, a captain in the US army as Annie later found out, first came into the Rovers she could see immediately that he was a cut above the regular enlisted GIs that had frequented the pub until now and that included Gracie's Chuck who was only a second lieutenant. He was tall, with a noticeably upright gait. Apart from the double silver bands of his rank that he carried with pride on his shoulders, there was something about the way he held himself erect, like an athlete, with a certain swagger when he walked, in the same way she fancied a professional soldier might. All that was missing was a swagger stick, she decided. Annie admired his handsome face as he strode towards the bar for he looked like a film star. Indeed, he had a Robert Taylor-style moustache and wore his hair in the same way as the star had when she saw him recently playing a US army captain in the revived version of the film *Waterloo Bridge*. The sides and back were short but the top was much longer than that of most of the junior men and was brushed back with not a hair out of place. He had such a wholesome look about him she couldn't help wondering if he had ever actually been in combat.

As he approached, she saw another soldier following him and she recognized Gracie's young man. Gracie's face lit up with a smile as he made his way to the bar. Annie left Gracie to attend to her soldier while she glided across to serve the officer.

'May I help you,' she said as Gracie began pulling a pint of mild for Chuck.

'That would be good, thank you,' he said. 'It's my first time in an English pub and I have to be honest and tell you I'm not quite sure what to order. What would you recommend?'

'You'd better be nice to him.' Chuck leaned over. 'I recommended he came here. May I introduce Captain Roy Farnworth, the general's senior aide de camp?'

'Allow me to introduce myself,' Annie said, beaming at the officer. 'I'm the landlady here, Mrs Anne Walker.' She offered a rather limp hand for him to shake. 'Welcome to Weatherfield and the Rovers Return.' She tilted her head slightly. 'As to what you might like to drink, that, of course, will depend on your taste, but if it's beer you're after, we basically have mild and we have bitter.'

The captain looked over to see what Chuck was drinking.

'I'm a mild man,' Chuck said and everyone laughed.

'Then maybe I should try bitter,' the captain said promptly. 'I think bitter sounds good.'

'Our best bitter is the local brew, Shires, and that's really popular,' Annie said.

'Is it true you drink your beer warm over here?' The captain's face was quizzical.

Annie's laughter tinkled. 'All I can say is that it's true we don't keep it on ice. Why don't you try it? I can give you a small glass of Shires. See what you think.' She filled a half pint glass and waited for the head to settle then wiped the froth that had spilled over the sides before she slid it across to him.

'You might be more comfortable over there.' She pointed to one of the booths. 'The banquette seats there are so much better upholstered than the bar stools.'

'That's right, you tell him. We have to be nice to him.' Chuck spoke in a stage whisper as the captain turned to look at the seats Annie had pointed to. 'He's the guy who's responsible for sorting out the billeting round here, so if you've any complaints he's the one to see.'

'Oh, but I don't have anyone billeting here,' Annie said.

At that the captain turned to her and smiled. 'Maybe you should,' he said.

'I've no spare room. I do have two young children, you know.' Annie let her eyelids flap like butterflies

179

wings. She paused to allow time for a compliment, but when none was forthcoming she added, 'They may be small but they do seem to take up an awful lot of room.' She was thinking back to this morning when she found the wallpaper in her bedroom had changed. Up to the height of Billy's arm's reach the blue wallpaper had been heavily scored over in red and carmine polish had been applied to the white painted skirting board.

'Perhaps you'd be willing to let them share if ever we get really pushed for billets,' he suggested.

Annie didn't reply immediately, but then she said, 'It's certainly something to think about if there's to be another wave of allies landing in Weatherfield.' But she had been sidetracked while they were talking, listening to his voice and looking at his hands. She was fascinated to notice, as he reached for his glass, how well mani-cured his nails were, and from the way that he spoke she discerned that he was obviously a man of culture.

It wasn't a busy night at the bar and while Gracie saw to the few customers, Annie spent most of the evening engaged in pleasant conversation with Captain Farnworth. He told her about his home in Nebraska, about his wife and three children, two boys and a girl, all now in their teens, and about his rather boring job as an accountant.

'It must be fascinating being an innkeeper,' he said. 'Isn't that what they call you guys over here?'

'Why yes, I believe that is one of the terms used for those of us who run a hostelry.' Annie gave a little laugh. 'And it can be so enlightening, meeting all sorts of different people and hearing about their lives.'

'And there have to be some perks, like: "Will you let me buy you a drink?"'

'Well, that is very kind of you.' Annie blushed. 'I don't usually partake while on duty.' She looked at her watch. 'But good heavens, it's nearly closing time. We're closing a little earlier these days to make the beer go further.' She gave a little laugh. 'Gracie, would you be so kind as to call time?' Annie helped herself to a small sherry and pulled a whole pint of Shires for the appreciative captain.

'You know,' he said as they clinked glasses, 'you remind me of someone and I can't think who. Have you ever been on the stage?'

Annie preened. 'Actually, I was once,' and she began to tell him about her days in the dramatic and operatic society when she was young.

Roy grinned. 'Well, it just goes to show,' he said. 'I must have known some of that, all along. Once a star, always a star.' He chuckled.

'I'll drink to that,' Annie said with a laugh and she finished the remains of her drink in one go.

After that night, Captain Farnworth took to coming into the Rovers often. It brightened Annie's evening as soon as she saw him and she felt as if he brought a kind of charm to the place that was very appealing. She liked hearing American accents, she decided, because they never sounded common. Realizing how much she enjoyed his company, and how stimulated she felt by their conversations, Annie made a point of trying to spend as much time as she could talking to him whenever he came in. They talked about everything and she began to feel almost as if she could confide in him; it was as if he were a really good friend. They talked about the current battle of the Atlantic, where the German stranglehold on merchant shipping was preventing vital supplies reaching Britain from the US, and on a lighter note about films like *Gone with the Wind*, about books they had read and the relative merits of some of their favourite writers such as Eugene O'Neill, John Steinbeck and Ernest Hemingway. Annie felt herself coming alive during their discussions. She began to look forward to his visits and felt bereft on the evenings he was missing. Whenever possible, on the evenings he did appear, she contrived to serve him herself. On evenings when he was definitely expected, she put on an extra dab of make-up, just in case. They became such friends that Annie seriously began to think that she might be persuaded to experiment with Billy and Joanie sharing a bedroom should the captain require it, even though she firmly believed it would cause even more havoc than usual behind the scenes in the Rovers.

Occasionally Roy, as he'd invited her to call him, came in with Chuck or one of the other junior officers, but most often he came alone. One night, when Annie knew Gracie was seeing Chuck after hours and had given her permission to leave early, she asked Roy to stay on for a private drink after closing time. She felt nervous approaching him, for it was a bold move with innocent motivation. To her relief, he didn't seem to read more than she had intended into the invitation, although he politely declined as he had duties to perform back at base. But he added, 'I'll take a rain check if it's all the same to you.'

Annie looked puzzled.

'Old baseball expression,' Roy explained. 'If a match is stopped part way because of inclement weather they give you a chitty so you can come back when it's rescheduled. The whole point is, you don't have to pay again.'

'Now that's a sensible idea,' Annie said. 'Though of course it wouldn't apply in this country, except in cricket. Football or rugby games are never stopped part way through because of the weather.' She thought of Jack, who had followed his favourite football club, Oldham Athletic, and who looked surprised when she suggested he might be home early if rain was to stop them playing. 'Nothing short of a hurricane or a sudden blizzard would stop a game at Boundary Park,' Jack had said with scorn. 'What's a bit of rain to us?'

'Truth is, I think they enjoy revelling in the mud.' Annie flashed Roy a smile. 'But I'll remember that expression in future, thank you.' She caught his gaze and was shocked to feel a sudden spark of the mutual attraction as they made eye contact. She lowered her lids, coyly. 'So, do let me offer you a rain check, Captain Farnworth,' she said. 'And you are welcome to cash it in at any time.'

It had been a long time since Annie had felt so flirtatious. She had forgotten how much fun it could be as it was something she had got out of the habit of doing. Life had become very hard for her, particularly since Jack had gone away, running the pub on her own at the same time as trying to keep the children in check. She didn't want to complain because she knew it was the same for most people in the street, even though everyone tried their best to put a brave face on things. But the light had gone out of people's lives as they struggled to manage the devastating effects of such things as shortages, rationing and sporadic air raids, while their loved ones, if they were lucky enough to still be alive, were serving their country thousands of miles away. The glamour that this soldier brought into her life against the background of the everyday drudgery was as exciting as it was irresistible. Her friendship with Roy had brought a little light back into Annie's life, and she made no excuses for embracing it wholeheartedly. After all, he was so very charming, and of course it was strictly platonic. She could never lower herself to respond to the Americans in the same way that women like Elsie Tanner had done, even if the GIs were Britain's allies – that would be shameful. But surely there was no harm in indulging her imagination a little so long as she always knew where to draw the line.

Chapter 8

1929

Life at Fletcher's Mill became easier for Annie once she began stepping out with Archie. The Bradshaw girls backed off when they saw the two of them constantly together. Archie, being so tall and brawny, could look quite formidable, and Annie liked to think that the dreadful tormentors kept their distance because they might be a little afraid of him.

'Let's face it,' Annie's friend Nancy said, ''e's not someone as you'd want to be messin' with on a dark night now, is 'e?'

Annie often wondered if he had threatened the sisters in some way, although he never would admit to anything.

'I don't need to bully anyone,' he said. 'One look at me and they realize who they're messing with.' It was true. They couldn't know he was a gentle soul at heart. So they still pulled faces at her and whispered behind their hands, but the open taunts became a thing of the past and Annie no longer had to be escorted to and from work by Nancy and Lilian although the three remained good friends and often did walk home together. They also began to visit each other's houses, although Annie still avoided inviting anyone round to Alderley Street if possible, because her mother was such a bad manager and the house always looked a mess. There was rarely a fire to make tea and never any food she could offer a visitor.

Florence had taken in some work eventually as Annie had suggested, mostly sewing for the neighbours, for which she was paid a pittance. Annie didn't want to discourage her, however little she contributed to the family pot, but whenever she had a piece of sewing to complete Florence claimed she didn't have the time to see to the shopping or do any cooking or cleaning. So Annie mostly visited her friends' houses and was interested to see how their mothers managed to run their households so efficiently, even though they were probably no better off financially than the Beaumonts.

Annie was tired of not eating properly. She put her ill health down to poor nutrition and blamed that on her mother's unwillingness to come to terms with the family's situation. She had tried everything, including, as a frantic last resort, offering to cook for the family herself when she came home from work if only her mother would do the shopping. For the next few days she left a shopping list and some money from her wages to enable Florence to do this. But within a week the arrangement had broken down.

Annie returned home from work one Friday night to find there was not enough food in the house for her to cook anything that would make a decent meal for the three of them. She was staring in despair at the empty shelves in the kitchen cupboard when her father arrived home from work, as tired and hungry as she was. She knew as soon as she saw his face that the situation would not be allowed to continue.

'What is the matter with you, Florence?' he asked. His voice sounded calm but Annie could see the warning signs of a major outburst in the tension of his neck muscles and the way he kept clenching and unclenching his fists.

'Nothing's the matter with me, Edward. It's you. You're the one who seems to be expecting miracles.' Annie couldn't believe that her mother sounded almost unconcerned.

Edward rolled his eyes heavenwards. 'I don't understand what the problem is. Annie has given you enough money from her wages to buy food and I believe she's even provided you with a shopping list. Yet it seems that a miracle is required for you to produce a meal for the two workers in the house when they come home at night. Do you really expect me or Annie to manage on bread and cheese after a hard day's work?'

'Oh, come on, you're only a clerk in an office, stop exaggerating.'

Annie thought her father was going to explode. He went red in the face as his neck muscles tightened, and he puffed out his cheeks. Even his eyes were shot with blood. 'Only a clerk?' he shouted now. 'How dare you, woman. At least I'm contributing towards this household, not leeching it like a parasite. Who do you think is providing the money for the rent and for the clothes on your back?'

'Clothes? What clothes? When did I last have anything new?'

Edward ignored her pathetic accusation and continued to rant. 'While poor Annie here is literally working all the hours God sends to provide food for us – or she would be, if you could be bothered to buy any.'

'Are you implying I'm lazy?' They were both shouting now.

'I'm not implying anything, because I can't fathom whether you are lazy or just plain stupid. But you can't expect Annie and me to come home from a day at the mill, whatever you might think of our jobs, and have to cook our own meal when you've been doing nothing but lying around the house most of the day.'

At this Florence began to cry. 'I'll have you know I've been taking in sewing from the neighbours, work

I've practically had to beg for. Do you know how humiliating that is?'

'Don't talk to me about humiliation, madam. How do you think a squire feels being bossed about in a stinking, overheated cotton mill by his inferiors? Or your daughter working her fingers to the bone to put food on the table? Don't ask *me* for sympathy.'

'Oh, Edward, how can you be so cruel when I'm doing my best?'

'Well, if that's your best then your best is obviously not good enough.'

'I don't know what you want me to do,' she sobbed.

'I want you to bloody cook, woman. When a man comes home from earning the rent money and he's starving he wants his wife to prepare a meal for him, and his daughter is entitled to the same treatment when she's been slogging her guts out all day too. Surely that's not too much to expect?'

Annie had never heard her father swear or use what her mother called gutter language before and she was shocked, though she knew he was right. She hated such confrontation, but she was pleased that it was coming out into the open at last and her mother was being taken to task by Edward in a way that Annie couldn't have done. Florence began to snivel and Annie almost felt sorry for her, but she knew she had to stand firm with her father on this.

'Shall I go around to the corner shop and fetch some eggs? I can at least make an omelette for us all,' Annie offered, not sure on what level to interfere while her father was still incandescent.

'You can make a bloody omelette for thee and me, though I swear I'd be happy to see her starve until she understands the meaning of the word.' Edward pointed his finger in Florence's direction and Annie could see his hand was shaking.

'Oh Edward, you can't mean that?' Florence whined.

'Why not? That's what you're doing to us. You're making us starve by your – your crackpot ways.'

'I don't mean to. I'm just so tired and miserable all the time. I mean to go out shopping, and I intend to cook, but often I forget what I'm doing and somehow the day just slips away. But I can change. I know I can. Give me another chance, please.' Florence got down on her knees and tried to hug Edward's legs. Annie couldn't look at her, it was so humiliating. But, she thought, maybe her father was right and that was the only way to make Florence understand the consequences of her inaction. Annie and her father had lived off starvation rations long enough. It was time for it to stop.

For a while after that night things did begin to change. Florence became more reliable about shopping, although she would often not stick to the list Annie had carefully worked out to match their limited budget. She would come home with some luxury item like a chicken breast that would barely feed one instead of the offal that Annie had reckoned on to serve the three of them. No matter how Annie tried to talk to her, Florence didn't seem to understand the economics of running a house-hold at all. But at least a variety of ingredients began to appear in the kitchen cupboards and the meat larder usually had something fresh in each day.

But the next problem was that Florence was not a natural cook and didn't seem to understand some of the basic skills required in the kitchen. Despite Annie's coaxing and the offers of help from their neighbour, she refused to take instruction or even to acknowledge what she was doing wrong.

'It's a bloody waste of money,' Edward yelled when, for the third night in a row, the food had been rendered almost inedible by Florence's culinary attempts. 'There's no point in doing the shopping if you're not going to learn how to cook the damn food properly.' He picked up with his fingers the latest charred offering on his plate and stared at it in scorn. 'I wouldn't give it to the dog if we had one,' he said with derision and he tossed it onto the fire.

'Edward, don't!' Florence shouted. 'That meat cost good money.'

'So, you've learned one bloody lesson at least,' Edward sneered. 'But it doesn't matter how much it cost if it's uneatable. What's the bloody use of buying it if you aren't going to learn how to cook it properly?'

After much shouting and swearing, name-calling and recriminations they came to an uneasy truce. Florence promised to take some instruction and to try to improve but Annie feared each night what she might be coming home to and the palpable tension round the dinner table was at times unbearable.

'Maybe we could advertise for a cook,' Florence suggested one night when Edward had declared himself to be sated for once.

Annie stopped what she was eating with her fork halfway to her mouth. She glanced at her father, who once again looked fit to burst.

'Daddy, you'll pump yourself into a heart attack, if you don't take care.' Annie was genuinely concerned.

'It's that stupid woman you call your mother who'll be the death of me,' Edward spluttered. 'Will she ever understand the seriousness of our situation?'

Annie glanced at her mother, whose eyes had begun to brim, and she sighed. 'Probably not,' she said, and she understood at that moment that getting angry was not going to provide a solution either. At least for the near future, housewifely chores were going to be an on-going battle but as Annie was becoming more skilful on the looms she was offered a better position and she received a slight increase in pay. It meant working longer hours and involved overseeing others but she readily accepted, thinking it would make things easier at home. To help Florence she decided to use the extra money to take on someone to clean the house.

Mrs Brockett, their neighbour, recommended Moira Beattie from the next village and, to Annie's relief, the young woman said she could start right away.

Florence protested when Annie told her what she had

done. She didn't see the necessity to have someone in to clean.

'It's a waste of your hard-earned money spending it on a charlady, Annie,' she said. 'You're young. If you're earning more money now you should be spending the extras on going out and enjoying yourself; buying pretty clothes and make-up, not worrying about the house all the time.'

Annie sighed. Her mother never had adjusted to their reduced circumstances. 'You don't seem to want to clean it, Mummy, and quite frankly I'm too tired when I get home after a hard day's work.' She tried to be patient. 'All I want to do is eat something and put my feet up with my friends and, at the moment, I can't do either of those things.' How could she explain without hurting her mother's feelings? 'It's not very nice,' she said at last, 'when the house I come home to is in such a state that I feel ashamed to invite my friends in.' She had tried to spell it out many times but Florence never seemed to understand. Now her mother looked shocked. She opened her mouth as if to protest but Annie plunged on. 'You don't have to worry about it, I'm quite happy paying someone to clean so that I can invite my friends round. I don't like having to go to their homes all the time and I hate feeling so ashamed of my own.'

At that Florence began to cry. 'What have we come to that you want me to be a cleaner? How can you expect me to stoop so low? That's maid's work. I don't know what you're suggesting. I was never born to be a maid, Annie, and neither were you.'

'No, Mummy, I agree and that's why I'm prepared to buy in help.' Annie put her arm round her mother's shoulders and was shocked to feel her bones so close to the surface. 'Unfortunately, it doesn't matter whether we were born to it or not, that's the situation we find ourselves in. I'm just trying to be practical. So, I'll happily pay for a cleaner then you can concentrate on your sewing and the cooking and I can do my new job at the mill.' She smiled, but Florence was too busy mopping up her tears to notice and as soon as Moira started working for the Beaumonts, Florence began grumbling, finding fault with everything the young woman did.

'I can't get on with the cooking because she's under my feet all the time,' was the first complaint.

'But she only comes in for a couple of hours a week,' Annie argued.

'It doesn't matter. I feel the house is not my own.'

'That's because it's not.' This time Edward intervened. 'You share it with us and Annie's right to want it to be respectable enough to be able to invite people in. So, unless you want to do the cleaning, and I mean proper cleaning, then you'll have to put up with Moira Beattie. And I don't want to hear any more arguments, understand?'

'You two are just ganging up on me,' Florence protested. 'You think yourselves so much better than me because you go out to work while I have to work in the house.'

'Oh dear. Poor Cinderella, are you?' Edward jibed. 'Well, I can tell you something for nothing, woman, this Cinders won't be going to any balls ever again, not unless there are some drastic changes in this house.'

Annie was grateful for her father's intervention. He was doing his best to come to terms with their situation. In fact, she had been wondering lately how he would react if she suggested that he might look for a better job. She knew that work was not always easy to come by, but it would help her enormously if he could add more money to the household coffers. Till then, however, she was glad of his support, however limited, and maybe one day he would once again become the squire of the manor he once was.

Chapter 9

April 1943

Roy Farnworth, or Captain Roy as Annie called him, had taken up his 'rain check' for a nightcap at the Rovers just before Christmas in the old year of 1942. He had become a regular visitor at the pub from the day Chuck had introduced him to it and he and Annie spent many an evening happily chatting together. But it took him several months before he had taken up Annie's offer of staying on for a drink after closing. After the first time, however, he regularly stayed late whenever he could. They always remained in the pub by the bar and Annie treasured the evenings that they would sit and, in his words, 'shoot the breeze' together. She really enjoyed talking to him and a comfortable friendship began to develop between them.

She knew he was in charge of arranging the billets for all the soldiers under his command, but Annie was sure he had other more mysterious responsibilities as well. Like Chuck, his work seemed to take him away from Weatherfield and all around the country so often that she was convinced she had been right in surmising that the two were involved in some kind of intelligence work. However, that was not a question she wanted to ask. Careless talk cost lives, after all.

When they were together, Annie felt free and different in a way she found difficult to describe. She enjoyed his company – it was innocent fun, and for an hour or two she felt like a young girl again. For her, there were no strings attached and she could forget she was a mother and the landlady of the pub. She was sure he felt the same way. He talked easily about his family in America and she hoped he also felt free to switch off from his responsibilities for an hour or two and relax.

In the first week of April of the New Year, Annie issued Roy with a different kind of invitation, which she thought seemed perfectly reasonable as they had become friends. 'I thought you might like to join me "behind the scenes" on Sunday night,' she said. 'I shall be closing the pub early and I thought we could listen to some Duke Ellington records. You said he was a favourite of yours too.'

'He is indeed. That would be swell, thank you.' Roy seemed pleased she had asked.

She expected him to come into the bar for a drink beforehand and when he didn't appear she was disappointed. She had just seen the last customer off the premises when there was a tap on the windowpane of the door. 'It's me, Captain Farnworth,' a voice called. 'Sorry I'm so late.'

When she opened the door, he rather sheepishly thrust a bunch of flowers into her hand.

'You didn't have to bring these,' she laughed, 'just because you're late.' She gave an embarrassed laugh.

'That's not the reason I've brought them,' he said, 'though I do apologize again for being so late. But I hope you like carnations.'

'I love them, thank you,' she said. 'Do come in. I'm intrigued to hear the real reason you brought them.'

'A little birdie told me it was Mother's Day here in England today,' he said, grinning.

'Well, yes, it is. But isn't it Mother's Day in Nebraska too?'

'No, not at all. My—' He checked himself and added instead, 'We don't celebrate it till May.'

'Oh, well then, double thanks for your undercover research. The flowers are very much appreciated.'

Annie went into the pub and then straight through into her private quarters. Roy followed.

Suddenly she felt almost shy and she didn't know what to say so she busied herself putting the carnations into water. She was aware that Roy was staring down at the wall. 'My little boy Billy wanted to give me a Mother's Day card.' She laughed. 'The only thing is he insisted on painting it over the wallpaper.' Roy laughed too. 'Just the kind of thing my oldest monster would do,' he said and, to Annie's relief, that first awkward moment was over.

Monday evening was mild and after Roy's visit the previous night, Annie was feeling particularly sprightly. The public bar at the Rovers was crowded, for once filled with more regulars than GIs and Canadian servicemen. Both Chuck and Roy were attending meetings in London for at least a week and somehow, for Annie, the pub felt quiet without them. However, feelings were running high about the war and its repercussions and several lively discussions had taken place already during the course of the evening, enough to entice Ena Sharples and her cronies to come through from the snug to join in. Some people were nursing their drinks as they had been warned there would be no more beer available that night, but others were switching their allegiance, even ordering soft drinks. Annie was on her own behind the bar, so she'd had no time to join in any of the discussions as she often liked to do. But she could hear the lively debates raging on the other side of the counter.

And then Ida Barlow arrived. There was a lull in the conversation while she ordered her drink and moved her port and lemon across the countertop.

'Did anyone see what nearly happened this afternoon?' she asked, filling the momentary silence.

'We won't know until you tell us what did happen now, will we?' Ena sounded like her usual sarcastic self.

Ida wasn't fazed. 'It was when the children were out playing by the Field, you know that deserted bit of flat land down by the viaduct.'

'And that's news, is it?' Ena cackled.

'Give her a chance!' Elsie Tanner chimed in. 'Go on, love,' she said encouragingly to Ida.

'You know how the kids love to play in and out of the Anderson shelters on the Field?' Ida continued as if there had been no interruption. 'Well, suddenly, out of the blue, there were a couple of planes flying overhead. I could make out they were German, I could see them swastika thingies on the side and I think they must have been lost. There were just the two of them and they were flying quite high, thankfully, because of all the barrage balloons out there.'

'Glad to hear they were doing their job.' Annie was surprised to hear her friend and neighbour Albert Tatlock pitching in to this one, though it had started off essentially as another discussion among the women.

'Suddenly, I saw one of those firebomb things,' Ida said. 'One of the planes dropped it, just like that.' She made a gesture with her hand, opening it palm down like she was dropping an egg. A gasp spread round the group.

'They can be terrible, them things,' Albert said, 'do rotten damage to houses and the like. And kill a lot of people.'

There was silence for a moment while everyone digested what he had said.

'What happened then?' Elsie asked, breaking the tension.

'It didn't do much damage as it turned out,' Ida continued, and relief showed on everyone's faces. 'It just fell on a bit of waste ground where there was nothing much to catch fire. It soon burned itself out.'

'So, I was right it wasn't really news after all.' Ena looked smug.

'No, thank goodness. But that's not the point. The thing is, it was right near to where them kids were playing. They could have been hurt in a flash.' She clicked her fingers in emphasis. Looks of fright and disbelief were exchanged once more. 'I'm telling you, two of the kids took off at a lick they were so terrified and it took us ages to find them afterwards.' She looked distraught as she relived the nightmare. 'Fortunately, the rest had the sense to crawl into the shelter. But the point is, and this is bloody news for you two . . .' Ida pointed her finger at Ena and Albert as she said this, 'I hadn't heard a siren going off.'

Albert scratched his head. 'That's very unusual,' he said. 'I'll have to report that. Someone wasn't doing their job right.'

Ena nodded, but for once she didn't say anything.

'I can tell you, it was enough to make me want to evacuate my kids right here and now. I hear there's a new drive to get people to move out of the cities.'

'Another one?' Vi Todd, Sally's mother from number 9, had come over to join the group. 'There were loads of kids sent away from Weatherfield at the beginning of the war. The government were desperate to convince us it was much safer for the kids to go and live in the countryside, far away from all the bombs.'

'I know,' Ida said, 'and I hadn't had my kids then, but now they're saying mothers of children under five can go with them and I'm seriously considering it.'

'What? With my husband away, go and leave behind all my friends and the little bit of family what's left when they're the ones who always help me out? Why would I want to go and live with strangers? Not on your nelly.' Elsie was adamant. She was thinking also of the hand-scribbled piece of paper she'd received that was supposed to be a Mother's Day card from her three-year-old daughter Linda that was still standing proudly on the mantelpiece at number 11. Would she really want to give up on such treats?

'I agree,' Vi said, whose children were now grown up.

'I don't know,' Albert said. 'Imagine being able to live on a farm or in a country village. I bet my Bessie would have loved to go with our Beattie when she was evacuated with her school class at the beginning of the war.'

'They say there's still people willing to offer board and lodgings to any children from the cities who might be in danger.' Ida was still open to the idea.

'But are they in danger? That's my question,' Elsie said.

'If Ida's story is anything to go by, I would say they are,' Albert said.

'You can't send your kids away on the strength of one firebomb, come on, Ida.' Elsie still managed to sound scornful as she looked directly at her friend.

'I can only tell you what happened. It was damned frightening, and . . . well, I don't know. I no longer feel that it is so safe here, for the kids especially,' said Ida, defending her position.

'Not an option for me,' said Elsie, shaking her head. 'And I'm disappointed. I thought you were with me on that one, Ida.'

'I was till I saw what I saw.'

'I can understand you being concerned,' Elsie reasoned. 'I am too.'

'Any mother would be,' Ena put in.

'But do you mean to tell me, on the strength of that, you'd be willing to let your two go off to live with strangers?' Elsie ignored the interruption. She still didn't believe Ida's change of heart was total.

'As long as we all went together it might not be too bad,' Ida said, 'but David's still a babe in arms. He's only nine months; he'd have to stay with me and Kenneth could be sent somewhere else?'

'You don't know where you might all end up. It's not bad enough your Frank's about to be sent back overseas?' Elsie wouldn't let it go.

'Well, I've not made my mind up yet, I was just saying, like . . .'

Elsie cut in, 'Well, you can "just say" all you like. I know that I've no bloody intention of letting either of my two out of my sight. We've no way of knowing how long they'd be gone for and I'll be damned if I'd let any Tim, Dick or Harry bring them up without me.' She poked Ida's shoulder, 'And neither should you.' Elsie folded her arms and confronted her friend. 'You were right with me and quite determined not twenty-four hours since.'

'I-I know. It's just that I'm not so sure now.'

'I would always want to put my child's safety first.' Ena's quiet comment brought her back to centre stage in the conversation as everyone looked at her.

'What, and I don't?' Elsie was outraged. 'I just happen to believe my kids are as safe here with me as they would be in the country with a stranger.'

Nobody spoke as, not for the first time, the two women squared up to each other.

Annie was itching to join in the argument. For once she sided with Elsie. She would never let either Billy or Joanie go away without her and she wouldn't dream of deserting the pub. For as long as it took for the war to be over she would happily keep on popping up and down to the shelter in the cellar if it meant that they would be safe, so long as she could keep the children with her. She was about to say so but then a customer called her away.

It was Elsie who broke the deadlock. 'What we really need, if kids are to stay here, is some proper nursery facilities.' She looked straight at Ena. 'The local nurseries round here are all full so I've been thinking we should open one of our own and I happen to think that the Mission of Glad Tidings would be the ideal place for it.'

'What would I be doing opening a nursery?' Ena Sharples' voice suddenly soared over the hubbub in the pub. 'You must be soft in the head. My kids are all grown up. What would I want with a nursery full of little ones?'

'Where's your community spirit then, Mrs Sharples?' Elsie sneered. 'You'd be doing it for the safety of our children, not yours.'

'If you really want safety, then in my opinion you should be sending them a long way out of Weatherfield.'

'Huh! I'd like to see you send a toddler and a babe in arms off somewhere you've never heard of, with a woman you never met, to a family you don't know from Adam.' Elsie was quite clear where she stood on the matter. 'I'm telling you, I'm not letting my children out of my sight.'

'So you'd rather I opened a nursery at the Mission so's you didn't have to do that? And whose bright idea was that in the first place, may I ask?' She looked round the group accusingly and ended up glaring at Elsie. 'You certainly couldn't have thought of owt like that all by yourself.'

'It *was* my idea, actually,' Elsie said, 'and although I say so myself it was an extremely bright one.'

'Oh, and how do you make that out?' Ena looked bored as she scratched her head without disturbing either her hairnet or her hair.

'For a kick off, if all our kids were together in one space then we'd know where they were every minute of the day that they weren't with us. No kids would be left wandering about on the street getting lost; none of them would be in danger from bombs whether the siren went off or not. But even the slightest peep from a siren and they could be downstairs in a flash, safely sheltering in the cellar.' Everyone in the group was nodding their heads now but Elsie hadn't finished. 'And the other thing is, it would free up all us women and maybe some of the older girls to carry out war work. Whatever's needed, just like in the nurseries that are already established. We would get money from the ministry and support to do it, just like they do.'

'And that support would include looking after the children, I presume?' Ena said, her jaw set in a firm line.

'Of course. To me, safeguarding our future is just as important as working in a bloody munitions factory. Then girls like your Vera, for instance, or anyone who'd enjoy looking after kids, could feel they were contributing. And for those already working in the factories, we'd be able to work longer hours than we can manage right now, because we wouldn't have to worry about looking after the kids. It makes perfect sense to me. We'd all be able to feel we were doing our bit. Isn't that what they're always shouting about? *Your country needs you!* and all that.' She pointed a finger directly at Ena, like she'd seen in the old Kitchener posters.

'Get off with you,' Ena said, 'that were the Great War, not this one.'

Elsie shrugged. 'All the bloody same to me. The thought's the same, isn't it? So, if you organize that the kiddies are looked after, then we can get on with our jobs, knowing the kids are safe. My friend Sarah's a qualified Nursery Nurse. She wants to go into the WRENS but she's not allowed to – she has to work in a nursery. I bet I could persuade her to help us. If she comes on board I don't think there'll be any problem getting some money from the Ministry of Health.'

Ena nodded her head as though she was at least considering Elsie's proposal now.

'And just think, you'd be able to sing hymns to your bloody heart's content. The kids wouldn't know any better.' Elsie giggled and took a large gulp of her gin. 'Maybe lots of hymn singing will help to bring this bloody war to an end. That can't come soon enough for me. Then we'll all be able to get on with our lives.'

'Hear, hear,' murmured Ida.

'So, what do you say, Mrs Sharples?' Elsie, well-fortified, challenged her nemesis.

'All I can promise is that I will go away and think about it.'

'Well, don't take too bloody long. The factories are crying out for us to work full time, even those of us with babbies. How long do you reckon it would take to get it set up?'

'I don't rightly know,' Ena admitted. 'Not long, I shouldn't think. We wouldn't need much if we can get financial support from the Ministry of Health for our setting-up and maintenance costs, though I'd be after your ration books if you expect me to provide owt in the way of food.'

'Don't worry,' Elsie said, 'we can all muck in with a bit of what we've got.'

She looked round and there were nods of agreement.

'Even if it is only powdered bloody eggs,' Albert said and everyone laughed.

'See, even Mrs Walker agrees, don't you?' Elsie suddenly turned her attention to where Annie was standing quietly by the bar. Annie gave a weak smile. She had stopped listening when they got on to nurseries and had no idea what they had been talking about. Her thoughts had been elsewhere. She had been thinking about Captain Roy and about the evening they had spent together the previous night. They had sat side by side on the sofa in the living room, listening to Duke Ellington playing softly on the gramophone, and she had offered him a tot of her best brandy. There was not much left, but she did consider him to be a special guest that night as he'd taken so much trouble to find flowers for her on her special day. He talked openly about his family in Nebraska in more detail than he had before. His wife was called Ellen and they had three children, sixteen-year-old Mary-Jane, and fourteen-year-old twins Barney and Peter, and they lived in a large single-storey detached house in a plot on the outskirts of the town. She showed him pictures of Jack and the children and they laughed as they exchanged stories of what the children got up to. He had stayed later than he usually did – there seemed to be so much to talk about. The record had finished playing and, apart from the click of the needle as it continued to spin, there was a strange silence in the room which neither rushed to fill as they exchanged glances. Then Roy drank what was left in his glass and stood up to leave. Annie had stood up too and suddenly he had put his arms round her and brushed her lips with a kiss. It was so unexpected it had quite taken her breath away. He had never done anything like that before. But when he began to apologize she found herself stopping his words with her own lips, pressing them firmly against his. 'Let's not say anything we might regret,' she had whispered as she'd reluctantly pulled away. He had hugged her briefly, then, and squeezed her hand before heading for the door without another word.

'Will you be sending your kids to the nursery once

it's up and running?' Elsie brought Annie right back to the present.

'Er, I-I'm sorry, I-I don't know about that. We'll have to see . . .'

'Please yourself, then,' Ena said as if brushing Annie aside. She sounded as if she had already made up her mind about the nursery but she said, 'I'll post a notice on the board at the Mission tomorrow to let you know my decision, either way.'

It took a week to sort out the paperwork and set everything up once Ena had decided she would run the nursery, and by then the Glad Tidings Nursery was ready to open its doors. Elsie Tanner was the first to drop her children off so that she could get to work in time for the early morning shift.

'Amazing how fast the town hall can shift themselves and move official bits of paper across their desks if they really want to,' she said to Ena. She peered into the room where three-year-old Linda was tearing round, dodging between the child-sized chairs that were laid out in a circle. Dennis was lying drowsily in a large cot where no doubt he would soon be joined by other babies. Ena's going to have her hands full here, she thought, but at least her Nursery Nurse friend Sarah was there to check things were working smoothly.

'If it's something the council think they'll benefit from, it's incredible what they can do,' Ena said. 'For once, they all seem to be working together and the money is actually going through.'

'This will benefit everyone in Weatherfield,' Elsie said. 'I really think you're doing the right thing.'

'Do you now?' Ena said, not without scepticism.

'And it was all my idea.'

'Aye, so it seems. You'd best make the most of it, though, because it might be the last one you'll ever have. Now, are you leaving both of them kiddies of yours here or what? Because if you are, you'd best get them registered.'

Elsie looked down the list that was on the table and put a tick by Linda's and Dennis' names.

'Now be good for Mrs Sharples, won't you,' she called out to Linda who was already lying across two of the chairs looking exhausted.

'I'm sure they will.' Ena looked Elsie straight in the eye and for once it was Elsie who looked away first.

The negotiations and the paperwork were dealt with, but it had taken a little time to convince all the other mothers in Weatherfield that the nursery was a good idea and to persuade them to sign up. Having glanced at the list, Elsie could see why it had taken so long for there were a lot of names.

It only goes to show, she thought, as she scanned it again to see how many people she knew, and we thought it was only Ida and me who wouldn't let go of their precious babies. Ena snatched the paper out of her hand and turned it over so that Elsie couldn't read it.

'Are you off to sign on at the munitions factory, then?' Ena asked.

'Aye, and I better get going. I'm doing extra hours now,' Elsie said. 'I'm glad so many people have signed up.'

'Not everyone has,' Ena said.

'Oh? Anyone I know?'

Ena smiled. 'Lady Walker, of course. It seems it's not up to her exacting standards.'

'Really? What excuse did she give?'

'She thought it best for little lord Billy to stay with her all day. Seems he's not far off school age, so she reckons she can be teaching him proper school stuff meanwhile. And she'll get her way as usual. At least until his dad comes home. I believe he's due some leave soon.'

'That's not before time.'

'No, and won't we see some fireworks fly then?'

'What do you mean? Like sparklers and Catherine wheels?' Elsie joked.

'More like rockets and bangers. I mean the full works.' Ena had a wicked glint in her eye.

Elsie's eyebrows shot up.

'Happen you've not been there of a night when she's been, shall we say, "entertaining" the . . . whatever rank he is.' It was obvious Ena was enjoying the telling. 'Some say he's a captain.'

'Go on with you. Annie Walker? Now you're talking daft.' Elsie was incredulous.

'Don't believe me, then. But I've seen it with my own eyes. Making cow's eyes at him, no less.'

'And a real captain? And I thought I had the pick of the bunch.'

'You, you'd take on the whole blooming bunch at once given half a chance. We all know about you, Elsie Tanner.'

Elsie sniffed. 'And *you* don't know half as much as you think you do.'

'I do know he's one of them Yanks. And he spins her a line about his being in charge of billeting out the soldiers.'

'But she doesn't take soldiers in. Talk about a dark horse.'

'I know.' Ena let the two words hang in the air. 'I've been thinking of writing to Jack, to tell him all about it.'

'What, sneak off telling tales like you did to my Arnold? Look where that got you.'

'It got you what you deserved.'

'You're the cow, it seems to me.'

'I'm not the one making the muck, I'm just enjoying raking it,' Ena chuckled.

'You're a right little snitch, that's what you are. You'd sell your own mother for the price of a cup of tea.'

'I don't have anything to hide,' Ena said, a self-satisfied smile on her face. 'But if Jack really is coming home on leave soon, then I don't need to bother telling him beforehand. He'll soon find out for himself.'

* * *

Annie was sitting in the kitchen on her own, thinking about Roy as she often did of an afternoon when she was expecting him to drop by in the evening. But today, although she wasn't expecting him, there was much for her to think about given what had happened before they had parted on that Sunday night. She had been aware that she liked him and she valued his friendship. It was comforting to have someone to talk to like that while Jack was away. If she thought about it, it was not surprising that, as their friendship deepened, so the warmth of her feelings towards him would increase. But until that Sunday night she had not thought they were anything more than good friends. That night, not only had she found Roy's move towards her shocking, but she had been even more shocked at her own response to it, though she had been careful to hide her feelings from him. She loved Jack, she knew that, just as she knew Roy loved Ellen, and she would do anything to protect her marriage. But Jack and Ellen weren't here and she and Roy were. Right from the start she had delighted in the rather glamorous companionship he offered, his conversation, his interest in her and the lightness and laughter he brought into her otherwise sombre life.

'You know, I can never guarantee anything.' That was what Roy always said when she asked him when she would see him next. And he had said that it would be at least a week before they could meet again. She had been left wondering if things had moved to a different level, but he wasn't here to discuss the new situation with her. That one moment of madness had sent warning signals flashing in her head. She needed to see him, to talk to him. She needed to know that one kiss hadn't put an end to their friendship.

She closed her eyes to block out the sun that was still streaming through the kitchen window, trying to conjure up pictures of Jack. But all she could see was Roy. Roy laughing, Roy serious, Roy bending to kiss her tenderly as he had done last night.

She shook her head. Now was not the time. She was tired, exhausted indeed, after trying to keep Billy amused all day. She was proud that she had managed it, even though the morning had got off to a terrible start, and she tried to concentrate on that to keep her thoughts from straying back to a certain US army captain.

Billy had run off to play out in the street as he usually did in the morning but when he met some of the other children he liked to play with they had told him they were starting at the Glad Tidings Nursery. Billy came flying back into the house, demanding to know why he wasn't going there too.

'I want to go!' he had begun chanting and would only stop when she promised him he could have a precious sweet at the end of the morning if he sat quietly and listened while Annie read him a book she had taken out of the library specially for him.

'Joanie can't listen,' he had insisted, 'only me.' And Annie had agreed for the sake of peace.

After that he seemed to calm down and Annie was relieved when he didn't mention the nursery or the other children again. She hadn't seen him for an hour or so now and presumed he was playing in his room with his cars where she had left him. Joanie, thankfully, was asleep. She still needed her afternoon nap.

Suddenly Annie felt something plop onto the top of her head. Thinking it must be from the washing hanging on the rack that was suspended from the ceiling, she looked up and saw, to her horror, that a bubble was forming underneath the wallpaper. It was getting bigger as she watched and the paper looked as if it was about to give way. She went cold, her mind beginning to race. What on earth could be happening?

'Billy!' she called as she went to investigate, and when all she could hear was the sound of running water she started to run up the stairs. The water noise grew louder as she neared the bathroom. The Rovers was the only place in Coronation Street to have an upstairs indoor bathroom, even though the toilet was outside, but at this moment it felt like a mixed blessing. A stream that was quickly turning into a river met her at the door and was beginning to flow down the stairs. When she opened the bathroom door the sudden rush of water soaked her dress and she jumped back. But not before she saw Billy and Joan sitting on the wet floor, their clothes saturated, playing with their plastic ducks and a little boat in the pools that were forming in the hollows of the sodden lino. Billy beamed at the sight of her. 'Look, I'm helping you, Mummy. I'm giving Joanie a bath,' he said.

She didn't know whether to laugh or cry. Was there any point in scolding him? She didn't want to think about how he might have dragged his sister out of bed. She leaned over and turned off the taps immediately but the bath was overflowing at an alarming rate and she could see where it was pooling in the corner that had been dripping through to the kitchen.

She fished both children out of the puddles of cold water they were sitting in and quickly wrapped them up in bath towels that were hanging just clear of the water level by the door. She carried them into their bedroom and went back to see what she could do. By the time she had cleaned them up and got rid of the worst of the water, it was close to evening opening time. She needed a plumber or a joiner or a decorator, or all three; she couldn't even think straight who it was she needed first, but she knew she wasn't likely to find anyone at this hour. Not that there were many tradesmen left to call on these days, but she would have to do something.

Ned had arrived for the evening session and she was grateful when he offered to go upstairs to see what he could do to help. Unfortunately, as he tried to find out the extent of the damage, the bubble on the ceiling burst and the water swamped the clothes on the drying rack and cascaded over the range and the chairs, splashing just about every item on the dresser and all the remains of food and crockery that had been on the kitchen table. She had to call Gracie to give her a hand.

Chuck was there earlier than usual and offered to help. Fortunately, Lottie who had come in for a drink was able to lend a hand behind the bar. By the time the worst of the mess was cleaned up and as much as possible had been dried, the children were in bed. Annie felt ready for bed too and she suggested that they closed the bar early as it wasn't very busy and it had been a long day. It was only as she sat down for a moment before going upstairs that she realized that Roy hadn't appeared all evening although he should have returned from his latest trip. When the phone rang she felt almost too exhausted to answer it, but she roused herself with the thought that it might be him.

There was much crackling and an echo on the line so that at first she didn't recognize that it was an English voice, not an American one, and it took a couple of moments before she shrieked, 'Jack! Oh, Jack, is that really you?'

'It's me.' He sounded cheery. 'But you don't sound yourself. Are you all right?'

For the first time in several hours Annie managed something like a laugh. 'I'm fine,' she said. 'All the better for hearing your voice, my love. But tell me, where are you? I wasn't expecting you yet.'

'No, we got what you might call an early ride. So I'm in London waiting to get on a train going north as soon as there is one. I'll probably have to change to get to Weatherfield.'

'It can't be soon enough for me,' Annie whispered.

'Me too. I don't know how long the journey will take, so long as it isn't all of my leave.' He gave a chesty chuckle.

'How long have you got?'

'Seven whole days. See you soon Annie, my flower.'

There was a click as the line went dead and then all Annie heard was the dialling tone.

When Jack finally arrived, it was long after midnight and he embraced Annie like he never wanted to let her go. It felt strange for Annie to have her husband back in the flesh, when for so long he had existed only in her thoughts and their letters. She kept touching him to make sure he was real. He was obviously exhausted and all he wanted was to crawl into bed to sleep, but he had one thing he had to do before he did that. He couldn't wait till morning to see the children who for so long now he had only seen in photographs. They were changing and growing up and he wanted to see them for real. As they climbed the stairs together, he insisted that they wake them up to greet their father. They went into Joanie's room first and as he picked her out of her cot she woke up and began to cry. She was bleary-eyed and rubbed at her eyes with her little fists, woken from a deep sleep.

'What a beautiful little girl you are, and you're *my*

beautiful little girl.' He clicked his tongue in what he hoped was a comforting noise. 'I've heard all about what you get up to. Yes, I have,' he cooed. 'And I carry a picture of you in my wallet. You're my good luck charm. You and Billy. How are you getting on with your big brother?'

In his own room, Billy heard the mention of his name though he didn't open his eyes. Having been aware of the earlier commotion downstairs when Jack arrived, Billy had woken up fully as soon as Jack entered Joanie's bedroom but lay without speaking. Still holding Joanie, Jack went into Billy's room and approached his son's bed, then bent down and put his hand out to touch his son's face.

Billy's eyes shot open and he immediately tried to move down inside the covers as he curled into a ball and started to cry.

'He doesn't recognize you in your uniform,' Annie said, putting her hand reassuringly on Billy's shoulder. 'You remember Daddy, don't you, darling?' she asked softly. 'I told you he'd be coming home soon to see you.'

'He smells,' was all Billy said.

Jack threw his head back and laughed. 'You're probably right, son. I hadn't thought of that. I suppose I've got used to it. But it would be lovely to have a scrub down. I'm sure I need it, and then I'll smell nice again and I'll be able to put on my own clothes.'

'I'm not sure they'll fit you.' Annie looked him up and down. 'You've lost so much weight.'

'True enough. But you haven't, thank goodness. You still look as gorgeous as I remember. Come here and give us another kiss.' He pulled Annie towards him. He was still carrying Joanie so that she was warm lying between them as he leaned in to kiss his wife firmly on the lips.

Billy suddenly threw off his bedclothes and jumped out of bed. 'No!' he shouted. 'Leave my mummy alone,' and he tried to prise them apart. Then he began beating Jack's legs with his fists and pulling at Joanie. 'And I don't want you holding Joanie, either. She's *my* sister and I want her all to myself.'

Jack looked a bit shocked at first, but Annie did her best to calm Billy down. 'He'll be better tomorrow, don't worry, dear,' she told Jack. 'He'll have forgotten all about this by morning.'

It felt strange having Jack in the double bed beside her after all this time. She didn't tell him about the flood, and now that most of it had dried out she hoped he wouldn't notice. Later on she could tell him, when it had become part of the family history. Now it didn't feel right to tell tales on her son the moment his father appeared. He was used to being only with his mother and sister, needed to adjust to having a man about the place. It wasn't as if he had meant any harm, and no real harm had been done.

'Do you want anything to eat?' Annie asked Jack after she had persuaded Billy to get back to bed. Jack had tucked Joanie into her cot, aware that Billy was watching his every move.

'Night, night, sleep tight,' Annie whispered to Billy through the crack in the door as she and her husband stood a little awkwardly on the landing, unsure what to do next.

'What I want now is to fall asleep with my arms wrapped tightly round you,' Jack said eventually and he began to move towards her, his arms outstretched. Then he stopped. 'Though maybe Billy's got a point. Maybe I should have a bit of a wash first.'

Annie smiled. That was her Jack, always so considerate, and yes, she was glad to have him home. 'Well, I think it's time we both went to bed. I know I'm more than ready,' she said, stifling a yawn. She hesitated, but only for a moment before she said, 'Oh Jack, it's so good to see you.' And this time she took the initiative. She stretched out her arms to embrace him and planted her lips firmly on his.

The moment she did so she was swamped with guilt, remembering another time when she had done the same thing recently, only with another man. She felt a little foolish now, thinking about Roy, when this was her husband, the man she was bound to, the man she had vowed to stand by for better or worse, the man she loved. She hadn't meant to betray him, not even in her thoughts, and yet she had fooled herself into allowing another man to almost enter her heart. But it was not too late to make amends. *I'll make it up to you Jack,* she cried silently in her head, *when I next see Roy.* And she said a silent prayer of thanks, adding a special request for Jack's ultimate safe return.

Jack wasn't up yet when she opened the bar for the dinnertime trade. Gracie had asked if she could come in a little later than usual as she hadn't known Jack was expected so imminently, but Annie could manage on her own and she thought it best to let Jack sleep as long as necessary. If Billy's shouting and carrying on over breakfast about who should finish the family's ration of marmalade didn't wake him then Annie decided nothing would. He obviously needed to sleep.

Annie, on the other hand, had not slept so well, worrying about Roy and what she would have to tell him. For her, things didn't improve, even when Jack was up and about. If she'd thought that looking after the children while she was alone was bad enough, she could not have imagined that trying to keep them under control once Jack was back would be even harder. He tried to give them a stern look every now and then, but she could see his heart wasn't in it. When she thought about it, it didn't seem fair to expect him to start disciplining the children when he was only going to be home for a few days, so she didn't pursue it. But they seemed to be as aware of the temporary nature of the arrangements as she was and consequently they were all on edge. All Jack wanted to do was to relax in the bar with some of his old mates and regale them with stories about the fighting and it seemed cruel not to let him play the role of the returning hero for a few days, so the last person Annie wanted to see in the bar as she unlocked the doors was Ena Sharples. But Ena Sharples it was who turned up like the proverbial bad penny and ordered her favoured milk stout. Annie knew she couldn't afford to antagonize any of her customers, and certainly not a regular like Ena, no matter what her personal feelings might be.

'So, is your *man* home then? There was enough racket going on in the street last night to wake the dead,' Ena said. A familiar spiteful look came into her eyes. 'But then, I'm supposing you know *which* man I'm talking about. Seems like a woman can't have too many up her sleeve these days.' She stared at Annie long and hard until Annie felt uncomfortable and went into the washing-up area to fetch some clean glasses. What was the woman driving at? Annie thought. Surely she didn't think . . . ? Could she possibly be alluding to Roy?

'You can try to fool as many people as you like, Annie Walker!' Ena's tone was jeering as Annie moved away. 'You can even fool yourself, if you've a mind, but you can't put one past Ena Sharples. Never could. Never will. And I know what I've seen.'

Annie returned, furious and indignant. The woman couldn't have seen anything. She had treated Roy like any other customer when they were in public. She was clutching as many glasses as she could hold between her fingers and had to concentrate on putting them down safely before she spoke. 'You haven't seen one thing,' she said, her lips tightly drawn, 'because there was nothing there to see. And there never has been.'

'But you know who I'm talking about, at any rate,' Ena responded in a flash.

Annie felt the blush rise to her cheeks. She had fallen right into the trap and only had herself to blame. She'd always vowed never to respond to Ena's barbs as she could never best her in any exchange and she should have stuck by her own maxim.

'Who knows what twisted way your mind works?' Annie said. She had to try to retrieve the situation. 'You are perfectly capable, as we all know, of innuendo of the first order. You can start a rumour going and make up stories when none exist, to suit your own purposes. But I won't be drawn into anything so tawdry.'

'I've seen you making eyes at that Captain What's-his-name; don't think that your flirting went unnoticed. And I've seen him sneaking out of here at all hours too. Goodness only knows what you got up to in between.'

Annie was shocked. The woman really was capable of bringing two walls together with her false accusations.

'Just remember . . .' Ena wagged an accusing finger as she always seemed to enjoy doing on such occasions, 'I'll be watching you. Like a hawk. And if you put one step out of line I shall waste no time in telling your husband, believe you me. He deserves better than the likes of you.'

Annie was shaken by the implications of Ena's tirade but she refused to trade insults. Her hands began to tremble so she found things to do behind the bar. She had always tried to keep her meetings with Roy away from prying eyes and maybe by the very nature of its secrecy their friendship hadn't been a good idea, but she was done with that now. Jack was home and thank goodness she had been able to see the folly of her actions in good time. She would tell Roy the next time they were alone together. The irony of that thought brought a smile to her lips. She seemed to be trapped by secrecy at every turn. But seeing Jack had brought her to her senses.

Several other customers had come in by now, though thankfully Roy was not among them, and, glad of the distraction, she began to serve them. She was very relieved when at last Gracie appeared and she was able to slip upstairs with the excuse that Jack needed her.

By the time Jack had been home for a week, Annie had recovered her poise. And though she still found she was looking out for him in the bar each night, she was relieved that Roy didn't put in an appearance throughout the whole of Jack's leave. She would have introduced him to Jack as a friend, as she'd rehearsed many times in her head, for despite Ena's insinuations, they had done nothing wrong, but it did make life easier that the necessity for the introduction never arose.

Billy didn't forget the scene he'd made at his father's

arrival and he remained wary of Jack for most of the week. It was as though he had forgotten how being part of a family worked and he couldn't get used to sharing his mother and sister with someone who to him looked like a stranger. He was also wary of Jack because the name 'Daddy' was the one he had always been threatened with when he did something naughty. During the week that Jack was home, however, Annie didn't use Jack as a threat to Billy and nor did she tell Jack about any of Billy's bad behaviour. There would be time enough to sort that kind of thing out when Jack was home for good. For now, she allowed Jack to indulge him and eventually, to Annie's relief, Billy did accept Jack's offer to play football with him outside in the street. The final barriers came down, however, one day when it was raining and Jack helped him to build a crane from the pieces of Meccano that had been part of his own childhood and which he'd packed away for the hoped-for time when he had a son.

'Building that crane made me feel like a real father, I must admit,' Jack said proudly to Annie that night. And she was satisfied that her plan was working, at least in the short term.

'I'm so glad, dear,' Annie said, and she had just got used to having Jack around the place once more and was aware that they were slipping back into some of their comfortable familiar patterns when, all too soon, his leave was over and it was time to say goodbye.

Saying goodbye this time seemed even harder than ever before.

'You will keep writing, won't you?' Jack begged. 'Your letters are what keep me going. I reread them if I'm having a tough time.'

Annie blushed at that, remembering some of the personal details she had written, usually late at night, using language she never could have spoken to his face.

'I read yours again too, if I can't sleep,' she said.

Jack laughed at that. 'And they put you to sleep, I suppose?'

Annie blushed then. 'In a way.'

Not wishing for a public display of emotion, Annie and Jack agreed to say goodbye at home.

'Take care my love,' Annie whispered when the final moments came.

'Be good,' Jack said. His comment was benign, she knew that, but her eyes misted nevertheless.

She stood at the door and waved as he trudged down the street weighed down by his oversized kitbag and she realized she didn't know if she would ever see him again.

'I heard your husband was on leave. I didn't want to make things more awkward for you than was necessary,' Roy said when he suddenly reappeared in the Rovers the following week.

Annie was angry with herself but she couldn't help glancing round to make sure Ena Sharples wasn't watching when she saw him coming in. But Ena was in the snug and for once was not facing the door. Annie smiled and led him to the other side of the bar where they would be under public scrutiny but if they spoke softly could keep their discussion private.

'That was a very gentlemanly gesture,' Annie said, 'and I thank you. I've come to expect nothing less from you, but it wasn't as if we were up to anything, now was it? Nothing I wouldn't tell my husband about.'

Roy stared at her intently, frowning slightly. 'We weren't up to anything physically, no. But you must know I have feelings for you.'

Annie stiffened. She felt her stomach twist as he said this. Did she too have feelings that she had been denying all this time? Maybe Ena was right and Annie had been kidding herself. Had Ena seen more going on between the two of them than Annie had been aware of?

His eyes were looking directly into hers and Annie could feel herself paling. 'Maybe we'd better not get into that kind of analysis,' she said stiffly. 'I think this is where our friendship has to end.' This really was not a conversation she wanted to have in such a public place and yet she couldn't invite him into her private quarters right now.

He sighed, a resigned look on his face. 'I see,' he said. 'Your husband's leave really had an effect.'

'It made me realize a few things, yes. But that doesn't mean I didn't value your friendship. I must say I've always looked forward to our evenings together and enjoyed our little talks.'

'Me too,' he responded quickly. 'I really appreciated your company and our discussions. A beacon in a tunnel, if I may say. It was good to talk to someone who understood.'

'My only worry is that I led you on to expect more. If I did, then I'm sorry. It was never my intention.' She kept her voice soft and lowered her eyes as she spoke.

He shrugged. 'Maybe it was my fault that I thought there was more on offer. I am a long way from home and I'll admit I was – am – lonely at times, so things can happen. Your mind can play foolish tricks on you, for one.'

'I never meant . . .' she began.

'Stop!' He gestured with his hand. 'Enough recrimination. I think we both get the point. No more blame game. You're one hell of a woman, you know, Annie Walker. And I'm sure your husband won't mind me saying that. I'm only sorry it has to end like this. But a man can dream.'

Now Annie could feel the heat returning to her face. There wasn't much left to say. She could never knowingly be unfaithful to Jack, she knew that now. He was a good man. And she didn't think Roy would ever want to hurt his family intentionally either. But it would be better to put temptation aside before anyone really got hurt. She was aware he was talking again.

'I'm being posted elsewhere,' he said. 'Ironically, that's

what I came to tell you. They need my skills in other parts of the country. I wasn't sure when I came how we were going to manage that scenario. Now I know. It seems like perfect timing.'

Annie hoped her churned-up feelings were not on display as she nodded. 'Perhaps it's for the best,' she said.

'It's been great knowing you.' He put out his hand and she felt the warmth of his fingers as he clasped hers. 'You'll always have a special corner in my heart,' he said so softly she almost didn't catch it, but when she realized what he had said, she felt tears welling. Annie withdrew her hand quickly and turned away. When she turned back, he was gone.

Chapter 10

Lottie had fallen in love with Tim Lucas almost from the first day she met him at the dance hall when she was bowled over by his boyish charm. She had never had a regular boyfriend before but knew Tim was the one for her, right from the start. She never told anyone at home about him, not even her sister, for she didn't want them to make fun of her or to nag her to bring him home. She was grateful her father didn't drink in the Rovers. He gave his custom to the Nags Head, so she never had to worry about him bumping into her new boyfriend by chance when she popped into the Rovers with him for a drink.

When orders came through that Tim's unit was to be shipped abroad, Lottie felt like her world was coming to an end. Unlike many of the men in his battalion who couldn't wait to get in amongst the fighting, Tim was reluctant to go but they both knew he had no choice. For his sake, when he made the announcement she tried to hold back the tears though she long remembered the feeling of devastation she experienced that night, knowing they would soon have to say goodbye. It was the first time she had felt truly loved.

They met in the Rovers that night, as they'd taken to doing, and Lottie could see from his face as soon as she saw him that something was wrong. Then he told her and she felt her heart sink. 'I suppose we sort of knew this was coming,' she said, trying to be realistic.

'But that doesn't stop it hitting you hard when you know it's really going to happen.' Tim sounded glum.

'Others have had to face it. We're not the only ones. So I'm sure we'll get through it too.' Lottie tried her best to perk him up.

'I know, but it doesn't make it any easier.' He picked up her hand and as soon as she felt the warmth of his touch her fingers began to tingle. He was staring at her intently. 'I want to ask you something,' he said, his voice serious.

Her heart fluttered and she looked at him eagerly.

'Will you wait for me?' he said.

Lottie swallowed hard. 'Of course I will. You don't even need to ask. I promise I'll be faithful till you come back,' she said. Then she smiled. 'Gosh, but that sounds all very heavy and serious. You've not even gone yet.' She gave a little laugh. 'And, in the meanwhile, we can keep in touch. There are such things as letters, you know.'

Tim nodded. 'I'll write as often as I can.'

'And I'll write every day,' she said squeezing his hand.

He leaned forward and kissed her fully on the lips. 'That's my girl.'

Lottie pulled away. She didn't want to spoil things now when they had managed to be discreet for so long. She couldn't afford anyone seeing them kissing and reporting back to her parents.

Suddenly he pulled her to her feet and she felt the tickle of his breath in her ear. 'If you really love me this would be the perfect time to prove it,' he whispered. 'Why don't we slip away and seal that vow?'

'What? Now?' Lottie was so shocked she spoke more loudly than she intended and several heads swivelled in her direction. She felt a flush rise to her cheeks. She didn't need everyone knowing her business. She tilted her head, indicating they should continue the conversation outside. To her relief, Tim hurried to follow her out.

'It has to be now,' Tim said when they were safely out of earshot of the pub. 'I've got to catch a train in the morning. Do you know of a small hotel or somewhere we could go?'

'Of course I don't. What kind of a girl do you take me for?' Lottie snapped. She felt angry and let down. This wasn't how she'd pictured his last night.

Tim turned to face her, picking up both of her hands

in his. He looked down at her solemnly. 'I'm sorry. I didn't mean it to sound so sharp. I was just thinking that this might be our last chance of being together . . . like that.'

Lottie wondered how she could say she was saving herself for marriage. It sounded so trite, given the circumstances. But when she didn't answer him immediately he said, 'You don't have to worry about it being your first time, if that's what you're afraid of. I'll be gentle.' He was very persuasive and Lottie had to admit she was tempted, for what he said was true. Who knew what horrors the war might inflict on them? They needed to make the most of today. And yet she couldn't bring herself to say yes. She just stared at him. In truth, it wasn't the act itself that terrified her but the thought of the possible consequences if things went wrong; and she was too shy to ask if he had any johnnies.

'Do you not trust me?' Lottie said finally, trying to turn the tables. 'Is my word not good enough when I say I'll wait for you?'

'Of course I trust you,' he hastened to assure her. 'That's not the point. Surely you can see it from my point of view? I want to take away an everlasting memory of you, of us, together. After all, who knows when we'll be together again?' He kissed her one more time. 'It can be your parting gift,' he whispered, letting go of her hands and slipping his inside her coat. 'If you really love me you won't deny me. It might be my one last pleasure on this earth.'

'Oh, don't say that.' Lottie clung to him. But she had to face the facts. What he said was true. He was about to be shipped off, probably to the front line, where anything could happen; where he could even be killed. What if he didn't come back? She glanced up and watched his face, her feelings in turmoil. They were standing so close she could see the disappointment slowly creep into his eyes as the moments ticked by and she still failed to respond. Eventually, he pulled away and dropped his hands by his sides. 'Well,' he said, 'it was just a thought.' His voice was rough now and he took out a cigarette and prepared to light it.

Lottie bundled the matches back into his hand. 'You shouldn't be doing that out here,' she warned.

'Why?' He laughed. 'No one can see me from up there.' He pointed skyward.

'Never mind that, I still think you'll have Albert Tatlock or worse still Ena Sharples on to you. They're the ARPs round here and I assure you, you don't want to tangle with them.'

'Okay, just to please *you*,' Tim mumbled. 'Come on. I'll walk you home.'

They walked the whole way in silence and Lottie felt wretched. She had spoiled their evening. But wasn't that better than ruining their lives?

The following morning Lottie was up far earlier than usual, though she had hardly slept. She knew the south-bound troops' train was due to leave very early and she had to see Tim before he left, before she went to work at the factory. She hurried down to catch the bus to the station, overwhelmed by the need to apologize; she wanted to explain why she hadn't felt able to do as he'd asked the previous night. She desperately hoped that he would understand. But it seemed many other people also wanted to get to the station and the bus was delayed. In the end, while they were still on the edge of town, she got off and she ran the rest of the way. But when she finally arrived she was met by a tide of women, mostly mothers with young children, streaming away from the platform as she was entering the concourse and she realized she was too late. She could just make out the shape of the large brown engine in the distance, enveloped in smoke and steam as it chugged its way out of the station. Within minutes the crowds inside had dispersed and she was left standing on the platform alone.

Lottie wrote her first letter to Tim as soon as she got home from work that night. In it she apologized and explained about the bus. Then she begged for his forgiveness that she hadn't felt able to give him what he had wanted. She sent the letter care of the British Forces Post Office service and hoped that it might eventually reach him wherever he was, even though she didn't really hold out much hope, so she was overjoyed when a few weeks later she received a reply. She kept it, still sealed, in her pocket all day, until she could open it in the privacy of her bedroom at home. It was later that evening when she gingerly tore at the flimsy paper of the envelope, careful not to destroy one word of his small sloping handwriting, and she read it over several times before she ultimately kissed his signature which merely said, *Best wishes from Tim*. Then she folded it away, but not before she had practically memorized its content, for he wrote as he spoke and she fancied she could hear him speaking the words as she read. *I understand your dilemma,* he wrote, *and honestly, Lottie, I don't blame you one bit for the stance you took. I know I was disappointed at the time, any man would have been, but you don't always get what you want in this life! I'm delighted that you took the trouble to write and hope that you'll continue to do so. It's so great to get letters out here. (I'm not allowed to say where I am.) But always remember you're my girl.* How she treasured those words.

She felt so encouraged by his response that she wrote again almost immediately, and when no reply came she put it down to the understandably poor postal service that was doing its best to fulfil its commitments to Britain's soldiers. Undeterred, she wrote again, and again. She wrote many more letters after that, but they all went unanswered and by what she counted to be the tenth rejection of her communication attempts, she no longer knew what to think. As she didn't know anything about his family, except that they were a long way away in Portsmouth, she had no idea how to contact them, so her first thought was to see if she could find out anything about Tim through the war office. She wasn't sure if they kept lists of names of those who had gone missing but the only response she received was a curt note saying if she was immediate family she would receive notice of such an event. However, if she wasn't immediate family then they were unable to help her. Lottie had to accept that Tim had been killed, or else he was missing in action. Or maybe he had changed his mind and decided he didn't love her any more. Whatever had happened, she had to accept that he had gone from her life, probably forever.

Heartbroken, she blamed herself for not making his final night in Weatherfield a happier one. If only she had said yes. But it was too late now. At first, Lottie felt as though she would never be able to forgive herself and she tried to concentrate on her war work and keep her mind on other things. She declined any invitations and refused to let Gracie chivvy her into going out dancing again.

She was only glad that she'd never told anyone at home about Tim. At least she didn't have to put up with any teasing or nagging about him from her sister or her parents. And, though it was scant consolation, unlike her friend Gracie, she didn't have to worry about her parents finding out she had a sweetheart they didn't approve of.

Gracie and Chuck had been to the cinema to see a Humphrey Bogart film called *Across the Pacific*. It had been Chuck's choice of film and Gracie was not happy as they made their way home in the dark.

'We're going to see something I want to see next time,' she said, 'that was all pretty horrid.'

'I agree it was not one of his best.'

'That's not what I'm complaining about. I've had enough war stuff. I'm reminded of the bloody war every waking minute at home.'

'What, do you mean you'd rather see something soppy and romantic?'

'What's wrong with that?'

'Nothing, except that it's not real life, is it?'

'Life would be a whole lot better if it was.'

Chuck stopped and suddenly pulled Gracie close. He opened his great coat and wrapped it round her so that the two of them were cocooned together. Then he kissed her like he had never kissed her before.

'What the—' Gracie was taken surprise.

'I'll give you real life.' He sealed his lips onto hers for what felt like an amazing age until they were forced up for air.

'So, how do you like real life now?' he murmured stroking her hair.

'Oh, Chuck, it's marvellous. If only life were like that all the time.'

'It could be. When you come to America.' They walked on.

'You say that like it could really happen one day.' Gracie suddenly felt let down.

'It could. We could make it happen.'

'How? When I never know where you are from one moment to the next, never know if I am going to see you again. I can't plan to do anything – and we certainly can't plan to do anything together, because you never know where you are going to be from one minute to the next. I'm not sure I can go on much longer like this.'

'Hey, what's brought all this on?'

'Nothing's brought it on. It's there all the time, only you don't usually get to see it.'

'I want you to know something.' They had reached the Field, though neither of them noticed, they were so engrossed in their discussion. 'I love you, Gracie Ashton,' he said.

'Do you? Oh Chuck! And I love you. But it's impossible, can't you see that?'

'It doesn't have to be – we can make it possible.'

Gracie began to cry.

'Sometimes I feel as if I don't really know anything about you.'

'I know it's hard but . . .'

Gracie's voice grew stronger. 'I don't think you realize what it does to me when you promise me one thing and then you don't keep that promise. Sometimes I don't hear from you for ages. I try to get on with my life while you're not here, but half the time I just don't know where I'm up to.'

'I'm sorry I can't tell you when I'll see you next, but

that's the nature of my job. I'm not just an ordinary foot soldier, you know. I have certain responsibilities.'

Gracie couldn't accept the simplicity of his explanation. 'It feels sometimes like you're just messing me about. Like you're keeping things from me, not telling me the whole truth.' She turned to him and put her finger on his lips. 'I do love you, you know, but I get so frustrated sometimes it feels like . . . like I don't really know you at all.'

Chuck held her tightly. 'I'm sorry but . . .'

'No buts. If you're not prepared to be honest with me when we're here together, how can you expect me to travel to be with you halfway round the world?'

They had reached the doorstep of Mallard Street without realizing where they were and suddenly they were bathed in light and there was a loud roar as her father appeared. Chuck immediately apologized for disturbing him and, as he spoke, the older man's face changed from red to purple. Mr Ashton grabbed Gracie's collar and hauled her inside the house.

'Oh my God, he'll kill us both,' Gracie screamed. 'You shouldn't have spoken. Chuck, please, just go.' And the door was slammed in Chuck's face.

Lottie wasn't usually a curtain twitcher, particularly since the enforcement of the blackout, as it was difficult to see what was going on in the street at night unless there was a full moon. Tonight there was only the smallest crescent of a new moon, but when she heard the angry shouts floating across from what she guessed must be the Ashtons' house she dashed upstairs to try to look out of the window. She made sure all the lights were off before she flicked back the curtain a little way and peered out into the darkness. The voices were definitely coming from the direction of Gracie's house, she was sure of that, but she had to rely solely on her hearing because until her eyes adjusted to the glimmer of moonlight she couldn't see anything.

She heard Gracie's father yelling something about dirty Yanks and, when she heard Gracie crying, realized immediately what had happened. She saw a momentary streak of light as the front door opened and then was shut again seconds later. Lottie sighed as she heard as well as saw the slam of the Ashtons' front door and the street was plunged into pitch darkness once more. She thought she saw the moonlight illuminating the silhouette of a figure sneaking off into the night and all she could hope was that Gracie was all right. She knew Bomber Ashton, as Gracie's father was known in the street, could be handy with his fists, but according to Gracie, it seemed he did more shouting than hitting these days, unless his injuries were giving him gyp. She only hoped that was true tonight.

Lottie sat on the stairs, wondering if there was anything she could offer to do for her friend, or whether her meddling would only make things worse, when suddenly there was a knock at the door.

'Lottie, please let me in.' It was Gracie's voice,

sounding so distressed Lottie opened the door immediately. Gracie was shaking from head to toe as she stood there, trying unsuccessfully to cover up the beginnings of a black eye.

'My father caught us on the doorstep,' Gracie sobbed when Lottie quickly pulled her inside and shut the door.

'You're lucky, I'm on my own tonight,' Lottie said, leading her friend into the kitchen. She quickly soaked a dishcloth in cold water and offered it to Gracie to hold against the darkening bruise on her face. Then she indicated they should each sit on one of the battered-looking chairs that stood round the kitchen table while she put a pan of water on the gleaming gas stove to heat. The Kemps were one of the few families in the street to have such a modern convenience and, as the water began to hum almost immediately, Gracie could see why Lottie was so proud that they had one. But it wasn't gas stoves that concerned her right now.

'It was all about Chuck an' me as you might imagine.' Gracie began to tell Lottie the story. 'We was getting right careless because the old man hadn't bothered us before. He's been wrapped up in himself of late and I don't think he realized I even had a boyfriend. But tonight he suddenly popped open the front door while we were in the middle of a kind of row. It was stupid really, I should have known better than to be talking about it on the doorstep, but we had been walking and I didn't realize we were home.'

'What kind of row?'

'Well, Chuck messes me about something shocking sometimes. He says he'll come and then he doesn't turn up. Sometimes I don't see him for ages without any real explanation. I never know when he's telling me the truth. He doesn't seem to think I've got any kind of a life going on when he's not there. I hate it when he makes promises he can't keep and I don't know where I am. It must have sounded louder than I thought, but honestly, Lottie, I swear we weren't making much of a noise. The thing was, I didn't even hear the old man begin to open the door.'

'Hmm.' Lottie didn't know what else to say. Her illusions about men were gradually being shattered.

'The thing was, when the old fella came out and saw us together, he started shouting the odds as only he can. Unfortunately, Chuck made the mistake of trying to apologize for the noise and of course Dad could tell that he was a Yank, soon as he opened his mouth, couldn't he? I've always told Chuck to keep his trap shut no matter what and to let me handle things, but bloody men. They have to be on top. You should've seen my dad's face when the penny dropped.'

'I can see your face right now and that's enough,' said Lottie dryly.

Gracie managed a snigger but then carried on with her story. 'Well, he only dragged me inside and slammed the door shut in poor Chuck's face, didn't he? I tell you, Lottie, it was awful.'

'What about your mum, what did she say?' Lottie asked.

'She tried to haul him off me. Honestly, though, she's always trying to defend him, telling me that his bark's worse than his bite; that I should make allowances because he's in constant pain from his injuries; that sometimes he has to lash out at whoever's closest to him at the time. But she could see for herself tonight. There was no excuse for him hitting me like that. Mind you, he's not done owt like that since he's come back from the navy.'

'No, that's why I thought it might just be a shouting match,' Lottie said, 'though I could hear him all the way over here. But I didn't think you'd be in any danger.'

'I don't know if I was in danger or not after the first clout. I think he shocked himself and wouldn't have hit me again, but I decided the best thing I could do was get out of the house, and quick. So that's what I did. I left him shouting at the wall.' She gave a little laugh. 'But once I was outside in the street I realized I didn't know where to go. It was all very well getting out of his way but where I thought I was going to, I've no idea.' She gave a deep sigh. 'Of course, Chuck wasn't there. I told him to leg it as soon as my dad started on him because I knew he had to get out of the situation or there could have been some real damage done.' She held her head in her hands. 'I'm only sorry I'm involving you, now, Lottie. I do hope you don't mind that I came here, but I quite honestly couldn't think of where else to go. I could hardly run to the Rovers, now could I?' She finally managed a little smile. 'Could you imagine Annie's face if I had? Goodness only knows what she'll say when she sees this tomorrow. I hope she doesn't think it were Chuck.' Gracie took the wet pad away from her face and went to look at her eye in the small piece of broken mirror that hung from a hook on the wall. It seemed to be swelling up as she looked at it.

'I see what you mean,' Lottie said, watching her. 'But what you were arguing about wasn't worth all this.'

Gracie shook her head but then clasped it between her hands and held it still, as the gesture was too painful. She sat down again at the table. 'Honestly, Lottie, I don't know why I'm even thinking about me ever going over to America and meeting his folks when he can't even get across our doorstep to meet mine.'

Do you know much about his family and his home in America?' Lottie asked. Gracie shrugged. ''He's told me a few things but sometimes I begin to wonder if he's telling me the whole truth.'

'What on earth do you mean? Why should he lie about a thing like that?'

'I don't mean he tells lies exactly, it's more like he's holding something back.'

Lottie was thoughtful for a moment. 'Well, you do hear some funny stories about some of these soldiers. And it's not only the ones from overseas. They take up with local girls and somehow manage to forget to tell them that they've got a wife and kids back home.'

Gracie looked horrified. 'Oh thanks, Lottie, that makes me feel a whole lot better.

'I'm sorry, I didn't mean it to come out like that but . . . well, you know, how do we know we can trust them? One minute we don't know them from Adam and then suddenly . . .' Lottie's voice cracked and she stopped as if she had just thought of something.

'Gosh, Lottie, what's up? Is there something wrong?'

Lottie began to cry and Gracie jumped up and put her arm across her friend's shoulders. 'It just struck me that that's what could have happened with Tim. Maybe that's why I never heard from him again. He's already married and was too much of a coward to tell me.' Lottie swiped the tears away with her sleeve. 'I haven't heard from him for weeks now.'

'Oh gosh, I'm sorry. I hadn't realized. And here's me so full of myself,' Gracie apologized.

'No need to be sorry.' Lottie got up and mashed some tea in a pot with the water that was now bubbling on the stove. She poured two cups and pushed one across the table towards Gracie. Sorry we've no sugar or milk,' she said.

'You never let on,' Gracie said. 'About the letters, I mean. In fact, you haven't mentioned Tim for ages so I just thought . . .'

'I know. It's okay. But I think it's time for me to be realistic and give up hoping for bloody miracles. I have to accept that he didn't mean anything that he said, so it's a good job I didn't give in to him. I bet he's most likely one of them with a wife and kiddie at home so there's absolutely no point in me waiting for him.' She made a sound of resignation and shook her head. 'I suppose it's possible we've both been led up the garden path.'

'Instead of being led up the aisle you mean!' Gracie spluttered, the hot liquid shooting out of her mouth as she laughed at her own joke and they both ended up giggling.

Then Gracie looked serious again. 'But you know, you could be right, of course. About Chuck, I mean. Though I can't bear to think of it but maybe he has got a wife in New York that he's not telling me about.'

Lottie sighed as she took a sip from her steaming cup. 'Just because we fall in love with them it doesn't mean they automatically become good marriage material, does it? In fact, I'd say the opposite. Once they join the army, something seems to happen to them and they definitely don't become the kind of men to make good husbands.'

'I'm sorry it hasn't worked out for you with Tim.' Gracie put out her hand and patted Lottie's arm. 'Though for what it's worth, I thought he was nice.'

Lottie shrugged. 'And I like Chuck. I think you two go well together.' She sighed. 'Maybe you should put yourself out of your misery and ask Chuck if there is someone back home. At least you'd know where you stand.'

Gracie nodded and smiled. 'You're right. Maybe I should.'

'Now,' said Lottie, suddenly businesslike, 'will you be wanting to stop over the night? If so, you'll have to share the bed with me, I'm afraid. Our Madge won't want to be giving up hers.'

'That's very kind, but I think I'd best go back when I've finished my tea. Hopefully things will have had time to calm down by then. Me mam will only worry if she doesn't know where I am.'

Once Jack had gone back to the army, Annie had little time to brood. She was fully occupied during the day looking after Billy and Joanie who, together, were proving to be a handful; and at dinnertime and in the evenings she was kept busy supervising and serving in the bar. She still refused to let Billy go to the Glad Tidings Nursery even though he had cried and begged to be allowed to go on several occasions. As far as Annie was concerned he was rough enough in his play without the influence of all the young ruffians he would be rubbing shoulders with there. And he was a companion for Joanie who she felt was too young to be going to a nursery, even if there had been one she approved of. Not that Billy was setting his sister a good example, if his recent behaviour was anything to go by. But unfortunately, Annie now found that the threat of 'telling Daddy about it when he comes home' no longer had any scare value. Now Billy clearly remembered who Daddy was and could only think of him as a gentle man who played football and built Meccano

251

cranes, not as some kind of ogre to be afraid of, which might have been more helpful.

Maybe I should have let Jack deal with Billy while he was at home, Annie thought now. He might have benefitted from Jack wielding a firm, fatherly hand to keep him in line. But each time she'd thought about threatening him while Jack was on leave, Billy had given her one of his sweetest smiles and her heart had melted so that she'd relented at the last moment, but now she was paying the price. It had been bad enough the day after Jack had gone back, when Billy gleefully told her that he had helped her by picking all the vegetables from their tiny victory garden. When she went into the kitchen she found he had pulled the top leaves off the potatoes and carrots and the first shoots of the other vegetables that she had been coaxing to grow. But today was the final straw. He had wanted single-handedly to get Joanie dressed and downstairs for breakfast before Annie had opened her eyes, but his best efforts had only resulted in bringing the high-sided cot crashing down on top of both of them. When Annie woke up to hear them screaming like the house was on fire, she realized she had to do something, as each escapade was getting more serious. His behaviour was spiralling out of control and he could have hurt them both badly. Yes, she wished she had told Jack about what his son had got up to while he'd been away, but it was too late now and she would have to think of some other solution.

It was then she realized there were a lot of things she hadn't told Jack. She had convinced herself a week wasn't long enough to begin burdening him with her petty problems. But were they all petty? After all, she hadn't told him about Annette who had paid that unexpected visit over a year ago.

Was that because of all the memories Annette had stirred up, reminding her of her years at the mill, a period in her life she had never wanted to talk about to anyone?

She thought about Annette. The poor child who had only ever known life from the inside of an orphanage. Annie felt a sudden flutter of fear. Was Annette any closer to finding out about her mother? Had Annette had any more luck in tracing either of her parents? She hadn't ever told Jack about her friends Nancy and Lilian, and certainly not about Archie. They were from a past she had spent years trying to forget.

'Old boyfriends are definitely not something one tells one's husband about,' her mother always said. 'It's much more pragmatic to maintain an air of mystery and mystique about the past,' Florence had counselled. Annie didn't agree with everything her mother tried to teach her, but that was one piece of advice she had been willing to heed.

Recently she hadn't had much time to think about anything, she had been so busy pulling pints, collecting empties and watching the till. The GIs were now coming over in greater numbers than ever and that in turn brought an increase in local trade. Women like Elsie Tanner, Ida Barlow and Sally Todd came in even more regularly than usual, eager for the free stockings, cigarettes, bars of soap and even chocolates the American soldiers brought with them to hand out in the pub. Chuck and many of his mates became regulars as it became quite clear that he and Gracie were falling for each other in what Annie considered to be quite an alarming way and she wondered if she should counsel Gracie about what difficulties such a romance could involve. As more men arrived, a new captain in charge of billeting details introduced himself to her, but although she greeted him warmly, Annie maintained a distance between them and kept him at arm's length.

Working so hard had its advantages as there were nights she was so tired that when she finally crawled into bed, she passed out like a light. But reaching exhaustion point also sometimes brought on attacks of the blues. Then she would toss and turn, unable to clear her mind from dark thoughts, and that was when her darkest moments hit her. All she could wish then was that she was no longer on her own. When the black mood seemed as though it would never lift, she tried to keep herself going with her dream, that she and Jack would one day be tenants of a Tudor-style country pub in leafy Cheshire. The war would be over and peace would reign once more. That is, if Mr Hitler didn't invade Britain and spoil everything.

What she really needed in the meantime, she decided,

was a holiday, and that made her smile. For all she could then think about was the one holiday she had taken during her time at the mill. When she was a young child her affluent family had taken the spa waters in Buxton, and Harrogate and even once in Bath, but none of those trips were as memorable as the wakes week she'd spent in Blackpool with the other mill hands during the three dreadful years she had worked at Fletcher's. Indeed, it had been one of the highlights of those years – until it was ruined, before Mr Hitler had even come into power.

Chapter 11

1929

Most of the workers from Fletcher's Mill went for their wakes week holiday to Blackpool in summer every year. They put by a few pennies each week for the Christmas Club for half the year and for the Wakes Saving Holiday Club for the other half. They had no choice but to take a week's holiday in the summer for the factory closed down. They were offered no wages, so most of them saved up to enjoy a few days away and going to Blackpool had become a tradition. Normally, Annie wouldn't have entertained the idea of joining them, but when Archie told her he was thinking of going she changed her mind.

'How will they be able to do without you in the

loom sheds?' Annie teased him. 'I thought all the mechanics had to stay behind to overhaul the machinery.'

'Na, I'm working so hard on my machines all the rest of the time they don't need me during wakes week,' he quipped back.

The truth was, Annie found out from her father, Fletcher's didn't want to have to pay all the mechanics for the summer week's work, so they'd asked for volunteers to stand down and take the unpaid holiday leave instead.

Annie's mother wasn't pleased when Annie announced her intention of going to the seaside for a week with the other mill hands.

'How on earth can you think of going on holiday with . . . those kind of people?' was her mother's first objection when Annie made the suggestion. 'Goodness knows what your father will say, but I'm telling you that, on top of everything else, it would be a luxury we simply cannot afford.'

Annie smiled to herself at this. She was convinced her mother's motive for talking in this way was more about the fact that she would be losing the household's main meal-maker than about her mother's grasp of the family's financial situation.

'How would you get there?' Florence asked, by way of another objection.

'Like everyone else, I suppose, by train. Or there might even be a charabanc going from Fletcher's Mill.' Annie was not specific, as that was a minor detail.

'I won't be earning any money that week, anyway, so I thought I may as well go away on holiday and enjoy myself,' Annie said calmly, for she knew her mother had no chance of winning this particular argument. 'Once the factory closes for the week, no one but the mechanics who stay behind can earn anything.' Annie didn't add that she had, in fact, been putting a little by from her wages each week so that she could buy some new clothes. But now she intended to use that money to pay for a few days at the seaside.

'Besides,' Annie went on, 'it will be good for my health to have a breath of clean sea air, and maybe even a dip in the sea.'

'You sound as bad as those working-class girls you call your friends if you believe in all that superstitious nonsense.' Her mother was dismissive.

'It's hardly superstitious, and I don't know why it's nonsense to believe in the healing powers of sea water. And it certainly won't do me any harm to breathe in some fresh sea air for a change instead of all the muck I take into my lungs all day long at the mill. But you needn't worry,' she added, 'Mrs Beattie will still be here to clean up after you. And if you speak to her very nicely, for an extra bob or two she might be persuaded to cook your meals as well.'

Florence looked so crestfallen that she had no arguments left, that Annie didn't have the heart to tell her that she was not really seeking permission to go away, she was telling her mother as a courtesy, for she and Nancy and Lilian had already begun to plan the trip. Nancy had been in touch with the landlady of one of the boarding houses that was advertised as being 'a stone's throw from the sea, just off the Golden Mile'. They'd asked for a room with a double and a single bed in it for they'd heard it would be much cheaper if the three of them shared the accommodation.

Almost all the girls in her loom shed said they were going on the trip and Annie, for once, didn't even care if that included the Bradshaw sisters. As long as Archie was there to protect them, she and her friends would be able to make their own fun. Annie didn't tell her mother that Archie had said he was going, for she knew Florence didn't approve of her stepping out with him.

'Oh, darling.' Florence always spoke with a tired sigh whenever his name came up. 'You can do so much better than to be courting a working-class loom mechanic.' Florence looked down to the spectacles on the end of her nose as she said this. 'Really, Annie, you mustn't let your standards drop like that.'

Annie hated it when her mother spoke in that way. To her it showed that Florence had never been reconciled to their change in station. She still thought she was the Lady of the Manor and she acted accordingly. Even her lowly clerk of a husband would never be a working-class man in her eyes, and she refused to accept that he needed to be grateful for his job at Fletcher's now that unemployment was rife.

Annie, Nancy and Lilian went to Blackpool by train, not something any of them had done before, and the excitement as they climbed into the carriage was palpable. Annie insisted on giving a porter some coppers to help them hoist their luggage onto the overhead racks and she sat back with satisfaction when he had gone. Her mother would certainly have approved of that, she thought. They were packed into the carriage with a large family so that they could hardly move on the well-worn seats but that didn't dampen their enthusiasm. 'We're free at last!' Lilian shrieked. 'A whole precious week to ourselves with no one to tell us what to do.'

Annie joined in and she would have got up and done a little jig if she had had the room. Nancy had bagged a seat by the window and didn't say much, but her squeals as the train pulled out of Mayfield station were enough to indicate her levels of delight. Annie was sitting next to Nancy and she could see perfectly well out of the window. She watched with growing excitement as fields and houses sped by as the train picked up speed and began to fly through the countryside. When they pulled into Blackpool station they almost fell out onto the platform, but there was nowhere to fall for it seemed as if the whole station was jammed with people jostling each other as they poured out of the trains on every platform. Annie somehow bumped into Archie who she found had been travelling in the next coach. She didn't refuse when he kindly offered to carry the small leather suitcase that she had bought for a few pennies in a charity shop, as far as their lodgings; and he somehow managed to also balance the large canvas bag that Nancy and Lilian were sharing under his arm. The girls looked around them in awe as they left the station, for they had never seen anything like it. People, trams and motor cars filled the streets and, high above their heads, the super iron structure of the tower loomed just like it's sister tower that Annie had seen in the famous pictures of Paris. She could see one of the piers jutting out into the water with its amusement arcades and shops, and she looked with delight at all the people on the long stretch of golden sands, trying their best to make the most of the sun. There was another pier in the far in the distance and Annie drew in her breath as she caught sight of the Big Wheel. She couldn't wait to get started on their sightseeing.

They felt they were being very grand for mill workers, having booked to stay half board, with a light evening meal and breakfast as part of their tariff. If they wanted anything for supper after that, then they had to find their own bag of chips or snack to munch on before they went to bed, though the landlady made it clear she would not tolerate any crumbs or food remains in the bedroom. Despite the journey, they were not feeling tired at all, buoyed up by the thrills they could see awaited them. Once they had unpacked their few belongings and eaten the early meal the landlady had prepared for them, the girls were free to go out and enjoy themselves and, as none of them had been to Blackpool before, that is what they intended to do. Archie was staying at a small guest house in the next street with a couple of his mates from the mill that he had travelled up with and Annie had arranged to meet him at the nearby tram stop on the promenade.

Annie was with Nancy and Lilian when Archie arrived with his two friends, Kevin and Derek, and after a round of introductions the six of them started out together. Knowing they had the rest of the long, light summer evening ahead of them, they took a gentle stroll, following the tram tracks along the promenade so that they had a good view of the long stretch of sandy beach Blackpool was renowned for.

Despite the lateness of the hour and the breeze that was now coming off the sea, there were crowds of people still on the beach. The older members of the families were sitting in striped deckchairs with the younger ones stretched out on rugs on the sand. Less hardy souls were packing up and trudging back to their digs with all their belongings and the man in charge of the donkey rides had rounded up all the animals and thrown cheap blankets onto their backs. He was now leading them away down the beach. There were plenty of children who were carrying on digging with their spades and running back and forth to the outgoing waves with their buckets for more water to fill the elaborate moats they had built round their sandcastles. And all the while gulls were screeching overheard, swooping down every now and then to steal an ice cream, or a sandwich directly from the hand of an unsuspecting victim.

As the evening wore on, however, Archie and Annie drifted away from the others, deciding to explore the town on their own and they agreed to meet their friends later, back at their respective lodgings.

Nancy and Lilian seemed to be getting on well with Kevin and Derek and Annie was pleased that she and Archie would be able to spend time on their own. There was so much to see and do, Annie wanted to be out as much as possible; she hoped the weather would remain sunny and that there would be no threat of rain.

The next day, the two of them set off together after breakfast, Annie holding firmly on to Archie's arm. They didn't intend to return to their lodgings until the evening in time for tea.

'I'm here to have a good time,' Annie told Archie, gazing meaningfully into his eyes, 'and I want to make the most of it, so we've got to sample whatever entertainment is on offer.'

'And you don't care if you wear me out in the process,' Archie teased her. He squeezed her arm and Annie felt a warm, tingling glow. Archie Grainger might not be what her mother had in mind when she thought of an ideal suitor for her daughter, but Annie wasn't so proud. She already had a soft spot for him. He had confided in her about his dreams when they had first met and she felt she could help him achieve those dreams. She could help him to improve himself so that he could start to climb the social ladder; they could do it together. Indeed, over the course of the holiday she was looking forward to spending lots of time with him and getting to know him better.

They started out walking towards the more genteel end of the promenade, towards the North Pier.

'I've heard there's a small shopping arcade there, actually on the pier,' Annie said. 'I thought it might be fun to see it,' and they set off, heading towards the sounds of a military-style band they could hear playing in the distance.

It was a bright and sunny day and Annie wore the same light cotton frock that she'd worn each summer, whenever it was warm enough, since they'd lived in Weatherfield. Others also seemed to be relying on the good weather, for she could see the sunbathers already stretched out on the beach in their efforts to acquire a tan, and children were racing each other down to the water's edge then rushing to be first as they ran back with their buckets full of cold water to begin to build their sandcastles. Annie and Archie stopped to watch a puppet show on the sands, Annie cringing as Mr Punch bashed his poor wife Judy over the head with his truncheon and then battered their baby in no less a cruel way. But somehow the watching audience kept screaming for more. Annie turned away in disgust. They walked on to the North Pier where they found the brass band they had heard, 'oompah-pahing' by the entrance.

They found the shopping arcade but it turned out to be more exclusive than Annie had imagined.

'I wish I could treat you to that,' Archie said, pointing to a tulle, long-sleeved blouse as they pressed their noses against the window of a small shop that was advertising ladies' haute couture. 'I bet you'd look right pretty in that.'

'Not at that price I wouldn't,' Annie laughed, though it hurt her to know that once upon a time she would have been able to afford to buy something like that herself. And she was painfully reminded of the time when she couldn't even get a job in such a high-class ladies' retail shop.

They wandered back down the Golden Mile to the Central Pier in search of the amusement arcades, but it was not easy to walk along the overcrowded pavements. The streets were busy, no matter which direction they tried, and wherever they went they were jostled by the crowds; holidaymakers loaded up with suitcases and other baggage, and day trippers dragging beach paraphernalia in their wake. Everyone was vying for the limited street space and Annie wondered what it was like for those who lived in the town. Whenever they passed one of the railway terminals they could see hordes more people spilling out of the trains as they pulled into the platforms; old people, younger folk, children and babies. It seemed like the workers and their families from all the northern mill towns were descending on Blackpool at the same time.

As they passed so many souvenir shops, Annie suddenly thought it would be fun to send a postcard to her mother to let her know she was having a good time. She stepped up to the racks in the first shop they came to, to see if she could choose one. To her horror, all she could find were cards with large ladies showing off their enormous breasts and backsides, with some saucy comments underneath. She didn't like them at all, didn't find them amusing, and she was sure Florence wouldn't appreciate receiving one, so she hurried past the remaining cards and knickknack shops she saw.

When they reached Central Pier, Annie looked up in awe at the tower that soared into the sky high above them.

'It's supposed to have been inspired by the Eiffel Tower, you know,' she said to Archie.

'Where's that?' Archie asked.

'Why, in Paris, of course.' She wondered if he was joking and tried not to sound patronizing. But Archie wouldn't have noticed. He was too intent on finding the amusement arcades so that he could gamble his farthings and ha'pennies in a bid to win more. When he finally found the slot machines he'd been looking for, he found other kinds of stalls there too, and he became desperate to try his hand at shooting, or throwing, or trying to manipulate a mechanical grabber to cling on to a free gift.

'I bet I can shoot every one of them ducks down and win you a prize, Annie. You just see if I don't,' Archie boasted, as a man with a money bag strapped round his ample waist tried to woo them away from the coconut shy. Annie was relieved to find that Archie's aim was not as good as he claimed, as few of his throws or shots were on target. She wasn't sure she wanted to trail an oversized pink teddy bear around or wear a hat with 'kiss me quick' emblazoned on the front for the rest of the day.

It took a while before Annie could finally manage to drag Archie away from the amusement arcade.

'Let's find a café somewhere to get a cup of tea – I'm beginning to feel tired and a little hungry,' Annie said. 'I think we should stop and have a sit down.'

'If you're hungry, there's a stall over there with fresh cockles and whelks and I think they've got some jellied eels.' Archie pointed to where a line of vulgar-looking, assertive stallholders were shouting their wares.

'Or you could have some fish and chips?' he said. 'And we don't even have to sit down. See, everybody's eating with their hands as they're walking along.'

Annie had already noticed and hadn't wanted to draw attention to the fact. She shook her head, not sure she could face the thought of any of the items he had mentioned. The smell of the fat frying and the seafood bubbling in open cauldrons was already making her nauseous.

'Actually, I would appreciate a sit down even more than food,' she said.

'Then you won't mind if I have something to eat, I hope? I'm hungrier than I thought,' Archie said, and he bought a large bag of chips. They were cut into sizable chunks, more like scalloped potatoes, and were dripping in fat, but they had been so expertly wrapped that the newspaper absorbed most of it. When he offered one to Annie she had to turn her head away. She tried not to notice the grease that had seeped through to his fingers.

'Perhaps you'd like me to get you something sweet?' he said. 'Look, they're spinning candyfloss over there. Shall I get you some of that?'

Once more Annie shook her head. 'No, thank you. I'm not sure I'm feeling hungry any more. A cup of tea and a sit down will do fine.'

By the time he'd finished his chips and kicked the balled-up newspaper to the other side of the street, Annie had found a café that looked passably clean. It was beside the large open-air dance floor in the entertainment complex on Central Pier. She sat down with relief while Archie ordered them a large pot of tea. Within minutes a band struck up and couples began to whirl by. Annie recognized some of the Fletcher's Mill girls who had been with them on the train. Suddenly she saw Nancy and Lilian twirl close to where they were sitting, with Kevin and Derek hanging on to their arms, though she wasn't sure which of the boys was which. Archie's jaw dropped open as their friends waved.

'Why don't we try?' Annie said, suddenly coming alive again. 'Ballroom dancing is not difficult if there's a good band.' But Archie reminded her how tired she had been only a few moments since. She did manage to persuade him to his feet after they had each downed another cup of tea, and she was surprised how well he was able to shuffle in time to the rhythms of the swing band, even if he was a little clumsy with the steps.

Feeling refreshed, they headed down the Golden Mile towards Squires Gate and the Pleasure Beach on the South Pier. Once more Archie lost several of his precious coins in the amusement arcade there, in an attempt to win a prize for Annie, and Annie spent some of her precious money paying for a ride for them both on the dodgem cars and a spin on the Big Wheel.

By the time they got back to their digs, Annie was only just in time for tea, with the landlady threatening to remove the sandwiches she had laid out for each guest if Annie delayed by so much as one more minute. Lilian and Nancy were already there and had almost finished eating, but Annie was able to swap stories with them about their day before she had to rush off to have a quick wash and find a cardigan to put on for the evening.

That night Annie was exhausted because they had

walked several miles and seen so much over the course of the day. But it was a different kind of tired from how she felt when she came home from working at the mill. This was what she called a 'healthy tired'. She really did believe the air was doing her lungs some good. It was probably doing them all good. She noticed Archie hadn't smoked so much, something she hated to see him doing when they were at home. The other bonus was that there had been no Bradshaw girls to spoil her fun. Wherever they were in Blackpool, thankfully they seemed to be nowhere near Annie or any of her friends.

The rest of the week seemed to rush by and Annie mentally checked the list she had carried in her head to make sure she had seen everything she had wanted to see. The six of them had been to a variety show together on their second-last night in the Winter Gardens complex and that, for Annie, was the pinnacle of the trip. She had also been with Nancy and Lilian to look over the Littlewoods department store that they'd heard about.

'I'm sure we won't be able to afford to buy any clothes there,' Annie said, 'for all that they're supposed to be designed to suit everyone's pockets.'

'That doesn't matter,' Nancy said. 'No harm in dreaming.' A sentiment with which Annie heartily agreed.

Over the course of the trip, however, Annie became aware that something very special was happening and that her feelings towards Archie were changing. She had liked him since they'd first met at the mill and had started stepping out together. Despite her mother's disapproval, she had always been pleased to be seen out with him, arms locked as they walked along together sharing their thoughts and the occasional joke. No, he wasn't the kind of man she had once dreamed of, but then her life had changed and she had had to adjust her dreams. If there were changes that needed to be made, Annie hoped they could learn and grow together. There was something striking and commanding about his powerful frame and the way that he carried himself, and yet when he looked at her sometimes he made her feel like she was the only girl in the world. She had been thrilled when he told her he was coming on the trip and looked forward to spending time with him. But now she realized she had fallen in love and she didn't want the week to end.

She had loved all the things they had done together and she had really enjoyed his company. And, what's more, she had been surprisingly impressed by how attentive he was. Of course, he tried it on sometimes – she expected that in a man – but apart from that he was extremely attentive, always at her side being thoughtful, kind and considerate, displaying all the qualities she was looking for in a man. And when he had seen her to the door of her lodgings each night and kissed her, though sometimes longer and harder than she might have liked, there had been a strength about him that had made her suddenly feel breathless and her pulse rate quicken. He had seemed equally excited in a way only men could, and once or twice he had tried to press himself on her rather more than she cared for, but when she had resisted he had shown the kind of restraint and respect she knew she deserved and she liked him for that. But now she felt more. Suddenly she wanted to sing and shout and tell the whole world that she was in love and she wondered if he felt the same way. Maybe she would find out as they were about to spend their last day in Blackpool together.

'What shall we do today?' Archie asked when they met at the tram stop after breakfast. 'It's the first time we've nothing planned.'

'Maybe we should find somewhere where we could just sleep,' Annie said without thinking, 'we've been so busy until now.' Annie laughed at her joke and was surprised to find he was eyeing her intently.

'I tell you what, why don't we spend the day relaxing on the beach as the weather's nice. We haven't really done much sunbathing, have we? And then, later on this afternoon, we could go down to Stanley Park?' Archie suggested. 'It's supposed to be very nice and we've not been there yet.'

'Well, it looks as if the weather might hold, there's not a cloud in the sky at the moment, so it might be a good day for the beach. And then later on, as you say, we could have a stroll in the park.'

Archie took Annie's hand and tucked it into the crook of his arm as they set off walking south.

'It's a pity we can't stay long enough to see the illuminations,' Annie said, noticing some elaborate structures that had been attached to several lampposts. 'It looks like they might be preparing already.'

'I've heard about those. People come from all over to see them, don't they? When do they start?' Archie asked.

'Not till September,' Annie said and burst out laughing. 'We'd both be bankrupt if we had to stay on till then in our lodgings. We'd have to get jobs here.'

Archie grinned at that. 'Maybe we can save up so that we can come here again in September, just to see the lights.' As he said this, his eyes met hers and he covered Annie's hand with his own and held it for a few moments.

'That would be lovely,' Annie said and smiled up at him as she spoke. They walked on in companionable silence although Annie couldn't help noticing that Archie looked as though he had something on his mind. But he didn't say anything as they wandered down to the beach and for the rest of the morning they allowed themselves the luxury of hiring two deckchairs.

Stanley Park, when they eventually strolled down to it, was even more beautiful than Annie had imagined, for the gardens were extremely well kept. They reminded her of the grounds of her old family home when they had lived in Clitheroe. The large, sweeping stretches of woodlands criss-crossed by intricately interwoven pathways were, not surprisingly, well populated with visitors, given that it had been such a warm, sunny day. And yet it was not difficult to find quiet, secluded corners too. There were areas where small isolated gardens had been cleverly created, enclosed by tightly intertwining bushes and what looked like solid walls, except that they were made of shrubs and plants.

Inside one such intimate space was a small wooden bench and they sat down to enjoy the carefully crafted flower arrangements that surrounded them: the early roses, the late rhododendrons and a whole host of sweet-smelling flowering blooms. When Annie felt Archie put his arm round her and pull her towards him, she caught her breath. Had he been aware of a deepening of his own feelings too? Was this the moment he was going to tell her how much he loved her? She snuggled up to him and sighed contentedly as she rested her head on his shoulder. Archie had also edged closer so that their legs were touching, his thigh warm against hers.

'It's been a great day, hasn't it?' he said, 'even though we've not done much.'

'It's been a great week,' she said.

'Do you know something? I do believe I've fallen for you, Annie Beaumont,' he said.

Annie's heart began to sing. 'I think I've fallen in love with you too,' she said. 'Do you really love me?'

'Yes, I do,' he said and then, without warning, he

kissed her in a way she had never been kissed before. No longer tender, his lips pressed hard against hers so that they were painful against her teeth and she felt the roughness of his tongue as he pushed it inside her mouth.

'What are you—' she tried to ask but he silenced her by crushing the weight of his whole body on top of hers. She could hardly breathe. Then she felt the warmth of his hand as it swept up and down the length of her inner thigh beneath her skirt, pausing only when it could reach no higher. At the same time his other hand had somehow found its way inside the top of her dress and into her bra where he began to tweak at her nipple. Suddenly it was as if her whole body had been connected to an electricity meter and someone had put in a shilling. She had never before felt anything like the wave of burning sensations she felt now. It wasn't that she didn't like it, but it had all happened so quickly and unexpectedly she didn't know how to react. She didn't know what he might do next and she felt as if her own body was completely out of her control. Eventually she managed to pull away from him but it took a great deal of effort.

'What do you think you're doing?' she panted. She hoped she hadn't cried out too loudly, for although they were cocooned in their own little arbour she realized she couldn't be sure what could be heard on the other side of the dense shrubbery.

'I think I'm kissing you, and it feels rather good,'

Archie murmured, shifting his weight so that he was no longer smothering her.

'But you must know I'm not the kind of girl to be kissed like . . . like that!' Annie exploded. This time she couldn't stop herself and she managed to wriggle from underneath him and stand up.

'And what kind of girl is that, exactly?' His voice was teasing. 'From where I'm sitting you were enjoying it.'

'You know what I mean,' she snapped. 'I am certainly not the kind of girl who will give herself away cheaply to just anyone.'

'But I'm not just anyone. You said yourself that you love me.'

'Yes, I did, and I do, but that doesn't mean . . .' Annie blustered, sounding confused. 'What I mean is, I won't be treated like . . . no one will touch me like that except my husband. If I was to act like . . . like any common mill girl, how could I expect a man to respect me?'

'What's respect got to do with it? We were talking about love. And if you loved me then you'd let me kiss you and touch you in any way I wanted.'

'If you loved me you wouldn't want to treat me so roughly, not when—'

'You said you loved me and I believed you, stupid fool that I am,' Archie jeered. 'And if you really loved me like you said, then you would want me to make love to you.'

'And if you loved me like you said, then you would

understand and respect me and you wouldn't even ask me to make love to you before we were married.'

'Married?' Archie sounded like he didn't understand the meaning of the word. 'You and me?' He sounded incredulous. 'Some hopes.'

Annie stared up at him as if she didn't recognize him. There was a hardness in his eyes and a sneer on his lips that she had never seen before.

'What's so special about you that you can expect to save yourself for some man in the future that you've got hidden away in your imagination? You're no different from any of the others at Fletcher's. Girls like you are ten a penny and I can have any one I fancy, whenever I like.'

Annie was shocked when Archie's hand moved to button up his trousers. She hadn't realized till then that they'd been undone.

'Don't worry, I won't go crying around the town about not being able to get into your knickers. It's your loss not mine.'

Annie gasped at the crude vulgarity of his language. She had never witnessed that side of him before. How could she have made such a mistake and misjudged him so? What had happened to the gentle, respectful Archie she thought she knew? Her mother had been right all along.

'Do you know something?' Archie stood up now. 'You're a stuck-up cow. What people say about you is right.'

Annie stared at him, shocked and horrified.

'What do you mean?' she said. 'What do they say about me?' She could feel the blood draining from her face.

'Hmph,' he sneered. 'I don't think you really want to know.'

As Archie stormed off, Annie remained rooted to the spot, not able to believe what had just happened and she thanked God that no one seemed to have been around to witness her shame. She pulled down the skirt of her dress without thinking. She hadn't noticed before that it was where Archie had left it, high above her knees. She waited until she was sure he was not coming back before she allowed herself the luxury of crying, although tears had begun to trickle down her cheeks even before Archie had left. But now that she was crying in earnest she didn't think she would ever be able to stop.

It wasn't until she noticed it was getting dark and that she had begun to feel chilly that she realized how long she had been sitting there. She had missed the meal at the boarding house and even any chance of a late supper out because she had to get back before the landlady locked the front door. Tomorrow, thank goodness, they would all be going home. For now, all she had to do was to find her own way back to the boarding house and wish that she would never have to see Archie again.

Chapter 12

May 1944

Gracie had no intention of giving up her boyfriend just because her father didn't approve of Yankee soldiers for she knew by now that she really did love Chuck and needed to find ways of being with him. And Chuck had told her that he loved her just as much in return. Despite her misgivings that he wasn't being completely honest with her, she knew that whatever the future might hold she didn't want to stop seeing him now. The problem was that now that her father knew, and had forbidden her to see him, they had to be constantly on their guard to make sure they weren't seen together by someone who might tell tales to her parents.

Chuck came into the Rovers regularly whenever he

had a night off-duty, as did many of his fellow GIs, but Gracie was careful not to be seen to be flirting with him. Her father still threatened to throw her out of the house if she ever dared to bring an American soldier home again or if he heard that she had been going out with a GI behind his back. Thankfully, her mother showed a little more compassion.

'I know your dad doesn't like Americans after what happened to him out in the Pacific an' all that,' Mildred confided to her daughter, 'but what he's really worried about is that American soldiers have a reputation for "loving and leaving" women high and dry. I'm sure you know what I mean. They're not always known for their dependability, now are they? Or for their complete honesty when it comes to their families back home.'

'I don't know, Mam. I can't say as I knows enough of them to judge.' Gracie was not going to tell her mother about her own reservations regarding Chuck's stories of his home life.

'They tell you one thing, but the truth can often be something quite different.' Mildred sighed as if she'd had personal experience of such deception. 'I know you might think you love him,' she said, 'but do be careful, I'd hate to see you get hurt.'

Gracie was startled to think that her emotions were so transparent. She had hoped she was giving the impression that she and Chuck were no longer seeing each other. 'It seems like it doesn't matter how I feel about him,' she said. 'If it's up to you and Dad, I won't be seeing him at all apart from serving him the odd pint at the Rovers.'

At that Mildred smiled. 'But we both know that when you're in love you don't always do as you're told,' she said and she gave Gracie a knowing wink.

Gracie was surprised that Annie Walker was sympathetic too. When she finally broke down and confessed to Annie how she had received her black eye, Annie offered her and Chuck a bolthole.

'You know the two of you could sit in one of the booths in the pub after hours when everyone's gone home,' Annie said, 'if you ever need somewhere private to talk.'

'That's really kind of you, Mrs Walker.' Gracie hoped she sounded grateful enough. 'As it happens, there are several things me and Chuck need to get sorted.'

'Well, I know how difficult it can be when you've nowhere you can go, where you won't be disturbed. So long as it's only talking that you'll be doing,' Annie added as an afterthought, giving Gracie a knowing look. She suddenly frowned. 'I shall trust you – and please bear in mind that I don't expect you to betray that trust.' Annie sounded severe and her lips were set in a straight line. 'But you've got the keys so you can lock up as usual whenever you're ready to go home.'

And that's how things stood as the summer of 1944 approached, though they rarely took advantage of Annie Walker's kind offer, not wanting to arouse

Gracie's father's suspicions if she stayed out late too often. It was now May and Chuck had been away a lot during the previous few months but they had managed to snatch precious moments together whenever he was in Weatherfield. If it was raining they went to the cinema, but when it was nice out they preferred to go for long walks. Gracie's favourite was to hire a rowing boat on Heaton Park Lake. She would lie back while Chuck managed the oars and, if no one was looking, they would pull up at the tiny island in the centre of the lake and disappear into the bushes, hoping no one could see them. At times like that they could forget the war and pretend they had their whole lives in front of them without interruption.

There had been rumours flying around Weatherfield for several months after the successful campaigns in North Africa and on the eastern front, that the allies were planning an invasion elsewhere in occupied Europe to push the German lines back. Chuck had been hinting for some time that he could be called away at very short notice to be part of such an invasion, though there was no certainty about where or when that would happen.

There had been much talk in the Rovers about how quickly a round-up of all available serving soldiers might happen, given the limited time that would be available in order for the Big Brass to make their decisions. According to all the 'experts' in the pub there wouldn't be many times in the course of a month when all the conditions could be met that would be needed to make such an operation successful.

'It depends on the moon.' Albert Tatlock made it sound almost mystical.

'Course it does! But 'e's right you know, without bloody moonlight no one will be able to see a bleeding thing.' Elsie Tanner quickly demystified his comment and everyone laughed.

'You can mock,' Albert said, 'but it depends on the amount of clouds in the sky an' all if it comes to that. And the winds; not to mention the rise of the spring tides, if they want to land troops off boats.'

'I hope you realize that we shouldn't be talking like this,' the ever-practical voice of Ena Sharples said as she sat down and banged her bottle of milk stout on the table. 'You know what they say, "Careless Talk Costs Lives".'

'This isn't careless talk, this is a carefully thought out plan,' Elsie chipped in again with a laugh. 'If the allies are going to invade then it seems to me that the more the Germans are confused about the when, the how and the where, the better.'

'Well, we don't have to worry there, then,' Albert said. 'We're confused enough so I'm sure the blooming Germans will be too.'

The American soldiers were also buzzing with stories about a possible invasion, for it could mean that they would be shipped out at a moment's notice. But they didn't seem to know any more about it than the customers in the pub.

'Is it true, all these rumours I've been hearing about you lot dashing off abroad?' Gracie asked Chuck when the rumour-mongering threatened to get out of hand one night. She didn't want to be seen lingering over Chuck's order but she did take her time pulling his pint and wiping up the spilled froth from the countertop.

'I'm afraid so,' Chuck's mate answered for him. 'So, if you've anything special to say to any of us, now's the time to say it.' He seemed to be addressing the room at large.

He carried several pints of beer off to their colleagues who were squashed together in one of the booths but Chuck hung back. 'Actually, Gracie, there is something I want to talk to you about. Privately.'

Gracie looked round to make sure no one else was listening before she said, 'Stay on after closing, then.'

Chuck nodded as he picked up his pint and Gracie was wondering what on earth this could be about.

'Would you like another drink before I tot up the till?' Gracie asked when there were only the two of them left in the pub later that night. 'Someone bought me one earlier that I had no time to drink, so I'm going to make myself a port and lemon. Well, a port with a splash of soda anyway, I haven't seen a real lemon for years.'

'No, thanks,' Chuck said. 'I've had my ration for tonight.'

Gracie poured her drink and brought it over to the table in the booth. She slid in beside him on the bench seat and sat close enough so that he could put his arm round her shoulders should he choose to. But he didn't. In fact, he moved further round the table so that they were almost sitting opposite each other. She was surprised, then, when he directly met her gaze. His blue eyes were steady and serious looking.

He cleared his throat before he began to speak. 'Gracie, if I do get called away – as you know, it could be sudden – and I don't know when, or even if, I'll ever be back. So it's very important that we have this conversation before I go.'

Gracie felt a cold shiver run down her spine. She wanted to tell him to stop, she didn't want to hear any more, but she couldn't. He was speaking again.

'I know we've talked about the possibility of you coming Stateside some day to meet the family, and as far as I'm concerned that stands. I would still love to think you would do that. But before that happens I think there are a few things you need to know.'

Gracie closed her eyes. This was it. There *was* something he'd been holding back. So was this going to be the moment when he finally told her the whole truth?

'Are you all right?' he asked. 'Can I get you some water or anything?'

She opened her eyes. He looked genuinely concerned. 'I'm fine,' she said. 'I was just wondering what you're going to say, that's all. Go on.'

'I don't know how to say this so I'll just come straight out with it. The fact is – and I know I should have told you this long ago – but the fact is, I've been married before.' He rubbed his eyes between his index finger and his thumb, leaving wetness on his cheeks. Gracie sat in silence, shocked by his confession. That was not what she was expecting to hear. Was he still married? Did that mean he wasn't free to love her and everything he had told her, including how much he loved her, was lies?

'Eleanor and I were childhood sweethearts,' he said, 'and we got married as soon as we were out of college. Well . . .' He hesitated. 'Truth is, Ellie didn't actually finish college.' He had been looking directly at Gracie but now he looked away. 'We jumped the gun and she got pregnant and had to drop out of school when her parents washed their hands of her.'

Now Gracie gasped. It was one thing to hear about a wife, but a child as well!

'My parents were great,' he went on. 'This was going to be their first grandchild so they were quite excited and they helped me to finish college. We got married straight away, of course, soon as we found out, and my folks bankrolled us so we could rent a small apartment on the East Side.'

Gracie gulped back the tears. How could he expect her to sit and listen to him talking about another life she was no part of and another woman he so clearly loved?

'We'd always intended to get married and have a family, though maybe not quite so soon . . .'

He stopped talking for a minute and Gracie thought he had finished, but then she could see that his eyes had filled and he didn't seem able to go on. She took a deep breath, about to ask him where Ellie and her child lived now, but he was speaking again. 'When the baby was born—' He broke off and it was several moments before he could continue. 'Ellie died in childbirth,' he said at last, his voice breaking. A lump rose to Gracie's throat at the thought of the horror and she caught her breath. 'I'm so sorry.' She put out her hand across the table but he made no move to touch her.

'My son . . . my son's name is Donald, though everyone calls him Buddy.' He fumbled inside his jacket. 'Here, I'll show you.' He pulled out his wallet and produced a small, much-handled black-and-white photograph of a little boy in a sailor suit. He had a head of light-coloured bubbly curls and he was grinning into the camera. An older woman with shoulder-length dark hair was bending down beside him and waving.

Gracie stared down at the photo, not quite able to take it all in. 'How old is he?'

'He'll be four in January.'

'Does he live with you?'

Chuck nodded. 'I moved back in with my mom and dad after Ellie died. They've continued to help me in ways I can never repay. I mean, like, since I've been over here they've been bringing him up.'

There was silence while Gracie studied the picture for a few more moments then she handed it back to him. She was remembering the letter to his mother Chuck had been sending home the night they first met.

'Why didn't you tell me before?' she asked, finding it impossible to keep the accusation out of her voice.

Chuck looked away. 'I know, I should have done. But the truth is, I thought I was coming here to fight a war. I didn't expect to fall in love.'

Gracie couldn't look at him. 'And if I'm honest, I thought the fact that I had a child might put you off.'

'In other words, you couldn't trust me.' Gracie sounded scornful.

'Oh no! I do trust you. But, I suppose I thought that a dead wife and a child was more than I could ask anyone to take on.'

'Is there anything else I should know?'

'No. I swear that's it. I'm really sorry I left it so long to tell you,' he said. 'I can see now that it was wrong.'

Gracie pushed her drink away; she no longer had any appetite for it. Chuck spread his hands across the table, palms up, inviting her to place her hands within his. But she couldn't. She sat back and folded her arms until eventually he did the same.

'When I came here tonight I intended to ask you a very specific question,' he said.

'Oh yes? And what was that?'

'It doesn't matter. I can't ask it now. I realize it wouldn't be fair.' He leaned forward and took one of her hands in his. 'We could be shipped out at very short notice, and where would that leave you? Of course I'll do my best to come back, and at worst I'd write to you and send for you.' He gazed at her fondly. 'But I've only just dumped my entire life story on you. You need time to digest it.'

He continued gazing at her. Was she sure it was love she was seeing in his eyes? Gracie stared back at him, her eyes searching for the truth. He had told her what he claimed was all of his story, but could there be anything else he was hiding? She was no longer sure. She withdrew her hand from his.

'I'll admit it's been a bit of a shock and I'm glad you told me about Buddy now, but I wish you'd felt able to tell me before. I'm not sure what it says about us in the future. I really do need time to take it all in.'

'You're right and I understand. It's no more than I deserve. And seeing your parents' reactions to us Yanks has made me stop and think that maybe things are not as straightforward as I might like to believe. We both need time to let things settle. That's why I don't want either of us to say any more now, but I want you to know that I do love you, with all my heart. I've loved you from the first moment I set eyes on you. Oh, and you're nothing like Ellie, by the way,' he added as an afterthought. He suddenly grinned, so that his face looked like a schoolboy's.

Gracie didn't sleep much that night. She lay tossing and turning until it was almost dawn, and every time she closed her eyes all she could see was little Buddy's face in the grainy photograph. She loved Chuck, she knew she did, but could she trust him when he said that there were no more secrets? And did she love him enough to accept his son as her own? For that was what it would mean if they were ever to have any kind of future together. It would be difficult enough for his parents to cope with – what they might see as an English girl taking away their grandson – but what would her parents say to it all, she wondered? Not that she could let their prejudices get in the way of her life. Particularly as she would be moving to New York. But if that time ever came, could she really think of defying her parents by going halfway round the world to bring up another woman's child, for that's what it would mean. Did she love him enough – and did he really love her?

The following morning when Gracie finally woke it was at a much later hour than she usually emerged and she realized she had better move quickly or she would be late for her first shift at the Rovers. She ran to the corner shop to see if she could get some kind of milk for her breakfast. Not fresh milk, of course, she would have to settle for the condensed stuff that came in tins. But as she ran she was surprised to hear the loud revving of engines and to see men in uniforms rushing back and forth in all directions. There were none of the shire horses with their carts like there usually were at this time of the morning, leisurely trotting down the street as their drivers made their deliveries. Instead there was much more movement and bustle and the normally quiet Weatherfield streets were clogged with motor vehicles. She didn't know what to make of the trucks that had begun to pass by, rattling and bumping over the cobbles. But when she saw soldiers peering out from behind the rain flaps, waving and wolf-whistling from the backs of the trucks as they bounced around on the wooden bench seats, it soon became clear that it was the US troops that were on the move. Gracie was shocked. She had not imagined their departure would happen so fast. She scoured the faces of the soldiers as they passed by but she didn't see Chuck in any of the vehicles. She began to panic, and as she ran she worried whether she would ever see Chuck again – and what it might mean if she didn't. What if he had already gone? She didn't bother going home after she picked up the tin of milk, but ran straight round to the Rovers Return.

Annie ushered her into the pub through the private side entrance and immediately handed her a note that had been stuffed into an envelope addressed *To Gracie*. 'I've just found it on the doormat underneath my own letter,' Annie said. 'I don't know how long it's been there.'

Gracie looked at her anxiously, then she tore open the envelope and scanned the contents. Chuck's words were scrawled in his large, spidery writing across the page but the message was brief and to the point.

We are shipping out today – like now, this minute – even as I am writing this! I doubt I'll be able to see you before I go, but like I said last night, I hope I'll be back again before too long. Remember me fondly as always, as I will love and remember you. Your Chuck xx

She folded the paper as her tears splashed onto the words, washing them across the page in a web-like mess. She looked up, wondering what she should say to Annie, and was surprised to see that Annie's face was wet with tears too.

When Annie had picked up her own letter from the doormat she thought it was just one of Jack's regular weekly communications. She had begun to feel she could almost write those letters herself as he said the same things over again, using the same words and phrases each time. But this time, as she started to read, she realized it was different in tone from his usual letters and he was saying some very different things. She saw Gracie beginning to weep over the scrappy note she had extracted from the envelope that looked like it had been torn from a child's exercise book, but her hand was shaking too much as she read her own letter to pay Gracie much mind. Jack's words were unusually thoughtful, philosophical even, for him, and as she tried to absorb all he was saying it put her into a thoughtful mood too. Jack was reflecting on his role in the army, talking about how he would much rather be pulling pints with her at the Rovers than dodging bullets in some inadequate bunk hole hundreds of miles away. *But at least I can sleep well at night,* he wrote, *with a clear conscience as I know that I am doing the right thing. I'm doing my bit for my country and helping to keep safe all those I love and cherish. And that, of course, means you, dear heart.* He went on to tell her how much he loved her in words that made her blush to read them, and when she finally got to the end where he had signed his name with an unusual flourish she felt the wetness trickling down her cheeks.

She was glad Jack felt that fighting for his country was the right thing to be doing, for she felt that way too, even though she missed him and would have preferred to have him by her side. He had every right to be proud of the service he was doing on behalf of his family.

But was Annie's own conscience clear? Annie left Gracie in the hallway and went up to her bedroom. She needed some time to be on her own. She sat down in front of the cheval mirror and put her head in her hands. Yes, she had acted promptly and appropriately when she had admitted her naiveté and broken off her friendship with Roy. But how had she treated Annette? That poor young girl had pricked her conscience several times recently, even though it had been such a long time since she had seen her. She had come a long way, looking for her mother, and it couldn't have been easy. She had obviously had a hard life in the orphanage, and never known much in the way of love. Yet, had

Annie told her the truth? Had she really told her everything she knew?

She looked again at Jack's letter that he had written with such openness and honesty, and she thought of all the things that had happened since she had left Fletcher's Mill, things she had clammed up about soon after they had happened and had never discussed with anyone.

Chapter 13

After they came back from Blackpool, Annie thought she would never get over Archie and the shocking way he had treated her, but once work in the mill began again in earnest, she found she had far more important things to worry about and Archie Grainger no longer filled her thoughts. She began to see him for the common lout that her mother had warned her about, and she was able to forget that she had once foolishly thought that she'd loved him. Of course, the inevitable baiting and bullying began again from some of the other workers but she felt she was immune to the name-calling and vile words now and she was only concerned with avoiding physical conflict.

Lilian and Nancy remained her closest friends and they picked up once more on their old routine with the two girls calling for Annie each morning on their way to work and escorting her safely home again each night. After a few weeks, however, Lilian more often came alone in the mornings as Nancy was not very well and, although she could ill afford it, often had to have time away from work. Annie and Lilian worried about her and offered to help out if it was money she needed in order to see a doctor. But Nancy steadfastly refused their help, saying it was just a touch of influenza and that she would be all right soon. Annie was worried that, if it was a form of flu, she might catch it too, for she was feeling constantly tired these days and any benefits she might have gained from the sun and fresh air while on holiday were quickly forgotten.

However, big changes were soon to take over Annie's life that would make her forget about Archie and the holiday and would point her life in a different direction altogether.

Annie arrived home from work one night to find her mother and father having a cup of tea with a stranger in the front living room. The smartly dressed gentleman stood up when Annie entered and put forward his hand. 'I'm Mr Jackson from Jackson and Pollock, solicitors of Clitheroe, and I've come here to—' he began but Florence interrupted.

'Annie, this gentleman has come with some of the

most amazing news.' She grabbed Annie's hand and pulled her down onto the sofa.

Annie didn't know who to listen to first, and then her father joined in. 'Your mother has claim to an inheritance.' His face had broken into a beaming smile.

'Yes, Annie,' Florence agreed. 'What do you think? My old Aunt Victoria, my dear mother's sister, has sadly just died. Unfortunately, we never saw very much of her, but she has remembered me in her will. She must have been in her nineties.' She looked towards Mr Jackson.

'Ninety-two, I believe,' he confirmed.

'And of all things, she ran her own ice-cream factory, quite successfully,' Edward said, taking up the story. 'Apparently, she owned the buildings, the machinery and all the equipment so it should be worth a tidy sum – and she has left it all to your mother.' He shook his head in disbelief.

'Indeed,' Mr Jackson intervened. 'A tidy sum as you say. It is a going concern with profitable retail outlets besides. I have just come to advise you of your good fortune today, but the details of your mother's inheritance will be revealed at the will reading next Tuesday. I trust you will be able to attend?' He looked at Florence who nodded vigorously.

'Oh, I shall be available, most definitely. I always knew we were destined to be rescued from poverty one day. Didn't I always say we must never give in to it?' She looked about the room as if expecting a round of applause.

'The factory is situated by the canal in a place called Weatherfield,' Mr Jackson continued.

'So we'll have to move there,' Florence said eagerly. 'To a much nicer area and a much larger house.'

'And you and I will have to give up our jobs at the mill to run the place, Annie,' Edward said.

'Which will be much more fitting for both of you,' Florence concluded. 'Thank you so much for your kind visit, Mr Jackson, I shall look forward to seeing you on Tuesday.'

Life is definitely looking up, Annie decided as she showed the solicitor to the door, and she felt as if a weight had been shed from her shoulders as she thought of no longer working on the looms.

The only people Annie regretted leaving behind were her friends, Lilian and Nancy. They had been so good to her during the three years they had worked together that she didn't know how to tell them that she was going and she dreaded the thought of saying goodbye. She told Lilian about her good fortune one morning when they were on their way to work, shortly after the family had received the solicitor's letter to say that all the necessary papers had been completed and signed. Nancy was unwell and was not with Lilian that day so Annie decided she would call on her friend on the way home.

She was shocked when Nancy opened the front door, for she was looking so pale and thin it seemed as if she could hardly stand up. At first, she seemed reluctant to let Annie in, but Annie gave her no choice and pushed past her and into the kitchen so that they could both sit down.

'Are you checking up on me?' Nancy sounded defensive and ready to pick a fight.

'Well, of course I am. I've been really worried about you,' Annie said. 'I wanted to see how you are.'

Nancy's chin jutted out in defiance, but before she could say anything Annie said, 'But the main reason I've come today is because I've something to tell you. Only Lilian knows, but I shall be leaving Fletcher's at the end of the week.'

Nancy's eyes widened. 'But that's tomorrow!' She sat down heavily. If she'd looked pale when she opened the door, she looked even paler now.

Annie sat down too and told her the story briefly. 'You can imagine how I feel to finally be able to get away from here.' She couldn't help smiling.

Nancy's head dropped so that she was no longer looking at Annie as she nodded. 'I can understand that,' she muttered.

'You and Lilian would be the only reasons I'd have for staying,' Annie added quickly.

'Oh, but you mustn't do that,' Nancy cut in, grasping hold of Annie's hand.

'Why not? You two are my best friends.' Annie put her finger under Nancy's chin and tilted her face so that her friend had to look her in the eye. 'I'm sorry to have to say it, but you look dreadful. Have you been to see a doctor, like you promised?'

'No, not yet.'

'Why not?' You must.' Annie was insistent.

'There's really no need, that's why not.'

'How can you be so sure? Are you a doctor?' Annie was flippant but Nancy was looking directly at her.

'Of a sort,' Nancy said. 'Every woman knows when she's having a bairn.'

Annie looked at her friend in amazement. 'You mean to say you're pregnant? But how far gone are you?'

'Since wakes week. You can do the counting.'

'How can you be so certain it was wakes week . . .?' Annie began naively, then her voice trailed off as light dawned. 'So, who's the father?'

Nancy didn't answer. She just looked down at her feet.

'If it's one of Archie's friends, whatever their names were, I swear I'll . . .' Annie made a ball of her fist and looked as if she would have punched them on the spot if they'd been in the room right now. Nancy was still silent.

'But I didn't think you were so smitten?' Still nothing.

Annie clenched her jaw and looked at her friend once more. Now tears were gliding down Nancy's face, and her shoulders were shaking with silent sobs. She seemed to have nothing to wipe them with so Annie handed over one of her own white lawn handkerchiefs which she had once had to embroider as part of a school assignment. She had attempted, not very well, to entwine the initials AB in fine embroidery silk into one of the corners. She was fond of the handkerchief, but that didn't matter now. She had never seen her friend so distressed.

'I'm so sorry, Annie,' Nancy wept, 'I can't apologize enough.'

'Apologize for what? You haven't done anything to me. It's you who's in this sorry state,' Annie said, but that only made Nancy wail louder.

'I don't know what got into me. Honestly, I don't. You know me, you know I'd never do anything to hurt you.'

'Yes, of course, but Nancy, what is it that you think you've done to me?'

'We were all drunk, that was the problem. And you know what it's like when you're on holiday, away from everything and everybody that's familiar. You can forget yourself, get carried away. You sort of forget about real life, you just want to have a good time. Whether it's really a good time or not . . .' Her voice trailed off.

'Nancy, you are not making any sense. Will you please tell me, now?'

'I don't know as I can. Honestly I don't.'

'Why? I don't understand what's stopping you.'

'Cos he was your feller, that's why. You were sweet on him. I shouldn't have done it, no matter what he said.'

Annie stepped back now as light began to dawn. 'Nancy,' she began, 'did you . . . ?'

'I should have told you sooner,' Nancy said.

'What?' Annie asked with foreboding.

'It was Archie.'

Annie actually gasped out loud as Nancy said this and her hands flew to her mouth. She was silent for several moments, then she asked, her voice incredulous, 'When? I'd have hardly thought he had time.'

'That last night when you weren't with us.' Nancy wiped her eyes and went to sit down, resting her elbows on the table. 'Lil and Kevin and me and Derek had all arranged to go out for a drink. When they pitched up, Archie was with them. I was surprised and asked him where you were. He said you'd gone for a walk as you wanted to be by yourself for a bit and we'd see you back at the boarding house later on.'

Annie sat down across the table, not sure she wanted to hear the details, but knowing that she must.

'We went to this pub,' Nancy went on. 'It were very nice. The lads were buying so we kept drinking. We were on port and lemon and you know they can taste no stronger than a Vimto. It wasn't until Archie asked me to go for a walk on the beach with him that I realized that I was drunk. Archie was too. He was all jumpy, like he had ants in his pants.' Nancy paused. She looked over to Annie, then stared down at her lap. Her voice was soft as she said, 'I'm real sorry, Annie, that I never told you this before but I've always had a bit of a soft spot for Archie myself.'

Annie looked surprised. She shook her head. 'I had no idea,' she said.

'No, I realized that. So, as you weren't around and he'd asked me to go out with him, I thought there were no harm in it. I know it's no excuse but we hadn't had much for tea so what wi' all the drinks the lads kept buying, by the end of the night I didn't really know what I was doin'. Any road, it was getting dark and we ended up in this sheltered spot on the beach and at first I were really enjoying myself, we were having a laugh. Then he started getting a bit nasty, like. He suddenly started saying you was a stuck-up so-and-so and nothing but a tease who thought you were better'n 'im.'

'He actually said that?' Annie was stung by his double betrayal.

'I was frightened then,' Nancy continued, 'cos he sounded really angry. But then he flipped to being nice again and started saying things that made me feel good. Made it sound like I'd be the good 'un for givin' in to him. Like it was the right thing to do. And I'm ashamed to say I'd had too much to drink to be thinking straight, so I did, I gave him what he wanted . . . and you didn't come back till late that night, remember, not till we was asleep, any road. Or I might have said summat. But by the morning I had a dreadful hangover, and anyways I found I couldn't tell you.'

Annie remembered that night all too well. She shuddered, recalling how close she had come to giving in to him.

'Have you told your mother about . . . ?' She pointed

her eyes in the direction of Nancy's stomach, unable to put a final word to her sentence and unwilling to think any more about Archie's behaviour. 'What does she say?'

'I haven't said owt yet, though I'm sure she knows. They say women have an instinct for these things, specially once they've had kids themselves.' Nancy stopped to wipe her eyes and nose again with Annie's handkerchief because the tears were flowing freely once more. 'She'll be scared what my dad'll have to say so she's probably working up to throwing me out of the house.'

'Oh, don't say that!' Annie realized that, despite Nancy's confession, she felt sorry for the girl.

'Why not? It's true. I won't be able to stay here much longer.'

'Where will you go?'

Nancy shrugged. 'I'll think of something. I've got an aunt that might take me in. Whatever, I won't be welcome here.'

Annie looked round at the scantly furnished room. No family in these parts was willing to accept a child born out of wedlock.

When Nancy had first told her about the baby being Archie's, Annie's reaction was anger; she felt as if she had been betrayed. But as she looked at the sobbing, pathetic girl who, at this moment, looked more like a child herself, her anger faded and she found herself saying, 'I only wish there was something I could do to help.' Then a determined look crossed her face. 'You know what, there is something I can do. And I will. With any luck, by the time I've given him a piece of my mind, Archie Grainger will come crawling to ask if he can stick by you and do the decent thing.'

'Would you still do that for me?' Nancy sounded pathetically grateful. 'Only trouble is, I've already asked him and I think you can imagine what his answer was. He's not going to let the likes of a baby get in his way, now is he?'

'But he's got you into this mess, he should face up to his responsibilities.' Annie tried to sound strong though she didn't feel it. But she did feel sorry for Nancy. The silly girl had been caught out in a weak, drunken moment when she was far from home and not thinking of the consequences. Annie was only glad *she* hadn't given in and allowed him to have his way with her. The thought that she could so easily have been in this predicament made her shudder and want to cry, but instead she said a little prayer of thanks that she had been strong enough to spurn the tempta-tion Archie had placed before her and she was pleased now she had stuck to her principles. As for Archie, he was nothing more than an oversized worm. Her mind was working overtime to dredge up all the other awful names she could think of but she ran out of inspiration. She didn't know if she was doing her friend any favours by suggesting Archie should marry her. On the other hand, Nancy's mother was bound to make her get rid of the baby one way or another. Marriage was her only hope for hanging on to it.

Annie stood up and offered her hand to Nancy. Nancy and Lilian had been her first real friends and she was going to miss them dreadfully. They had come to her and offered their friendship, when she was at her lowest ebb. They had stood up for her against some of the most awful bullies in the mill and they had shown her how to live with dignity, and keep her spirits going despite suffering dire poverty. She didn't know how to express her gratitude to them for how she considered they had saved her life. But it was Nancy who spoke first.

'Thanks so much for coming to see me, Annie,' Nancy said with a weak smile. 'It means a lot to me to know you haven't deserted me.' She dabbed her eyes with Annie's handkerchief that was screwed up in a ball in her hand. Annie couldn't help noticing but didn't say anything. 'I can't tell you how sorry I am that you're going away,' Nancy said. 'We had some good times together, didn't we, you, me and Lil? I'll really miss you, you know. I think we both will.'

Annie could feel tears gathering in her own eyes and they threatened to spill over though she tried her best to hold them back.

'Who will we go off to work with of a morning and go home with on a night? Who will we stick up for in the canteen?' Nancy said.

Annie smiled at that. 'You've been a good friend to

me, Nancy, the best. And you were there when I needed one most.' Annie clasped her friend's hand as the tears finally rolled down her cheeks. 'You and Lilian took me under your wings when no one else wanted to speak to me. I want you to know how much I appreciate that. And if ever there is anything I can do for you . . .' Annie looked at Nancy hopelessly, her tears now swimming unchecked, for in that moment she knew that it was unlikely that their paths would ever cross again.

The next evening at Fletcher's Mill, as everyone was getting ready for home, Annie was looking forward to telling Mr Mattison that she was leaving. She waited until they had been paid at the end of the day as she didn't want to risk him getting mean and withholding her whole week's wages on some pretence. It didn't matter that she didn't need the money now – it was the principle of the thing. Then she marched into his office when the shift was over to tell him she was going. She walked purposefully, with her head held high, through the shed to his office, just as she had on her first day three years before. Only this time the tables were turned and she wanted everyone in the shed to know that.

'I shan't be working here any longer,' she announced while he ignored her intrusion and pretended to search for something in his filing cabinet. 'I'm leaving as of now.' When he heard her words, he spun round and glared at her.

'You're doing what?' he shouted. 'You can't just walk out like that and leave me an operator short.'

'I can do anything I want because I've earned it,' Annie said quietly. 'As of today, I am a free agent. I do thank you sincerely for giving me a job when I most needed it and when nobody else was willing to take on someone with no work experience. But, thankfully, that is no longer the case.'

'Why, you ungrateful . . . ! You won't find another job so fast, I'll make sure of that. Who'd put up with you and your toffee-nosed ways?'

'I'm delighted to say that you will have no say in my future employment because from now on I shall be my own boss. I'll no longer have to put up with these insanitary conditions, your total exploitation, or even your wandering hands.' Annie was delighted to see the man looking almost apoplectic. From his slanderous outpourings it sounded like he was equally furious and disbelieving but she didn't care. There was more she could say, but why waste her breath? So she just held her head erect and, looking neither to the right nor the left, walked out.

As she reached the door at the end of the shed, Archie suddenly emerged, spanner in hand, from where he'd been crawling about underneath one of the looms. The timing couldn't have been better if she'd planned it.

'Ah, Archie,' she said, trying to keep calm, 'you're just the man I wanted to see.'

'Well, that makes a change. Only sorry, you're too

310

late. You had your chance and you turned out to be nothing but a cock-tease.'

'Trust you to turn our friendship into something vulgar. But I wasn't referring to me, I was referring to what you did to Nancy. But I'm sure you would want to stand by her and do the right thing.'

Archie's eyes widened and he laughed out loud, far louder than was necessary. 'What? You're saying because she's up the duff that it's my fault?'

'You are responsible and that's a fact, as you know full well.'

'But she's just a slag and who knows how many men she's slept with? If she's got a bun in the oven there's no way to prove it's mine.'

Annie's heart sank. Unfortunately, he was right. Even though Annie believed her friend implicitly she had no means of showing that he had been the only one. And if Annie persisted he would only end up calling poor Nancy worse names. What if people believed him and some of the mud stuck? She hadn't thought of that, and that was the last thing she wanted to happen to her friend. Annie suddenly realized that there was no point in continuing the conversation. If he wouldn't own up to it there was nothing she could do. She felt helpless. But there was one thing that gave her some gratification. She had given him the opportunity and he had indeed shown up his true colours.

'You know that not one word of that is true,' she said. 'You should own up to your responsibilities. But that's a word that's obviously too long for you to understand,' she sneered. However, she knew it was hopeless, her pleas were falling on deaf ears. 'You're such a snake in the grass,' she spat out finally in frustration. 'But you mark my words, one day when you are least expecting it, Nancy and who knows how many more women will get their revenge on you.' It gave her some satisfaction that words had finally come to her to describe him, but that was the end of it, and she knew it. He would forever deny that he was the father and there was nothing more she could do. Holding her head high, Annie turned her back on him and walked out of the mill forever.

The Beaumonts' new house was in Weatherfield, close to the canal where the factory was, in a pretty area miles away from Fletcher's Mill. It was larger and in much better condition than the house they had left and, although the rent was dearer, Annie hoped that the factory would earn them sufficient to warrant it. There was a large living room, with a separate kitchen with hot and cold running water and an electric stove downstairs. Upstairs there were two good-sized bedrooms and a bathroom also with hot and cold water. The outside lavatory had a proper flushing mechanism and its own electric light. The spiders might be bigger but at least they weren't as scary as they had been in the dark. Even Florence was keen to set to work, sewing curtains and cushion covers and finding some cheap floor rugs to make the place feel homely, and it wasn't long before it felt more like home than their previous house had ever done.

It had already been decided that Edward Beaumont would take over the running of the factory, and the workers who had opted to stay on after the changeover of management were eager to show him the ropes. Annie happily went to work alongside her father in the production of ice cream.

It was hard work, but the business thrived under Edward's management and it all felt worthwhile.

'You might be exhausted but you look so much happier than in your previous job,' Florence commented one night when Annie came home late, complaining that all she wanted was a sandwich and to sit down in front of the fire.

'You've no idea, Mother,' Annie said. 'It's like chalk and cheese. No one is taking advantage of me here, except Daddy sometimes.' She gave an affectionate laugh.

'I do hope he's not working you too hard.' Florence looked concerned.

'Not at all.' Annie smiled. 'I love working with him.'

'Don't you miss your friends?' Florence asked.

Annie thought for a moment. She had often wondered what had become of Nancy and Lilian, but she'd thought it more prudent to assign them to the past. 'I did miss them, at the beginning, and I often think of them but I've got new interests now, and new friends.'

She sighed. 'Sometimes it's better to let the past go.' Then she laughed. 'Though I do sometimes wish I could meet some of my childhood friends from the old days. Who would ever have thought that Annie Beaumont would end up making ice cream!'

When Edward Beaumont died unexpectedly, sitting in his favourite chair in the office he had come to love, it felt as if the family had been dealt yet another crushing blow, for Annie had grown close to her father while they had worked together.

'At least he left us with no financial worries,' Annie remarked to Florence when the will was finally settled.

'No, bless him.' Florence sighed. 'He was a good husband and he tried to do his best for us. He wasn't a gambler or a bad investor. The previous disaster was solely your grandfather's fault, not Edward's. I've always been clear about that.'

'And thank goodness it seems that everyone likes the new strawberry and chocolate flavours of ice cream that we've developed.' Annie sounded justly proud.

The factory and the small retail shops where they sold their ice cream were their sole source of income, so it was important for Annie to continue running the business. However, she needed a partner and she soon realized that her mother was not capable of taking her father's place. And without him, Annie's heart was no longer in it and she knew she was no longer prepared to put in the long hours of work that were required if she was to run it single-handedly. So she appointed Neil Parkin as manager and major executive. He was a pleasant-looking, middle-aged man with a shock of iron-coloured hair and sensible notions of how the business might be developed. Annie was satisfied that she could take a back seat now and leave the running of the firm in Neil's safe and capable hands.

Free to start again to explore her own life, Annie wondered once more if she might consider a stage or screen career at last. But then she met Jack who mistakenly thought he had saved her from jumping into the canal, and they fell in love. Rather than ending her life she soon became aware that together they could embark on a new and fruitful life and when Jack asked her to marry him, she agreed.

Chapter 14

1944

'Is everything all right?' Gracie asked. Annie had come back into the bar and begun counting change into the till.

'Yes, why shouldn't it be?'

'Because you look so . . . solemn, I think would be the word.' She wasn't sure whether to confess that she had seen Annie's tears.

'I could say the same about you,' Annie said with a knowing smile. 'Was it bad news in your note? I presume it was from Chuck.'

Gracie nodded. 'He shipped out early this morning. All the GIs did.'

'That's what I heard. The street's been buzzing with

trucks and soldiers since before dawn. No one expected them to go so soon, though I suppose it's a good sign if there really is to be an invasion of Europe. Maybe it will mean an end to this wretched war. But I'm really sorry for you and some of the other girls round here who were sweet on some of the soldiers. You were really quite fond of Chuck, weren't you?'

'I'm afraid so.' Gracie looked away. 'Though nothing was ever agreed.'

'Would you have liked there to be?'

'I don't know.' Gracie shrugged. 'There's a lot at stake. He lives a whole world away and my parents are so dead against him, and there was no time to try to sort things out. Because he was away so much, it felt as though I hadn't known him for very long. Though I do know that I love him and I can't bear to think he's gone away and I might never see him again.' There was a catch in Gracie's voice. 'I was in love with him.'

Annie squeezed Gracie's hand. 'Chin up. If something's meant to be then he'll be back. You've got to believe that.'

'Did you get a letter from Jack?' Gracie changed the subject. 'Is everything all right with him?'

'Yes, thank you. Though I don't know if he'll be coming home on leave again. But his letter set me thinking, that was all.' A sad look crept into Annie's eyes once more and for a moment Gracie thought the older woman was going to cry again.

'Am I allowed to ask what you were crying about?'

Gracie said. 'I couldn't help noticing something had made you sad.'

Annie sighed. 'There was nothing specific in the letter but it did set me thinking about several different things. It made me think about that girl, Annette, for one. Do you remember when she came here looking for me, that time, though it's a couple of years ago now? You'd just started working here.'

Gracie nodded. 'Yes, I remember her. I'd seen her hanging around the place on several occasions before she actually came inside and asked for you. I've often wanted to ask if you'd heard from her again.'

'No, I haven't heard or seen anything of her but I've been thinking recently that I'd like to – though I know so little about her I doubt I'd be able to trace her even if I wanted to.'

'I don't know about that,' Gracie said. 'I believe you could find almost anyone if you really wanted to. Don't forget, she managed to find you.'

'That's true.'

'What do you know about her? That would be a good place to start.' She sounded enthusiastic about the diversion.

'All I know is that she was brought up in an orphanage,' Annie said. 'And for some reason she had her mind set that I knew who her parents were and that I could help her to find them.'

Gracie nodded. 'But you didn't know anything, did you?'

319

Annie hesitated and a guilty expression flashed across her face. 'That's what I told her.' Annie closed the till drawer though there were some sixpenny pieces and thre'penny bits still on the counter. 'But I've thought about her a lot since that day. And the fact of the matter is I'm not sure I told her the whole truth.'

Gracie stared at Annie, not wanting to say anything to interrupt, although questions were firing off in her head. Was Annie guilty in the same way as Chuck? Denying parenthood.

Annie turned to her and faced her full on. 'I think I *do* know who her parents are. And if that really is the case, then I would like to do what I can to help her find them.' Then Annie told Gracie the story of Nancy and Archie and the unfortunate wakes week in Blackpool and Gracie realized her suspicions were unfounded.

Annie remembered Annette saying she worked in Grant House that was not far from the orphanage on the edge of a large park somewhere in Cheshire. With the help of the street map and guide and the telephone directory, Gracie worked out the name of the orphanage and Annie was immediately keen to set off in her quest to find the young girl, but it was early June before they had the time.

It had been a wet summer so far and on the day they chose to go to Cheshire it didn't stop raining. A cold wind had also sprung up and Gracie felt chilled to the bone as she and Annie set off on their mission.

'I'm so cold it's hard to believe it's June,' Annie said.

'This wretched rain doesn't help,' Gracie said as she drew her coat round her and fastened the buttons up to the neck.

'Never mind, we'll feel a lot warmer if we're successful,' Annie said and she pulled on some fine cotton gloves and tucked her arm through Gracie's as they set off across the slippery cobbles to the tram. Gracie had insisted on accompanying Annie once she knew Annette's story. She had felt drawn to the girl the first time she had seen her and something told her Annie would prefer to have company on what could turn out to be a difficult day. Besides, Gracie was delighted to have something to take her mind off Chuck's sudden departure and the fact that she might never see him again.

Lottie had offered to cover the evening shift at the Rovers and Annie had decided it would be best if they closed the pub over the lunch period as it would help to conserve the diminishing beer stocks.

'And to think,' Annie said, 'here we are feeling so cold when only this morning I bribed Joanie and Billy with the promise of ice creams if they'd behave well and spend the day nicely with Grandma Florence.'

'What do they care about a bit of rain?' Gracie said. 'They're happy enough to be won over by the promise of something sweet any day of the week, particularly when they have so few other sweet treats at the moment.'

'I suppose children will do anything for an ice cream,' Annie said and Gracie laughed. 'And it is such a luxury these days,' Annie said.

'Though maybe not for much longer,' Gracie said. 'Can you still get all the ingredients?'

'Neil has just heard about a special recipe using goats' milk which isn't rationed, that we might be able to use, so all is not lost yet,' Annie laughed, then suddenly wrinkled her brow. 'I do hope I did the right thing asking Mummy to look after the children and that she'll be able to cope.'

'Don't worry,' Gracie assured her, 'I'm sure they'll all be fine.'

'I suppose they will, although I do worry that she's not up to looking after them both for a whole day any more. Billy can be such a monkey, and these days even Joanie can be a little minx as well. They'll probably run rings round her, the poor love.'

'Never mind, I'm sure you don't have to worry about them. It's us you should be worrying about,' Gracie laughed. 'We're the ones who are venturing into the unknown.'

'And I'm delving into a past I thought I'd been able to forget,' Annie said.

They caught a train from Weatherfield directly to the local Cheshire station which Gracie had worked out would be closest to the orphanage, then walked the last half mile till they came to a set of imposing wrought iron gates.

'I think this must be it,' Gracie said and Annie nodded. It looked like a typical Victorian building, an iron-framed construction with terracotta bricks and a fine slate roof, all of which looked in surprisingly good condition. Even the iron railings had not been removed to contribute towards the war effort although they would have benefitted from a coat of paint. They seemed to stretch all the way round the building, out of sight. There were two dark porch entrances, one marked 'Boys' and one marked 'Girls', and both looked equally forbidding. There were fine arched window frames but the plate glass windows looked as if they had not been cleaned since the building had been erected. They entered through the girls' entrance and Gracie was immediately hit by a smell of damp, tempered by disinfectant. She heard the sound of leather heels making sharp contact with the stone floor and almost immediately saw a young woman coming towards them. She was dressed for the country in a dark grey tweed skirt and a lighter grey twinset and she had an important-looking pile of papers tucked under her arm. She looked surprised to see them.

'Can I help you?' she said. 'Do you have an appointment?'

'We're looking for a girl called Annette, Annette Oliver,' Annie said, putting on her authoritative voice.

'Is she expecting you?'

'I shouldn't think so, but we would like to see her, if we may,' Annie said and smiled as she spoke.

'Maybe I should show you to the superintendent's office,' the woman said. 'She might be able to help you.' She sounded guarded, but just at that moment Annette came running down the passageway. A voice in the distance shouted, 'Stop running in the corridor!' Annette stopped almost immediately, not in response to the voice, if the look on her face was anything to go by, but because she had recognized Annie and Gracie.

'Ah, Annette. We were just talking about you,' the officious woman said, awkwardly shifting her pile of papers from underneath one arm to the other. 'These two ladies are . . .'

'Yes, I know who they are,' Annette said, cutting her short. A blush was on her cheek and there was a sudden light in her eye. 'I imagine they've come to take me out like they promised the last time I saw them.' She fixed Annie with a stare.

'We have indeed.' Annie picked up the cue.

'I presume that's all right, Mrs Rogers?' Annette turned to the woman in the twinset.

The woman glared at her for a moment. 'Yes, of course,' she said after a slight hesitation. 'I'll square it with the Principal. So long as you're back in time for late supper.'

'Oh, we'll take good care of her, and bring her back safely in good time.' Annie turned to Annette. 'Is there a nice teashop we could go to nearby?'

'Yes, there is, as a matter of fact,' Annette said, looking

really pleased. 'I'll just get my coat and umbrella if you don't mind waiting.'

'Then I'll bid you good day,' Mrs Rogers said and she didn't even glance round as the leather heels on her brogues click-clacked down the corridor.

'I presume we don't have to tell anyone else where you're going?' Annie asked when Annette returned dressed ready to go out.

'Not once old dragon Rogers knows. She'll make sure to tell everyone who needs to know, and a few who don't.' Annette smiled for the first time since they'd arrived and her whole face lit up. It was the most animated Annie had seen her and, despite her badly cut hair and uneven teeth, made her look almost pretty.

Annette asked how they had found her as she guided them to a small, cosy café only a few streets away from the orphanage. They were seated at a table in a recess, away from any prying eyes, and without delay a large teapot was placed in front of them and a plate with tiny portions of crumbly cake. Annette looked as if she would hardly be able to restrain herself from eating all three slices.

'I never would have found you without Gracie, you know,' Annie said, and she explained how the barmaid had wanted to help. Then, 'I've been thinking about you a lot since you came to Weatherfield,' Annie began, not sure how to start. 'I'm really sorry that I wasn't able to tell you the whole story when you came to the Rovers Return that day, but it was all such a shock, seeing the letter and the handkerchief that I'd embroid-ered. I couldn't work it out in my head where or how you'd got hold of them.'

'And now you've decided it's time to own up and tell me you're my mother?' Annette said, her voice matter of fact.

Annie's jaw dropped open. 'No! Is that what you think? Goodness me, you need to know right away that's not the truth at all.'

Annette looked confused. Annie reached out and put her hand on the young girl's arm. 'Oh, my dear,' Annie said. 'I had no idea that was what you thought.'

'Why are you so surprised?' Annette said, using a linen square from her pocket to wipe away the tears that had gathered in the corners of her eyes. 'It was your hankie and your name. What else could I think?'

'I am so sorry. It never occurred to me. But I do believe I know who your mother is. And your father,' she added.

'Do you know where either of them is now? Are they still alive?' Annette sounded lacklustre, as if her dream had been shattered.

'I'm afraid I don't.'

Gracie took her cue from Annie and leaned forward eagerly, 'But we thought maybe we could try to find out.'

Annette's face lit up but Annie, not wanting to build up her hopes, added, 'I've no idea what's happened to either of them since I last saw them – and that was the day I left my job at Fletcher's Mill. In fact, the last time I saw your mother she was set to leave her parents' house. Her name then was Nancy Warburton.'

'Nancy Warburton,' Annette repeated, rolling the words across her tongue. 'It would be wonderful to meet her after all this time,' she said, a dreamlike quality in her voice.

'Are you really sure that's what you want to do?'

Annette looked directly into Annie's eyes. 'I'm sure.'

'Then there is someone who might know where Nancy is. You see, I had two particular friends in those days, one was Nancy as I've told you, but there was also Lilian Vickers. If she still lives in the area then she might know of Nancy's whereabouts. They were very close friends.'

'Maybe we could go to where she used to live and see if we can find anything out,' Gracie said.

Annie looked at Gracie. 'I think we should try to locate Lilian now, don't you?'

Gracie nodded agreement.

'So, let's finish our tea and get a train back to Clitheroe. Then we can get a tram out to Norwesterly where I used to live. I can tell you at least the bare bones of the story on the way.'

It felt strange to Annie coming back to within yards of Fletcher's Mill after all these years, for she hadn't been anywhere near the place since she had triumphantly walked out on Mr Mattison that memorable afternoon. She was surprised how much of the area she recognized, although there were some parts where rows of back-to-back terraces had been flattened by bombs so that it looked completely different now. In fact, several streets had been hit pretty badly during the Blitz and all that was left was the odd wall and a pile of bricks. The mill was still standing, though no doubt it had been given over to munitions work since the start of the war. The whole terrace and the little house where she used to live was still intact and Annie paused outside for a few moments letting the memories wash over her.

A woman of indeterminate age was sitting out on the front step, peeling potatoes, while three young children were running in and out of the front door. Annie smiled at the woman but she seemed too involved in her task to notice so Annie walked in the direction of Lilian's house, past several unrecognizable streets that had been reduced to rubble and ash. But there were enough houses remaining that she could find her way to where she remembered Lilian had lived. Annie was surprised how apprehensive she suddenly felt, but thinking of her promise to Annette she knocked on the door before her courage deserted her. A woman opened it and there was only a moment's hesitation before Lilian's face lit up.

'I'd know you anywhere, Annie Beaumont,' Lilian said, and the two women fell on each other.

'Lilian, oh Lilian,' Annie said, her voice breaking.

'Well, I never thought to see you again and that's a fact,' Lilian said. 'Come in, come in. There's only me mam at home and she'll be right pleased to see you, I know.'

After all the introductions had been made and the kettle had been put on the hob to boil, Annie explained why they were there. Lilian stared at Annette in amazement. It was as if she had never seen a fourteen-year-old girl before.

'So you're saying you're the baby who . . . ?' Lilian was incredulous and couldn't even finish the sentence. 'And you've spent your whole life in an orphanage?'

Annette said, 'Until today I'd never even heard of Nancy Warburton, let alone that she was my mother. I only knew what they'd told me at the orphanage and that weren't much.'

'It's amazing.' Lilian was still staring at her. 'You look so much like her, I mean. She does, doesn't she just, eh, Mam?'

'She does indeed.' Annie spoke up, while Mrs Vickers continued to stare at the girl. 'That was what convinced me in the end. The more I thought about it the more I thought she had to be Nancy's daughter.'

Lilian turned to Annie. 'So, you never heard what happened to Nancy?'

'No,' Annie said, though she feared the worst seeing the expression on Lilian's face and reached out for Annette's hand as Lilian turned to the young girl.

'I'm afraid she died, lass,' Lilian said, 'giving birth to

you.' She paused, allowing Annette time to absorb the news. Then she turned to Annie. 'She went to that home for unmarried mothers that people used to talk about. It were right next to that building where the workhouse used to be. You might remember it, Annie, as a fair few of the girls from the mill ended up there. You see Nancy was a Catholic, which made things worse in a way. The home was run by the nuns and we used to hear all sorts of stories about what happened to the children left with them. Some say they were sent to be skivvies in the laundries they ran and that others were sent off to far-flung places, like Australia, never to see England's shores again. Nancy had told me she was terrified of what might happen to her little mite if it was left without a mother to look out for it. To be honest, some of the nuns who were helping Nancy with the birth seemed like kind people, but all I could think of was her face begging me to help. Those places couldn't wait to whip the babies away from the poor young lasses and take them away to God knows where. Poor Nancy, she just had rotten luck, didn't she?' Lilian turned away while she wiped her eyes on her apron.

Annie remembered the place well. It had been one of the veiled threats that had hung over young girls at that time and the one that had made her more determined than ever to be a respectable girl and to save herself for marriage, no matter how much a boy like Archie had pleaded.

'God rest her soul,' she said. 'What a sad end, though

at least you came through safely unlike some poor unfortunate little souls. But it was no thanks to her family. Would you believe, I was the only one ever visited. I pretended to be her sister, else they wouldn't have let me in. But I was able to be with her right to the end.'

'Did her family disown her then?' Annie asked. 'That's what she was afraid of the last time I saw her.'

Lilian nodded. 'She was too ashamed ever to tell them. But she was probably right, because when they did find out she'd died they spread the lie that she'd had peritonitis after a burst appendix. Daft thing to say, really; everyone knew it wasn't true. But then everyone tells lies when they are ashamed.' She turned to Annette. 'And I'm afraid I'm a liar too . . . and a thief.' Annette stared at Lilian.

'I'm going to tell you something now that I've never breathed a word of before.' She paused before continuing. 'Having told them I was Nancy's sister that made me her next of kin. Not that I waited around for anyone to challenge my story once the baby had been born. Whatever had gone wrong for Nancy, it was serious – as bad as it could be. In all the kerfuffle, no one seemed to notice the baby swaddled in a cot next to the bed. I still don't know what got into me or how I managed it, but I just picked you up, Annette, and calmly walked out with you, No one stopped me – I imagine women must have been coming and going with babies all the time from that place. Nancy had already given me the letter she'd written . . . in case anything happened,' she said sadly. 'She'd given me your hankie, Annie, that had somehow got left behind on your last visit and which I think she'd kept to remind her of your friendship. She also had an old bit of a rattle she'd kept from her own childhood and a dummy and she begged me to do whatever I could to help the baby if it came to it – I think she must have had some sort of premonition. I put all them things in that box.' She paused. 'And it was me that wrapped you up warm and put you in that basket. I don't think I had any idea what I was going to do with you, but all I could think was to take you to the orphanage and leave you there. I was terrified that folk would think you were mine, so I never went back, but I knew that Nancy wouldn't want you to be sent away, but to keep you close to home, in case one day someone should come to claim you.' Tears spilled over her cheeks. 'I'm so sorry, but I didn't know what else to do.' Lilian began to sob. 'I couldn't look after you myself, Nancy's family didn't want to know and I know she was afraid of where them women at the home might send you. You were so pretty, I really hoped that if I left you at the orphanage, you'd be adopted by some loving family.'

Annie could see Annette was trying hard not to cry and she squeezed her hand. Then she smiled at Lilian. 'I don't think there was anything else you could do. You were Nancy's best friend right to the end.'

Lilian lifted the corner of her apron and wiped her eyes, giving Annie a watery smile.

'Is Mrs Warburton still alive?' Annie asked. 'Maybe we could go to see her? After all is said and done, she is Annette's grandma.'

Lilian smiled. 'Yes, I believe she is, though not old man Warburton or Nancy's brother. Sadly, their house took a direct hit during the Blitz. As you may have noticed, quite a bit of the scenery has changed round here. Nancy's father and brother were killed when the house was hit, but Mrs Warburton was out at the time so she was all right. Afterwards, she went to live with her sister who lived only a few streets away, but I've no idea what kind of a state she's in.'

'You mean I have a grandmother who's still alive?' Annette's eyes opened wide. 'A real relation?'

Lilian nodded. 'Your mother's mother. Why? Are you thinking you might like to go to see her?'

'Yes, I would.' Annette answered before Annie had time to say anything, but then she added, her voice filled with anxiety, 'Do you think she'll want to see me?'

'I'm afraid I wouldn't count on it,' Annie said. 'After all, as we were saying just now, she never acknowledged that Nancy ever had a child, so there's no saying how she might react if you turn up on her doorstep claiming to be Nancy's daughter.'

After a slight hesitation Annette said, 'I'm willing to take that chance.'

'But what if she rejects you?' Annie cautioned. 'You must consider that possibility. It could be very painful for you. I'm not sure I'd like for you to be hurt in that way.'

'I appreciate that, and thanks, Mrs Walker, but I've waited all these years to find some member of my family so having found one I think I've got to know that at least I tried.' She was staring down into her lap and playing with the buttons on her coat. 'She's probably my only living relative so surely it's got to be worth a try.'

Annie, however, was not so sure but what more could she say? It was up to Annette, when all was said and done, although right now it felt as if the weight of the responsibility was sitting firmly on Annie's shoulders.

'If you're serious, she's not moved far away; a couple of streets, no more. I can tell you where to find her,' Lilian said.

'What do you say, Gracie?' Annie turned to the other girl who had been sitting quietly, taking it all in.

'I say that if Annette wants to do it then she should do it. She might always regret it if she doesn't. We're here now, anyways. She's got this far, so she may as well go to see her while she's at least got the two of us she can count on for support.'

'So, what do you say Annette? Have a think about it,' Annie said.

'I don't need to think, cos I agree. And if the worst comes to the worst and she doesn't accept that she's got a granddaughter it won't matter much. Any road, I've never had a granny in my life, so I haven't really got one to lose.'

'On the other hand, if she does accept you . . .' Gracie said.

Annie couldn't deny the young girl's logic though she was still afraid Annette could be terribly hurt by Mrs Warburton's rejection in a way that couldn't be imagined just by talking about it. Her mind drifted back to her last meeting with Nancy. How afraid she had been of her mother finding out about the child. Annie sighed. From her own point of view, it would be strange to see Nancy's mother again after all these years.

Lilian had gone over to the stove where she was busy making drinks for everyone. The conversation lapsed for several minutes as they were all bound up in their own thoughts and memories and Lilian took the opportunity to serve up thick cups of hot, black tea. 'I apologize that we've got no milk nor sugar,' she said. 'Though I do have some dried biscuits you can have. They're a bit hard but are fine for dunking in your tea.' She passed round an old Huntley and Palmer's tin, shaped like a pack of books bound together.

Annie declined the offer but Annette eagerly took her own and Annie's share.

'Have you any idea . . .' Annie began to say when Lilian had sat down again. 'I mean, do you know . . . do you know what happened to Archie Grainger?' She was hesitant to ask and concentrated on trying to hold the cup steady in her hand while she waited for Lilian to reply. Lilian didn't answer at once and Annie could see her looking at her intently. 'You do know he's Annette's father, don't you?' Annie asked.

Lilian frowned. 'Let's say I guessed as much. There were a lot of rumours flying around about that at the time, I must say, though he always denied it. But I never was quite sure.'

'Well, it's true. I've already told Annette,' Annie acknowledged. She wasn't sure whether she should go on and she felt herself blushing. It was not something she would normally have talked about in public, even to a small group of friends such as this, but she braced herself because she felt that she owed it to Annette. The poor girl had a right to know as much as she could about her heritage and Annie had held on to the secret for long enough. Maybe Lilian could tell her more.

'Tell me what you know about him. I want to know everything I can,' Annette pleaded.

'I'm not sure as I knows much, I'm afraid,' Lilian said. 'It must have been about the end of that wakes week holiday in Blackpool that they got together, isn't that right, Annie?'

Annie nodded agreement. 'That's exactly when it was.'

'The four of us agreed to meet for a drink, me and Nance and two of Archie's pals. You'd wandered off on your own somewhere, Annie, or so Archie said. We all got very drunk. Any road, while Nancy were dithering about whether she fancied his mate Derek or not,

Archie nicked in and asked her to go for a walk on the beach and I went off with Kevin down to the pleasure beach and Derek was left on his own. I didn't see Nancy again that night, not to speak to, she was snoring her head off by the time I came in.'

Annie hesitated. She hated the thought of hurting Annette more than was necessary but the girl seemed desperate to know as much detail as possible about both of her parents. And that was, after all, why she and Gracie had come, to help Annette find out whatever she could.

'When I went to tell Nancy I was leaving the mill and to say goodbye,' Annie said, 'she admitted what had happened between her and Archie that night. She only wanted to apologize.'

'Is that right? Then I've learned something. Whenever I asked her about that night she wouldn't say owt.' Lilian looked hurt.

'I was so naive, I confronted Archie,' Annie said. 'I told him he should accept his responsibilities, but of course he just denied it. He'd taken advantage of the situation and he didn't really want anything to do with poor Nancy even though she really fancied him, you know.'

'So, has he died too?' It was Annette's voice that piped up. It sounded thin, almost scared, in the silence that followed Annie's pronouncement and the cup in her hand was rattling against the saucer, slopping the tea into it.

Annie sat up, every muscle in her body tensing. Lilian

looked as if she was debating what to say but to Annie's relief she chose to tell the truth.

'I'm afraid he has.' Lilian's face was solemn. 'He wasn't long in the army when they heard that he was missing in action, presumed dead, as they always word it on the official telegram. Apparently, most of his regiment had been killed so I don't think even his mother is holding out much hope.'

A silence fell on the room for several moments, then Annette said, 'Annette Grainger. Just think, I could have been Annette Grainger.'

'How did you come by Annette Oliver?' Gracie asked now that the awkward moment had passed.

Annette shrugged. 'Just something the head of the orphanage dreamt up, I think, perhaps I reminded him of that orphan that Charles Dickens wrote about. Maybe I should change it now that I know.'

There was another awkward moment as no one commented. This time it was Annie who spoke first.

'If we are going to see Mrs Warburton then maybe we should go now,' she said quietly. 'We need to get Annette back to the orphanage in good time, otherwise she might not be allowed to go out with us again.' She smiled in Annette's direction as she pushed her half-finished cup onto the table and stood up. Then she turned to Lilian. 'It was lovely to see you again. Thanks very much for the tea.'

'I'm so glad things turned out well for you, Annie. Though it's not Annie Beaumont any more, is it?'

'No. I'm Mrs Jack Walker,' she said with some pride, 'innkeeper and publican at the Rovers Return on Coronation Street in Weatherfield.'

'Your new life obviously suits you better than working on the dreaded looms or, worse still, making gun parts.'

Annie laughed. 'You should ask Gracie about that. She finds pulling pints admirably better than making munitions.'

'It's true.' Gracie smiled. 'I refused to have anything to do with guns and bullets.'

'Then I take my hat off to you, lass,' Lilian said. 'I've not been so lucky, but it pays the rent for me and Mam. It was lovely to meet you, Annette.' She shook Annette's hand. 'Any time you feel like coming over this way we'd be delighted to see you. You can think of us as family, you know. I was very fond of your mother. She was like a sister to me.'

They were all tearful as they left Lilian's house. They kissed each other goodbye with promises to keep in touch.

Lilian had reminded Annie which street Mrs Warburton had moved to, where she now lived with her sister, and as they hurried up the hill it had clouded over, the grey clouds hanging low in the sky, and a considerable wind was picking up. It was Nancy's aunt, whom Annie had never met before, who opened the door and it took a few minutes for Annie to explain who she was. She didn't even try to introduce Gracie or Annette other than as her friends.

'I'm Eileen Henshaw,' the woman at the door said, 'and you'd best come in if you say you're a friend of our Nancy's. I'm sure my sister will be pleased to see you, though I must warn you, Wilma doesn't always have as good a memory as she once had. To be honest, she's a bit up and down.'

As they followed her down the dark passageway and into the large kitchen at the back of the house, Annie began to wonder whether it had been a wise move for them to come here. It was entirely possible that the whole visit would be a kick in the eye to nothing. If Mrs Warburton had for so long failed to acknowledge Nancy's situation why should she welcome Annie and, more importantly, Annette, now? And if her memory was failing would she even remember who Nancy was?

'Annie Beaumont!' Mrs Warburton said as soon as they entered the room and Annie was encouraged by the fact that the old lady seemed to remember her well. 'I'd have known you anywhere,' she went on, 'though you ain't half filled out since I last saw you. You look right bonnie.' Annie wished she could say the same thing, but in all honesty time had not treated her friend's mother kindly. The loss of her daughter, her son, her husband, and her own home had taken an obvious toll.

'I haven't had the pleasure of meeting your friends,' she said before Annie had a chance to say that her name was different now, and she invited them all to sit down. But her expression changed when she turned to show Annette to a seat. She almost lost her balance as she flopped back onto the sofa and she looked like she had seen an actual ghost.

Annie cleared her throat, not sure how to explain their visit, but before she could say anything Annette spoke up. 'I can see you looking at me, Mrs Warburton, so I think that you do know who I am. I suppose it's true, then, that I look like my mother. I've been told that before.'

Eileen Henshaw had followed them into the room and she sat down quickly on the sofa beside her sister. She picked up her hand and held on to it tightly. Mrs Warburton didn't acknowledge her sister's presence and continued to stare at Annette, her mouth slightly open, though she still didn't say anything.

It was Annette who spoke again. 'I'm the reason we're all here today, though I'd never have sussed you out on my own. It was Mrs Walker and Gracie helped me to find you.'

Mrs Warburton looked at Annie and frowned, the name Mrs Walker obviously adding to her confusion.

'The thing is, I was brought up in an orphanage in Cheshire,' Annette said, 'and until today I didn't think I had any family. But thanks to Mrs Walker and Gracie here, I now know that I have.' She paused as if to give Mrs Warburton time to respond, but when she didn't show any further reaction Annette went on, 'I do believe that you're my grandmother.'

At this, there was more of a response than Annette had bargained for. Mrs Warburton gasped out loud;

her colour changed from white to creamy yellow as if all the blood had been drained out of her face, and her whole body shuddered.

'How can that be?' she said eventually in a reedy voice, and she turned to appeal to her sister. 'My Nancy died from peritonitis many years ago and she wasn't even married.'

Eileen Henshaw had been stroking her sister's arm and she continued to do so. 'Now then, Wilma,' she said soothingly, 'maybe the time has come for you to stop saying that about her illness, for we all know that it's not true.'

Annette wasn't sure whether she wanted to weep for her dead mother when she heard that or to jump in the air to celebrate that she was finally getting closer to the truth. But the fact of the matter was that she could see now that she had been wrong; she did have something to lose after all. For in those few moments, she had lost her grandmother with very little chance of ever being able to get her back. Perhaps it would have been better to keep travelling in hope, she thought. She should never have insisted they come here, for she could see now how agitated the older woman had become and what it took for her sister to calm her down. She knew then that Wilma Warburton would never accept that Nancy had died in childbirth and, consequently, that she would never be able to acknowledge Annette as her own kin.

They sat for a little while longer but it seemed as if

this was the end of the road as far as Annette was concerned. The more she watched, the more her grand-mother's behaviour deteriorated. It was almost as if the old woman had become the child and had forgotten how to be an adult. Annette wanted to scream and rant that it wasn't fair. No sooner had she found what was probably her last living relative than the old lady had been snatched away from her.

Annie had done her best and Annette didn't want to let her down so she tried to maintain her composure and kept a tight rein on her emotions, though it wasn't easy. She felt as if Annie and Gracie were anxiously watching her all the time, no doubt regretting that they had allowed her to come this far.

'I'm so sorry, I should have warned you,' Eileen said after a few moments' awkward silence, when it became obvious that Wilma Warburton the adult would not be returning to them that afternoon.

'But she seemed so normal when we first arrived,' Annie said. 'I was convinced she knew who I was.'

'Oh, I'm sure she did,' Eileen said. 'There are lots of times when she's just like her old self, but then she goes off into a world of her own and she no longer remembers who she is or where she is.'

Annette felt really sad when she heard this, sad that she had arrived too late, although it sounded as though Mrs Warburton had been like this for a long time. But the day was not completely lost and Annette was reminded of the old saying that blood was thicker than water. She might have lost her grandmother, but what she unexpectedly gained that afternoon was a great aunt.

None of them had ever met Eileen Henshaw before, but by the end of the visit, in Annette's eyes, she had more than made up for her sister's shortcomings. Once Wilma had calmed down Eileen insisted that they stay for afternoon tea and it would have seemed churlish to protest that they had already had a drink with Lilian.

'You know you'll have to keep in touch with us, Annette, and come to see us whenever you like,' Eileen said when it was finally time for them to go. 'Now that you've found your family links at last, I'd hate for either of us to lose them again.'

Annette was surprised by the open invitation but she didn't refuse. 'That would be lovely, thank you, I'd like that,' she said, shyly. 'But what about . . . ?' Annette felt uncomfortable as she indicated her grandmother.

'Oh, you don't have to worry about Wilma; she enjoys having visitors even if she isn't sure exactly who you are. But I think it would be great fun to see Nancy's daughter from time to time. I've no children of my own so I'm delighted by the thought of having a great-niece. I think it's wonderful that I've increased the size of my family so quickly during the course of one afternoon.'

She gave Annette such an affectionate hug it was difficult for the young girl to resist. And as they pulled apart, she winked at Annette. 'Who knows,' she said, 'the day may come when your grandma will be able to acknowledge who you are.'

Annette found herself warming to the woman she hadn't known anything about at the start of the day, and by the time they were battling against the wind and the driving rain as they made their way down the hill to the tram stop she had accepted Eileen's invitation to return in a few months' time to spend Christmas with them.

There were some delays on the trains because of the unrelenting rain that was falling in some parts of Cheshire and when they finally reached the orphanage Annie was concerned that Annette would be late for supper.

'Don't worry, I'll be fine,' Annette assured them as they stood at the gates, 'though if you don't mind I won't hang around here, I'm getting very wet.'

'I'm sorry the day wasn't more successful,' Annie apologized.

'But it was,' Annette assured her. 'I've found out about my parents, I've discovered a friend of my mother's, and I at least know who my grandmother is, even if she isn't sure who I am. But, best of all, I've gained a great aunt. I think for me it's been a really good day. Thank you so much.' Gracie gave her an affectionate hug and then it was Annie's turn and Annie was surprised at how emotional she felt about saying goodbye to a girl she hardly knew.

As she drew Annette close she said, 'I hope you know that there'll always be a warm welcome for you in

Weatherfield at the Rovers Return.' She smiled. 'Though not in the bar, of course, at least not for another few years.' Annette laughed. 'And, you know, you'd be welcome to work there too should you ever fancy a job in a pub, once you're old enough. You don't want to be a scullerymaid a moment longer than you have to, even if it is somewhere as smart as Grant House. But please don't wait until then before you come to visit. You know you'll be welcome at any time.'

'Thanks so much, Annie, if I can call you that? I really appreciate all you've done for me. I know it wasn't easy for you.'

Annie and Gracie watched Annette go through the gates, her thin shoes squelching in the puddles, and waited until she had gone through the porch marked 'Girls' and into the cold-looking building.

'I have to thank you, Gracie, for coming with me,' Annie said. 'It wasn't an easy day for any of us, though I think it worked out better than we might have hoped in the end.'

'Between ourselves,' Gracie said, 'I think you did me a favour, actually. It was an interesting day meeting people I've heard you talk about and it helped to take my mind off brooding about Chuck.'

By the time they reached the Rovers, Gracie thought she should go straight off home as she was wet from the rain as well as cold and tired and Annie thought she would take the rest of the day off. Lottie was serving in the bar with Sally Todd and they were usually happy to be left alone. She would ask her mother to make something to eat while she put the children to bed. Then she would dry out, toasting her feet on the fender in front of the fire, and get snug and warm; she was sure she had left enough coal and hoped Florence hadn't used too much while she'd been out.

But the moment she put her key in the front door leading directly to her living quarters she knew something was wrong as she was met immediately by Florence, looking fraught and anxious, carrying Joanie, screaming, in her arms.

'Oh, Annie!' Florence all but sobbed, 'I thought you'd never get home.'

Tiredness gone in an instant, Annie was alerted by the panic and alarm she could hear in her mother's voice.

'Why? What on earth has happened?'

'It's Billy. He's gone missing,' Florence said.

'Missing?' Annie sounded sceptical. 'How big is the house? All we have to do is to search his favourite hiding places . . .'

'No, you don't understand. He slipped out of the house while I was making some dinner for him and Joanie. He had his coat on and I saw him go but I thought he would come back when it was time to eat. But he didn't. Then I thought I was bound to see him when he was tired or hungry, but I haven't seen him since.'

'You mean he's not been home since this morning?

He's been missing all day?' Annie had difficulty controlling the panic that made her voice rise an octave. 'Mother, how could you?' But Florence merely shook her head as if she couldn't believe what she was saying.

'I was seeing to Joanie, but you've got to have eyes in the back of your head with those two. He was like greased lightning, I swear.' She clicked her fingers. 'He was gone in a flash, just like that. And honestly, Annie, I've looked all over for him, but I can't find him anywhere.'

'What do you mean you've looked? Where did you look? Did you organize a proper search?'

'I went up and down the street calling his name and someone suggested I try the Field where there's some kind of a bomb shelter. I thought he might be hiding in there, but he wasn't and I don't know where else to look.'

Annie took a deep breath. 'Right, we need to be methodical and systematic about this.' She looked at her watch. 'I really can't believe you've left it this long.' She was beside herself with worry and didn't care how angry she sounded.

'It wasn't my fault,' Florence wailed. 'Don't get cross with me. You left me on my own, what was I supposed to do?'

Annie left her mother to whine while she went into the bar. She clapped her hands and asked for people's attention. As soon as she explained the situation everyone who was there seemed ready to swing into immediate action. Some ran off to rope in the rest of their family at home, and brought them back a few minutes later so that they could begin a well-ordered search. Albert Tatlock and Ena Sharples seemed to be vying for who had the most number of people on their team, but at least they did draw up sensible lists so that the most popular places in the neighbourhood where the local children liked to go were covered systematically. Everyone was willing to pull together and people lined up to receive instructions, prepared to fan out in all directions.

'Thankfully, it's June so we've got daylight on our side and it will be a full moon later which will help,' Ena said as she issued instructions to individual people. At the last minute, Ida Barlow ran into the bar where they were all congregating, carrying little David with Kenny running alongside, in wellington boots two sizes too big, panting to keep up with them.

'I've just heard about Billy,' Ida said. 'You must be frantic, Annie. What can I do to help?'

'Not much with two kiddies in tow,' Albert Tatlock grumbled.

'I know and I'm sorry about that but I've had to bring him. With all this excitement going on in the street and outside our house, I've no chance of getting him off to sleep until Billy's found. But don't worry, I'll keep him with me and he'll be no trouble.'

'I'll tell you what you can do, Ida Barlow,' Ena Sharples collared her. 'Why don't you go down to the Mission? There's plenty of places worth a look down there.'

'He won't be there,' Albert Tatlock said, his voice dripping with scorn.

'I'm glad you can read the mind of a five-year-old,' Ena said dismissively, 'because I know I can't. And let's face it, he could be anywhere, but you've got Kenneth with you who's almost the same age so he might be able to suggest places to look.'

'It's treacherous out there and slippery underfoot so please be careful how you go,' Annie called to the small groups that were about to set off. 'And you can come back to the bar for a free bottle and there'll be a special reward for whoever finds him.'

When everyone had gone, Annie realized Florence was still in the bar, with Joanie in her arms, not asleep but at last quietly sucking her thumb.

Annie looked at her mother with disdain. 'Can I ask you to put Joanie to bed? Do you think you can promise not to let her out of your sight until she's safely tucked in? That will at least be one less thing for me to have to worry about.'

'Oh, don't be cross with me, Annie, darling,' Florence pleaded. 'I didn't do it on purpose.'

'I should hope not, but you have been incredibly careless. Honestly, I can't believe how careless. If you thought they were too much for you, you should have said so, not jeopardized my son's life. You shouldn't have agreed to look after them in the first place. I told you we'd be gone most of the day.'

Annie flounced out of the room, wanting to shout

and scream so that she could release the tension caused by her own fears and anxiety, but she had to resist, telling herself her mother was getting on in years now and maybe she was the one who'd been remiss leaving her in charge of both the children when she was no longer up to it.

Annie desperately wanted to join in the search, but Ena and Albert both persuaded her that she should stay at home in case anyone telephoned with information or in case Billy came back of his own accord.

While she waited anxiously for news, Annie paced up and down and gnawed away at her fingernails; she didn't know what else to do. She didn't notice until it was too late that the fire had gone out. But she was too agitated to be aware of whether it was hot or cold. When Florence called her to say that Joanie was now safely in bed but was demanding a goodnight kiss from her mother, Annie ran straight up to the child's bedroom. But as soon as she saw Billy's empty bed through the open door to his room, all she could do was to run downstairs again and cry. If anything had happened to Billy how could she ever forgive herself? What would she tell Jack? Her mind went into overdrive as she tried to think of all the things that might have happened. What if he had got into some kind of trouble and was too afraid to come home? Or maybe he wasn't able to come home for some reason, could he have been abducted? What if he'd gone up to the Field as she knew he liked to do and had come across an unexploded bomb? She tortured herself, picturing him wandering lost, or worse still, being held against his will, and the tears continued to flow. She sat at the kitchen table, rocking back and forth in her misery, willing the telephone to ring.

At ten o'clock she could hear activity in the bar and ran through, praying for someone to tell her that the nightmare was over and that he had been found. But it was Ida Barlow coming back with Kenny. Gradually all the neighbours trooped back into the pub as they had agreed to reassemble in the bar at ten, frustration and disappointment etched into their faces. There was a general atmosphere of defeat which scared Annie even more.

Ena and Albert methodically counted off each member of the rescuers from their team as they returned, shaking their heads, unable to look directly at Annie as they had to admit that their search had been fruitless. There was no trace of him and, worse still, they were running out of ideas about where to look.

'Surely someone must have seen him?' Annie cried in anguish as she looked round the group who all stood miserably, not knowing what to say. The longer he was missing the more frightened she was for his safety. How long could he be without food or drink before he would be in real danger?

'Are you sure you called his name loudly enough for him to hear if he was hidden somewhere?' Annie asked, remembering how he loved to play hide and seek. She looked round the group in anguish, feeling completely at her wits' end.

'Of course we did.' Ida Barlow came and put her arm round Annie's shoulders. 'You must try and keep calm,' she said in a soothing voice.

Annie looked jealously at little Kenneth and David Barlow who had both fallen asleep on one of the banquettes and she wanted to scream at Ida, *It's all right for you, you've still got your son*. But she managed to hang on to her temper. After all, Ida was doing her best, as they all were, and she needed to keep her on her side. So instead Annie said as calmly as she could, 'Then there's really nothing more we can do except call the police.'

There was a shocked silence but no one contradicted her as she moved towards the telephone. 'You're sure you looked properly at the Mission?' Annie looked beseechingly at Ena Sharples.

'Of course we did; we moved every chair and even looked inside the piano.' Ena was dismissive until Annie said, 'No, I mean downstairs in the cellar. He had some kind of morbid fascination for that place.' Ena stared at her, then a little voice popped up: 'He wanted to give everyone a surprise.' It was Kenny Barlow who had suddenly woken up.

'What was that you said, darling?' Ida rushed over to him while Annie stood frozen, her hand on the telephone.

'I've just remembered! Billy said he wanted to come

to the nursery and he was going to jump out and give everyone a surprise.'

'Jump out from the cellar you mean?' Ida rushed over to him. 'When did he say that, Kenny love, can you remember?'

'It doesn't matter when he said it,' Annie interrupted. 'That's where he must be. In the cellar. I must go and find him.' And she rushed behind the curtain and grabbed her coat from off the hook. 'Billy, oh Billy, that's where you must be. Mummy's coming darling,' she cooed.

'You can't go on your own.' Ena Sharples jumped into action. 'I'll come with you. You all wait here,' she instructed the people in the bar and the two women ran out into the fading light. Annie was hardly able to see where she was going for the tears streaming down her face as she ran. Ena unlocked the door to the Mission and Annie raced across the large room that was filled with chairs. She tried the handle of the door leading down to the cellar and shrieked loudly when it came away in her hands.

Ena was tutting as Annie banged on the door, screaming, 'Billy, are you down there?' She was rewarded by a tiny voice calling, 'Mummy!'

'I'm here, darling. We'll have you out in a jiffy. Just stay calm,' Annie shouted through the door. Annie was frantic and when Ena arrived with a screwdriver she hacked at the lock like a woman possessed so that it didn't take long for her finally to be able to kick the door open.

She raced down the stairs to where Billy was lying at the bottom, his clothes filthy, his face streaked with black tears.

'I was waiting for the nursery to open,' he sobbed as Annie gathered him in her arms and squashed him with a giant hug, 'but then I couldn't open the door.' He held up the handle that had come away in his hand.

Annie shook her head in disbelief. 'Whatever were you thinking of? Oh, my poor darling, you must have been so afraid.' Annie was crying now with relief as she cradled him. 'Are you all right?'

'Nothing that a bath and a sandwich and a cuddle from his mother won't cure.' Ena was looking down from the top of the stairs. 'Shall I come down and fetch him up for you? It might help us get him up quicker.'

'No, you needn't bother, I can manage, thanks,' Annie said and told Billy, 'We'll get you home very soon.'

When she carried him up the stairs, Billy rubbed his eyes as he came into the light. 'Can I have something to eat before I go to the nursery? I'm hungry,' Billy said.

'Of course you can,' Annie laughed with relief.

'And I'll have a free pint of milk stout,' Ena said as she locked the Mission door and helped Annie up the street.

'You can have as many milk stouts as you like,' Annie started to say, then corrected herself, 'Or should I say, as many as supplies will allow.'

It was some minutes before they arrived back at the

Rovers and a shout went up followed by cheering as Annie came through the door.

'Why on earth did you want to go down to that awful cellar?' Annie asked Billy again, in between a shower of kisses as she carried him into the kitchen.

Billy swiped his face with the back of his hand as if to swat them away. 'I wanted to play with all the other children in the nursery, but they weren't there.'

Ena tutted. 'We'd been out with them for a walk to pick flowers and then when it started to rain so heavy we sent them home,' she said.

'So I thought I'd wait till they came back,' Billy said puffing himself importantly. 'But then I wanted to go home cos I was hungry, but I couldn't open the door. I shouted but nobody came.' His bravado deflated then and he began to cry.

'Hush, it's all right, darling.' Annie stroked his hair. 'And you won't have to worry any more about the nursery. If you want to go that badly, then you can go. You can play as much as you want with all the other children.'

'Can I?' he said, perking up immediately. 'Can I go tomorrow?' He climbed up and sat on her knees.

Annie nodded. 'And the day after and the day after that,' she said, but he was already asleep, curled up in her lap.

The news that a small group of GIs were back spread round Weatherfield almost as quickly as the news had travelled when they had disappeared and Gracie was anxious to find out if Chuck was among them, for this time she had received no letters from him since he'd been away.

'You can't expect him to write,' Annie told her, 'they're preparing for some major invasion in France, I believe.'

'We've been hearing about this for ages now,' Gracie said.

'I know, and I really think something is going to happen soon.'

Gracie didn't have to wait long, however, because in the early evening Chuck came into the Rovers with a small group of his compatriots, all looking very cheerful, and they grouped round the counter and ordered their favourite brew like they had never been away. At the sight of them, the general mood in the bar seemed to lift and the locals were eager to buy them a round and ask them questions about whether the invasion was really going to happen.

'Can't tell you much, I'm afraid,' Chuck said when he was asked, 'but things do seem to be hotting up.' Others peppered him with questions, and though his answers were always guarded, feelings of genuine hope and subdued anticipation spread throughout the pub. Everyone knew that no one could speak of what might happen for fear of helping the enemy, but the possibility of change for the better was on everyone's lips.

Gracie tingled from head to foot when she saw Chuck. The excitement was almost too much to bear.

She was, indeed, afraid of the strength of her feelings and it was impossible for her not to let her emotions show. Part of her wanted to rush to the other side of the counter and give him a huge hug, but she didn't have to because Chuck caught hold of her hand and reached out across the bar. He pulled her to him to deliver a passionate kiss square on the lips, not caring who saw, and then looked at her with so much love in his eyes she thought she was going to melt.

'I didn't expect to see you again,' Gracie managed to say, 'particularly after you all left so quickly, without so much as a by your leave.'

Chuck grinned. 'Sorry we had no time to say goodbye, but orders are orders.'

'So, lad, are things really on the up?' Albert Tatlock wanted to know, digging Chuck in the ribs with his elbow.

'I can't say anything for certain, Mr Tatlock,' Chuck said. 'And it would be great to think the end of the war is in sight but we won't start singing victory songs just yet.'

'Do you think this really could be an end to it all?' There was a general air of optimism and murmurings such as, 'Let's bloody hope so,' from some of the men, and 'I can't wait to have my hubby safely home again,' from some of the women. Gracie was rushed off her feet for the rest of the evening, so she was glad that Chuck made no move to go, even after Annie had called time.

'Can we have a word?' he said, 'when everyone's gone home?'

'I'll check with Mrs Walker, but I don't see why not,' Gracie said, suddenly feeling flustered. She still hadn't got over her surprise at seeing him. 'If you wait in that booth I'll be out as soon as I've dried up the glasses.

'I must admit I didn't think you'd be back,' Gracie said as she sat down later to join him.

'And I'll admit that neither did I. That's why I'm feeling like one helluva lucky guy right now, but a few of us are here on a special mission, though we won't be staying long. Captain Farnworth's with us too, but he didn't seem to want to come for a drink tonight.'

'I can't believe you're really here,' Gracie said, reaching over to touch Chuck's hand.

Chuck stroked her hand and sent a wave of electric shocks shooting through her. 'You better believe it. It's me, in the flesh, here feel my hand.'

'I don't know if I dare,' Gracie laughed, 'it will get me too excited.'

'Me too,' Chuck said softly. 'I could just hold you in my arms forever.'

'But we don't have forever.'

'Not this time, but there is something I want to say. I've been doing a lot of thinking while I've been away.'

'I'd have thought you were too busy for that.'

'Never too busy to think about you.'

Gracie smiled coyly. A lump had risen to her throat and all she could think about were the days in the park, the evenings at the cinema, all the lovely times they had snatched together despite the backdrop of the wretched war. Suddenly she felt as if her feelings were overwhelming her and she was afraid of what he might be about to say.

'I've had a long time to think about what I'm going to say next, so I don't want you to think I'm just talking on a whim. How long have we known each other?'

'A couple of years, it must be.'

'A lifetime, and yet no time at all. But Gracie, I want to ask you if you'll marry me.'

Gracie closed her eyes as he squeezed her hand.

'Are you serious?' Gracie didn't know why she felt so shocked. Weren't those the words she had been hoping to hear for so long? Why was she afraid to hear them now?

'Never more so.' He got up and came round to her side of the bench seat. He got down on one knee and grasped hold of her hands between his.

'Gracie,' he said, looking directly into her eyes, 'I love you now and I will love you always. Will you marry me?'

Her first reaction was to say yes, yes please, for she wanted nothing more in all the world. But she heard herself say, 'I . . . I don't know,' before she could take the words back. 'It's not that I don't love you, you know that I do, but I think you also know why I am hesitating.' How could she marry a man her parents refused to meet? That would involve her leaving everything she knew and loved and going halfway round the world to start up a completely new life, even though her heart was telling her to forget all that and say yes.

'You don't have to give me an answer right now,' he said. 'I know that you love me, and I love you more than life, but marriage is a whole different ball game and I want you to be sure before you say yes. We don't have time on our side for a long courtship, but we do have love. Bucket-loads of it. And when all this is over, if you say yes, then I'll send for you and we can start a whole new life together.'

She gazed down at him, where he was still kneeling, her eyes searching his face.

She withdrew her hands from his. 'Oh, Chuck, I love you so much. But please, let me have a little time to think before we rush into anything we might regret.'

'I can't have any regrets. But I'm not leaving just yet, so think about it – and think of me, and what sweet music we can make together.'

He had almost persuaded her but she felt she owed it to her parents to think carefully before she took such a dramatic step.

Chuck got to his feet. 'I know I've had time to think about it – I've thought of nothing else – but I'll go now and we'll talk again, soon.' He drew her to him then and gave her a long, lingering kiss, filling her mouth with his tongue, his hands lightly caressing her body until every nerve was tingling and she longed for him to take her right there in the pub. Trembling still, she pulled away. 'I love you,' she said.

*   *   *

Gracie slept badly that night, thinking about Chuck's proposal, wishing she could tell someone.

She was woken in the morning at eight thirty by a tentative knocking on her bedroom door.

'Gracie,' her mother called, 'are you awake?'

'I am now,' Gracie muttered, pulling the pillow over her head. She sat up as Mildred entered, clutching a telegram which she handed to her daughter.

Gracie felt her face pale with anxiety as she pulled out the flimsy piece of paper. The name at the end said CHUCK and she hastily read the contents.

JUST RECEIVED NOTICE OF TRAIN TO LIVERPOOL STOP LEAVES 09.00 STOP IF ANSWER IS YES COME TO STATION STOP IF NO WILL UNDERSTAND.

Gracie had been struggling with the question all night preparing what she would say to her parents and how they might react, but in that moment she suddenly knew that there could only be one answer. She remembered how she had felt the last time Chuck had gone away. Now he was off again and the chances were that this time he was never coming back. How could she bear the thought of losing him? She loved him too much to let him go forever. And yet here he was leaving Weatherfield almost immediately and it might be too late now to tell him that her answer was yes. She'd left it too late to tell him how she felt, that she did love him enough to face anything with him. How could she ever have doubted it?

All she could think about was the thrill and joy of starting a new life with Chuck, wherever he was, so long as they were together. It didn't matter that he already had a child. Where was her charity, her Christian spirit? Why shouldn't she become a mother to the boy? Chuck seemed to think Buddy would welcome it. Surely that meant that Gracie would be doubly blessed when she came to have children of her own? As for her parents, she knew her mother would accept her decision and she would bring her father round in time.

She looked at the clock beside her bed. It was twenty minutes to nine. She had to get to the station in time to tell Chuck her decision. She had to let him know that the answer was yes.

'I'm sorry, Mum, but I've got to go.' Gracie threw off the bedclothes.

'Is everything all right, dear? Is anyone dead?'

'No, Mum, no one's died. But I must go to the station, right now. Chuck's train will be leaving very soon and I have to give him my answer.'

Mildred looked bewildered. 'The answer to what? You're not making any sense.'

'To his proposal. He's asked me to marry him and I have to say yes, I *will* marry him when all this is over. I can't let him go back to America without him knowing that I love him. I love him, Mum, I love him!' she shouted.

Mildred stared at her, confused. 'You mean that American boy you were so keen on?'

'Yes! And I've got to get going. I haven't much time.

As it is, I'll have to run all the way. I'm sorry. I must go. I'll explain later. I love you too and I know you'll understand.' She leaned over and gave her mother a kiss on the cheek.

Mildred moved away from the door as Gracie threw on yesterday's clothes that were rolled up at the end of the bed and grabbed her coat from the chair.

I wonder if troop trains always leave on time, was Gracie's last sensible thought as she set off running as fast as she could.

Her breath was coming in short gasps and, as she saw the station up ahead, the pavements suddenly seemed to be filled with dozens of people. Several times she tried to stop as she had a stitch in her side but she was swept up by the crowds of all ages who were rushing in the same direction. When she finally reached the station, she was breathing hard but it was impossible to stand still for long as the large hand of the clock was inching past the Roman numerals marking nine. On the concourse people were milling in all different directions and it wasn't easy for her to move freely. Some were arriving, others were trying to leave and there was a general state of madness and confusion. Civilians and troops, Americans, Canadians, Poles, Brits, soldiers, sailors, airmen – there seemed to be no organization or sense of order as to who was diving in which direction for which train. How on earth was she going to find Chuck in all this mess?

She stood on a bench, hoping the extra inches would

help her to see over the heads of most of the crowd, but all she saw were the tops of the trains on the platforms and servicemen hanging out of the windows, all eagerly searching for their sweethearts and families. Frustrated, she jumped down and tried to push her way up and then down several of the platforms where the trains were preparing to depart, all the time straining to find Chuck. Several whistles pierced the bedlam but it was impossible to tell if it was the engines or the guards trying to make themselves heard above the din. Gracie realized that her cheeks were stained with tears of frustration and she brushed them aside angrily. She felt as if she had no chance of finding Chuck in all the madness but she couldn't give up trying.

Then suddenly she thought she heard someone calling her name and she spun round, not sure which direction it came from. She looked one way and then another and when she saw a soldier she thought she recognized, waving frantically, she began to wave back. His movements were the same as those of the soldiers in the other windows and he could have been waving to anyone but she settled her sights on him because she thought she recognized his face. His head and the top half of his body was hanging out of the window now and she knew she had found Chuck. She was on the other side of the platform, some way away from the train, but she began to push her way towards him. At that moment there was a loud hoot and the whole train shuddered as the engine began to pull the carriages slowly along beside the platform. Gracie ran as fast as the crowds allowed, pushing towards the train which was now beginning to chug slowly away. She could tell from the shape of Chuck's mouth that he was screaming her name.

Gracie cupped her hands round her mouth. 'Yes!' she screamed. 'The answer's yes. I *will* marry you.'

She saw Chuck throw his hands up in the air, giving the thumbs-up sign with both thumbs.

'I'll write,' she thought he mouthed, and he panto-mimed a writing gesture to make sure she understood. She stopped running then, satisfied that he had heard her. Their communication was over as the train picked up speed and pulled clear of the station.

Gracie set off back home, walking slowly. In her rush to get to the station in time she hadn't even brought any money for the tram, but the long walk gave her a chance to work out what she was going to tell her mother and father about the way she planned to spend the rest of her life.

When Annie heard that Roy had been in Weatherfield but hadn't come into the pub she felt a moment of regret, but she understood. No one had been hurt and it was better to let things rest and to leave it that way. Another time and another place, perhaps, but for them it was not to be.

Annie was alone on Sunday morning. She had been to church early and now she was rushing about the house tidying up, humming the old Great War song, 'Pack Up Your Troubles in Your Old Kit Bag' as she went. There had been a general air of excitement in Weatherfield since news had come through about the D-day landings in France earlier that week, and Annie too was infected by feelings of euphoria that at last an end to the war was in sight and Hitler was really on the run.

When the doorbell to her private living quarters rang, Annie touched up her hair in the small mirror in the vestibule and added a few dabs of lipstick to her already cherry lips as she always did before she opened the door. She was amazed to find Annette on the doorstep, a small bunch of freshly picked wildflowers in her hand.

She gave Annie an enthusiastic hug and Annie let the girl cling to her for a few extra moments when she realized that Annette was crying. Annie also felt tears trickling down her own cheeks.

'It's so lovely to see you, Annette,' Annie said. 'Is everything all right?'

Annette nodded but couldn't yet speak.

'I must admit you're the last person I expected to see,' Annie said, 'though it is a wonderful surprise.'

'I hope I'm not interrupting anything.' Annette was apologetic when she finally found her voice and she stood uncertainly on the doorstep for a few moments.

'Of course not. Come on in. I'm afraid the children are not here at the moment, so you won't be able to see them.'

'Are you sure I'm not intruding . . . ?'

'Not at all,' Annie tried to reassure her.

'The thing is,' Annette said with an embarrassed smile, 'I've just been to see Great-Aunt Eileen – and my grandmother,' she added hastily.

'Well, I'm delighted to hear that, Annette. Your very own family.'

'Yes, can you believe it? And I . . . I enjoyed it so much I thought it might be nice to come and see you and Gracie as well. I can't go and see my own mother, so I do hope you don't mind. I know it's not Mother's Day or anything but . . .'

Annie beamed. 'That doesn't matter a bit. I'm very flattered.' She took the flowers and went into the kitchen to look for a small vase. She showed Annette where to hang her coat.

'You know, you'd better hurry up and get to your eighteenth birthday,' Annie said with a laugh. 'We need you here to work in the bar because Gracie's definitely going to be leaving.'

'Oh?' Annette was surprised. 'I hope it was nothing to do with me?'

Annie laughed. 'No, indeed not. When the war's finally over she's going to America to marry her GI soldier, Chuck. She'll be going to live in New York with him. You'll have to save up and go to visit her one day.'

Annette smiled. 'Wouldn't that be wonderful?'

'Chuck's a widower and already has a son, so Gracie will become an instant mother.'

Annette's eyes widened and she smiled. 'How exciting. It's good to be able to think of someone as your mother, even if they aren't really.'

'Yes, it is,' Annie said.

'Like you and me.' Annette's voice was soft and she looked at Annie shyly. 'Just as it doesn't have to be Mother's Day to bring someone flowers. We can choose our own Mother's Day whenever we like.'

Annie blushed. 'That's exactly right,' she said as she sat down on the sofa and opened her arms towards Annette. 'Now, you come and sit down with me,' she invited, 'and we'll both think of Gracie and, of course, of Nancy.' She thought for a moment. 'If it wouldn't have been for Nancy there wouldn't have been you,' Annie said softly. 'And I'm delighted to find that we've added another member to our family.'

Coronation Street – Still the Nation's Favourite

Coronation Street was the creation of Tony Warren, a scriptwriter at Granada Television in Manchester. The story goes that Tony was frustrated with the scripts he was being asked to write and jumped onto a filing cabinet in the office of the Head of Drama, Harry Elton. Tony refused to come down until Harry allowed him to write about something he knew. Looking out of the office window towards the brick terraces of Salford, Tony said he could write about an ordinary street and the people who lived in it . . . and so *Coronation Street* was born.

It was initially rejected by the studio, who didn't believe that audiences would take to a drama about the ordinary lives of working-class Northern characters. It was Harry's idea to screen the pilot episodes to Granada staff, many of whom were 'ordinary' Northerners themselves. After proving the programme could connect with the target audience, twelve episodes of *Coronation Street* (it was originally called *Florizel Street* before being renamed) were scheduled and the first episode aired on ITV on the 9th of December 1960.

The critics did not immediately warm to *Coronation Street* but audiences didn't agree. It was the first time that genuine Northern accents were consistently used on television and viewers were hooked by the series' storylines, the portrayal of 'ordinary' characters and the brilliant acting on display.

Early storylines embedded strong female characters such as Ena Sharples (Violet Carson), Elsie Tanner (Pat Phoenix) and Annie Walker (Doris Speed) in the nation's consciousness; the squabbles and the skirmishes kept viewers glued to their screens along with storylines that featured a young and idealistic Ken Barlow, played by William Roache, who is now the world's longest running soap character to have been played by the same person.

Within a year, the programme was top of the ratings and stayed there throughout the decade, regularly pulling in audiences of 20 million viewers. As the programme headed into the 1970s, many of the older characters were leaving the series, allowing a new generation to sip their drinks at the Rovers Return. Bet Lynch (Julie Goodyear), Rita Fairclough (Barbara Knox), Deirdre Hunt (Anne Kirkbride) and Mavis Riley (Thelma Barlow) all started to carve out their own legendary statuses and the women who played them cemented their acting credentials with storylines showcasing their admirable talents.

Coronation Street, along with all ITV programmes,

was forced off the air for eleven weeks in 1979 as the whole country was caught up in industrial action. But this did nothing to dent the series' popularity and with barely any competition from the other channels, it reigned supreme until the 1980s when both the BBC and Channel 4 introduced hard-hitting new soaps *EastEnders* and *Brookside*. *Coronation Street* writers met the challenge head-on and some of the programme's most dramatic storylines were played out during the eighties. Who could forget the love affair of the decade between Deirdre Barlow and Mike Baldwin? The ensuing feud between Mike and Ken would last for years. Rita Fairclough's mental abuse at the hands of Alan Bradley and the dramatic conclusion which saw him fatally struck by a Blackpool tram has gone down as one of the defining plotlines in any soap. Hilda Ogden's poignant breakdown in the aftermath of the death of her husband, Stan, has come to be viewed as one of the most outstanding performances in the programme's history.

As the millennium approached, Bet and Alec Gilroy (Roy Barraclough) were manning the pumps at the Rovers but it was a time of upheaval for the show. The series had increased to three episodes a week. The show had relocated to a brand new set with new houses and shops and fresh characters had replaced some of the old guard and were taking root in the nation's heart. The touching but ultimately doomed romance between Raquel Wolstenhulme and Curly Watts (Kevin Kennedy) broke millions of hearts nationwide and made Sarah Lancashire a household name.

While the trademark humour of the series was much

in evidence, the show's plotlines reflected shifts in society and tackled modern issues such as drug abuse and transsexuality with the introduction of the character of Hayley Patterson. On the 8th of December 2000 the show celebrated its 40th year on air and the Prince of Wales made a cameo appearance. As the show entered a new century, new families such as the Battersbys and the McDonalds dominated the street. A new feud emerged between Karen McDonald, played by Suranne Jones, and Tracy Barlow, who had been played by a number of actresses over the years, though it was Kate Ford who embodied Tracy's most turbulent storylines.

In 2010, *Coronation Street* celebrated its 50th birthday, not long after it had officially become the world's longest running soap in the *Guinness Book of Records*. The show marked the occasion with one of its most dramatic storylines when The Joinery bar exploded, destroying the viaduct and sending a Metrolink tram hurtling down on to the street. There were seven episodes screened that week with a special live one-hour episode, which sent the programme's ratings soaring into the stratosphere.

In 2011, the character of Dennis Tanner returned to the street after an absence of forty-three years. As Elsie Tanner's son, Dennis' reintroduction into street life provided a tangible link to those early days, when Elsie, Annie and Ena held sway over Weatherfield life. The nation's favourite street has now dominated the airwaves for almost sixty years and seems destined for many, many more. The trials and tribulations of the people of Weatherfield continue to delight audiences the world over. Life is never simple for them but the good humour and witty one-liners have seen them through many a crisis. As Ena Sharples wisely observed, 'I don't expect life to be easy. I'd think very little of it if it was.'

It's 1939 and Elsie Tanner is moving into the
nation's favourite street

In Britain's darkest hour, this is one Christmas that
Coronation Street will never forget . . .

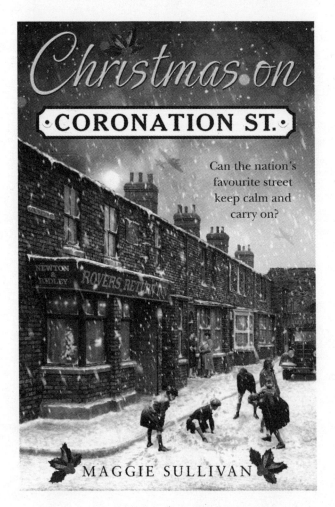

Available to buy now